Mistress
by Midnight

Mistress by Midnight

MAGGIE ROBINSON

KENSINGTON PUBLISHING CORP.
www.kensingtonbooks.com

BRAVA BOOKS are published by

Kensington Publishing Corp.
119 West 40th Street
New York, NY 10018

All Kensington titles, imprints, and distributed lines are available at special quantity discounts for bulk purchases for sales promotion, premiums, fund-raising, educational, or institutional use.

Special book excerpts or customized printings can also be created to fit specific needs. For details, write or phone the office of the Kensington Special Sales Manager: Kensington Publishing Corp., 119 West 40th Street, New York, NY 10018. Attn. Special Sales Department. Phone: 1-800-221-2647.

Brava and the B logo are Reg. U.S. Pat. & TM Off.

ISBN-13: 978-0-7582-5101-5
ISBN-10: 0-7582-5101-7

First Kensington Trade Paperback Printing: January 2011

10 9 8 7 6 5 4 3 2 1

Printed in the United States of America

Prologue

Dorset, 1808

Despite it being high summer, Con was so pale that he looked ill. But he had come to her at the ring of stones, and that was the important thing.

In a few days' time, he would belong to some other woman. He would stand in front of the altar at All Saints, and pledge his troth to Marianna Berryman, that sleek stranger who looked very like a cream-fed cat.

Laurette understood this rationally. Con had to enter this alliance for the sake of his estate and the people who depended on him. Two villages in his purview had suffered year after year from neglect. The prosperity of the local populace rested upon the shoulders of a nineteen-year-old boy. When others his age were out carousing, Con was promising his future away.

What she planned for the twilight was foolish. It would mean nothing in the wider world, but it meant everything to her. She smoothed the fabric of her beaded blue dress—the dress she had worn for her hopeless come-out—and almost enjoyed the shock on Con's face when he saw her. She had lowered the neckline—if her chest were the heavens, infinite constellations of stars were twinkling brightly.

But Con loved her freckles.

"I am considerably underdressed, I see." He wore a homespun shirt and breeches, clean but worn. New clothes were filling his closets, but she was glad he didn't come to her wearing Berryman largesse.

"This is a special occasion."

Con laughed a bit bleakly. "Yes, it's Wednesday evening. Bring out the fireworks."

"I didn't think of those. But I do have a bottle of champagne I pinched from my father's cellar."

"I'm not thirsty, Laurie." He collapsed onto the ground, but made no motion for her to join him. She could feel his retreat as though it were a living thing. Carefully she spread her skirts and sat beside him.

"You'll ruin that dress."

She shrugged. "I'll never wear it again. But I wanted to wear it for you tonight. So you would remember."

"I'll never forget you, Laurie, and that's the problem."

She clasped a hand. "This is to be my wedding dress, Con. I'm going to marry you tonight."

He pulled away. "Don't be daft. I've signed all the papers. Berryman will send me to jail if I renege now."

"You'll marry on Saturday, just as they planned. But your heart will always belong to me."

"You know it will, but what good is even saying it? This is over, Laurie. *We* are over."

His words were brutal. His thick black brows drew into an angry frown.

"Please give me tonight, Con. I want us to stand in this magical place under God's sky. To speak what's in my heart. To be your wife of the heart, if not in a church register."

She searched his face for a reaction. At first there was none. Then residual anger turned to incredulity, and, eventually, a faint smile.

"A pagan wedding for my pagan girl. It's not much to cling to."

"It's all I'll ever have," she said simply.

He kissed her then, too gently. She stole control and toppled him on his back, eating him up with hands and mouth as if she were starving. If she didn't stop she would make love to him before she said the words she had labored over so long. She broke the kiss, leaping to her feet.

"We shall continue all that in a moment, my Lord Conover. First I want you to stand up with me before the altar stone."

He shook his head. "You really are serious."

"I am."

"All right." Con got to his feet, brushing off his threadbare pants. "I wish—"

Laurette placed a finger on his lips. "No regrets. We have tonight, as the sun is sinking and the shadows loom. Now, hold my hands."

"Yes, madam." He brought them to his lips.

"That's soon to be Lady Conover to you. Oh, don't look so stricken. I know this is all pretense. But when winter comes, the thought of this summer evening will keep me warm."

"It's not enough."

"It will have to be. Now then." She squeezed his hands. "I, Laurette Isabella Vincent, do take thee, Desmond—"

"Thee?"

"Quiet. Your turn will come. Do take thee, Desmond Anthony Ryland, seventh Marquess of Conover, to be the husband of my heart, and the keeper of my soul and body for all eternity. Though circumstances may part us, nothing will ever break the bonds of our friendship and love."

The next part was tricky. She certainly was not going to promise to *obey*. Not Con or anyone.

"I do solemnly promise to be mindful of thy wishes in all things, even if I do not always agree. I will love you—*thee*—and support thee until I cease to draw breath. I pledge this to thee before the altar of the Ancients, in the sight of God our Father, whose ways may be a mystery at present."

There had been more, but her throat was becoming thick as Con looked down on her, his black eyes somber. "Amen."

He kissed the tear from her cheek. "I, Desmond Anthony Ryland, seventh Marquess of Conover, take thee Laurette Isabella Vincent as my wedded wife of the heart. I shall be true to thee until death. I love you so much, Laurie, my heart is breaking."

They held each other as the sun dipped behind the megalith, casting its last light on the sparkles of Laurette's dress. The champagne was forgotten, but the consummation of their union was not.

Chapter 1

London, 1820

Laurette knew precisely what she must do. Again. Had known even before her baby brother had fallen so firmly into the Marquess of Conover's clutches.

To be fair, perhaps Charlie had not so much fallen as thrown himself headfirst into Con's way. Charlie had been as heedless as she herself had been more than a decade ago. She was not immune even now to Con's inconvenient presence. She had shown him her back on more than one occasion, but could feel the heat of his piercing black gaze straight through to her tattered stays.

But tonight she would allow him to look his fill. She had gone so far as having visited Madame Demarche this afternoon to purchase some of her naughtiest underpinnings. Laurette would have one less thing for which to feel shame.

Bought with credit, of course. One more bill to join the mountain of debt. Insurmountable as a Himalayan peak and just as chilling. Nearly as cold as Conover's heart.

She raised the lion's head knocker and let it fall, once, composing herself to face Con's servant.

Desmond Ryland, Marquess of Conover, opened the door himself.

"You!"

"Did you think I would allow you to be seen here at such an hour?" he asked, his face betraying no emotion. "You must indeed think me a veritable devil. I've sent Aram to bed. Come into my study."

He *was* a devil, suggesting this absurd time. Midnight, as though they were two foreign spies about to exchange vital information in utmost secrecy. Laurette followed him down the shadowy hall, the black-and-white tile a chessboard beneath her feet. She felt much like a pawn, but would soon need to become the White Queen. Con must not know just how desperate she was.

Though surely he must suspect.

He opened a door and stepped aside as she crossed the threshold. The room, she knew, was his sanctuary, filled with objects he'd collected in the years he'd been absent from Town and her life. Absent from his own life, as well. The marquessate had been shockingly abandoned for too long.

She had been summoned here once before, in daylight, a year ago. She was better prepared tonight. She let her filmy shawl slip from one shoulder but refused Con's offer of a chair.

"Suit yourself," he shrugged, sitting behind his desk. He placed a hand on a decanter of brandy. "Will you join me? We can toast to old times."

Laurette shook her head. She'd need every shred of her wits to get through what was ahead. "No thank you, my lord."

She could feel the thread of attraction between them, frayed yet stubborn. She should be too old and wise now to view anything that was to come as more than a business arrangement. As soon as she had seen the bold strokes of his note, she had accepted its implication. She was nearly thirty, almost half her life away from when Conover first beguiled her. Or perhaps when she had beguiled him. He had left her long ago, if not quite soon enough.

A pop from the fire startled her, and she turned to watch sparks fly onto the marble tiles. The room was uncomfortably warm for this time of year, but it was said that the Marquess of Conover had learned to love the heat of the exotic East on his travels.

"I appeal to your goodness," Laurette said, nearly choking on the improbable phrase.

"I find good men dead boring, my dear. Good women, too." Con abandoned his desk and strode across the floor, where she was rooted by feet that suddenly felt too heavy to lift. He smiled, looking almost boyish, and fingered the single loose golden curl teasing the ivory slope of her shoulder. She recalled that her hair had always dazzled him and had imagined just this touch when she tugged the strand down.

She had hoped to appear winsome despite the passage of time, but her plan was working far too well for current comfort. She pushed him away with more force than she felt. "What would you know about good men, my lord?" She scraped the offending hair back with trembling fingers and secured it under the prison of its hairpin. It wouldn't do to tempt him further. Or herself. What had she been thinking to come here?

"I've known my share. But I am uncertain if your brother fits the category. A good, earnest young fellow, on occasion. A divinity student, is he not? But then—I fear his present vices make him ill-suited for his chosen profession. Among other things, he is so dishonorable he sends his sister in his stead. Your letter was quite affecting. You've gone to a great deal of trouble on his account, but I hardly see why I should forgive his debt." He folded his arms and leaned forward. "Convince me."

Damn him. He intended her to beg. They both knew how it would end.

"He does not know I'm here. He knows nothing," Laurette said quickly, and stepped back.

He was upon her again, his warm brandied breath sending shivers down her spine. She fell backward onto a leather chair. A small mercy. At least she wouldn't fall foolishly at his feet. She closed her eyes, remembering herself in such a pose, Con's head thrown back, his fingers entwined in the tangle of her hair. A lifetime ago.

She looked up. His cheek was creased in amusement at her clumsiness. "He will not thank you for your interference."

"I'm not interfering! My brother is much too young to fall prey to your evil machinations."

Con raised a black winged brow. "Such melodramatic vocabulary. He's not that young, you know. Much older than you were when you were so very sure of yourself. And by calling me evil you defeat your purpose, Laurette. Why, I might take offense and not cooperate. Perhaps I *am* a very good man to discourage him from gambling he can ill afford. But I *will* be repaid. " He leaned over, placing his hands on the arms of Laurette's chair. His eyes were dark, obsidian, but his intentions clear.

Laurette felt her blush rise and leaned back against her seat. She willed herself to stay calm. He would not crowd her and make her cower beneath him. She raised her chin a fraction. "He cannot—that is to say, our funds are tied up at present. Our guardian. . . ." She trailed off, never much able to lie well. But she was expert at keeping secrets.

Con left her abruptly to return to his desk. She watched as he poured himself another brandy into the crystal tumbler, but let it sit untouched. "What do you propose, Laurette?" he asked, his voice a velvet burr. "That I tear up your brother's vowels and give him the cut direct next time we meet?"

"Yes," Laurette said boldly. "The sum he owes must be a mere trifle to you. And his company a bore. If you hurt his feelings now, it will only be to his ultimate benefit. One day he will see that." She glanced around the room, appointed with elegance and treasure. Brass fittings gleamed in the candlelight. A thick Persian carpet lay under her scuffed kid slippers. Lord Conover's study was the lair of a man of exquisite taste, and a far cry from Charlie's disreputable lodging. She twisted her fingers, awaiting his next words.

There was the faintest trace of a smile. "You give me far too much credit. I am neither a good man, nor, despite what you see here, so rich a man I can ignore a debt this size. We all need blunt to keep up appearances. And settle obligations."

Laurette knew exactly what his obligation to her cost him and held her tongue.

Con leaned back in his chair, the picture of confidence. "If I cannot have coin, some substitution must be made. I think you know what will please me."

Laurette nodded. It would please her too, God forgive her. Her voice didn't waver. "When, Con?"

He picked up his glass and drained it. "Tonight. I confess I cannot wait to have you in my bed again."

Laurette searched her memory. There had been very few beds involved in their brief affair. Making love to Con in one would be a luxurious novelty. She was not prepared, however; the vial of sponges was still secreted away in her small trunk at her brother's rooms. She had not allowed herself to think the evening would end in quite this way. But she had just finished her courses. Surely she was safe.

"Very well." She rose from the haven of her chair.

His face showed the surprise he surely felt. Good. It was time she unsettled *him*.

"You seem to be taking your fate rather calmly, Laurette."

"Did you arrange it? That it would come to this?" she asked softly.

"Did I engage your brother in a high stakes game he had no hope of winning? I declare, that avenue had not occurred to me," Con said smoothly. "How you must despise me to even ask." He motioned her to him. After a few awkward moments, Laurette walked toward him and allowed him to pull her down into his lap. He was undeniably hard, fully aroused. She let herself feel a brief surge of triumph.

Con placed a broad hand across her abdomen and settled her even closer. "How is the child?"

Was this an unconscious gesture? Con had never felt her daughter where his hand now lay, had never seen her, held her. She fought the urge to slap his hand away and willed herself to melt into the contours of his hard body. It would go quicker if she just gave in and let him think he'd won. "Very well, my lord. How is yours?"

"Fast asleep in his dormitory, I hope, surrounded by other scruffy little villains. I should like you to meet him one day."

She did not tell him that his son was already known to her, as his wife had once been, improbably, her friend. "I don't believe that would be wise, my lord."

"Why not? If you recall, I offered you the position as his step-mama a year ago. It is past time you become acquainted with my son, and I with your daughter." His busy fingers had begun removing hairpins.

Laurette said nothing, lulling in his arms as his lips skimmed her throat, his hands stroking every exposed inch. In dressing tonight, she'd bared as much of her flesh as she dared in order to tempt him. She wondered how she could so deceive herself. Nothing had changed. Nothing would ever change. And that was the problem.

Laurette pressed a gloved finger to his lips. "We do not need to discuss the past, my lord. We have tonight."

"If you think," he growled, "that I will be satisfied with only one night with you, you're as deluded as ever."

An insult. Lucky that, for she suddenly retrieved her primness and relative virtue. She straightened up. "That is all I am willing to offer."

He stood in anger, dumping her unceremoniously into his chair. "My dear Miss Vincent, if you wish me to forgive your brother's debts—all of them—I require a bit more effort on your part."

"A-all? What do you mean?"

"I see the young fool didn't tell you." Con pulled open a drawer, fisting a raft of crumpled paper. "Here. Read them and then tell me one paltry night with you is worth ten thousand pounds. Even you cannot have such a high opinion of yourself."

Laurette felt her tongue thicken and her lips go numb. "It cannot be," she whispered.

"I've spent the past month buying up his notes all over town." Con's smile, feral and harsh, withered her even further. He now followed in his father-in-law's footsteps.

"You did this."

"You may think what you wish. I hold the mortgage to Vincent Lodge as well. You've denied me long enough, Laurie."

Her home, ramshackle as it was. Beatrix's home, if only on brief holidays away from her foster family. Laurette had forgotten just how stubborn and high-handed Conover could be. She looked at him, hoping to appear as haughty as the queen she most certainly was not.

"What kind of man are you?"

"Not a *good* one, I wager. I offered you my name once. I shan't do so again. Your refusal still rings in my ears. But I need a mistress. You once played the part to perfection. The position is yours if you want it."

Laurette considered. She could do it, but he would pay— far more than the price of her brother's losses.

She scooped up her hairpins from her skirt. "All right. The notes, if you please."

Con locked them into the desk drawer and pocketed the key. "Very amusing. You'd toss them into the fire and laugh all the way home. No, my dear. We are going upstairs. Now. As a show of good faith. The vouchers will be destroyed once I engage your services in a binding agreement. A year, I should think, will suit me."

Laurette's lips twisted in distaste. How had she ever thought to get around this man? She was as much an innocent as before. "But it will not suit me."

"Still full of misplaced pride, I see." Con ran a long finger down her cheek and she felt herself flush. "Six months, then.

Surely you can endure my lovemaking for that amount of time."

"I shall endeavor to do so." He might own her body, but never her heart. Not again. Six months would seem an eternity. "What of Charlie?"

"He's about to go on a Grand Tour. A trip to the Holy Land is in order, with a tutor, far from the gaming tables and whores. Yes," he added, as she stiffened beneath his fingers, "your brother has devoutly been studying all manner of carnal pleasures. I spoke with him this afternoon. He's actually most eager to get away."

She shivered. "Does he know what you plan for me? For us?"

Con raised another irritated eyebrow. "Come now. Give me points for discretion. I know how to be a marquess now. I'm not still some love-struck boy. I've kept my tongue this time." He cupped her cheek, almost tenderly. "It's all arranged, Laurie. A little house on Jane Street, not far from here. You may even have the child visit if you desire."

"Beatrix. Her name is Beatrix," Laurette whispered.

Con pulled her to him, kissing her forehead. "I know her name. I am her father, after all."

Chapter 2

Holding a taper, his heart flickering in rhythm with the candle, Con clasped Laurette's hand as they mounted the stairs. The circumstances were not ideal. She was not far wrong to think he'd orchestrated the swift sinking of young Mr. Charles Vincent, although Charlie had been floundering in deep water without any initial assistance from the Marquess of Conover. When the rumors reached Con's ears, it had been a simple matter to inquire about the well-being and solvency of his country neighbor and take him about Town. It was not Con's fault Charlie was such a complete mutton-head.

The boy couldn't match his sister for spirit or consequence. God had played a joke making Charlie the heir, not that there was much in the Vincent treasury to inherit. Con had done his research. Laurette would have a pittance when she turned thirty next year. Their guardian should be shot, but Con had planned a more subtle revenge for Sir Zachary Billington. He knew all about the perfidies of greedy guardians. His own had taught him well.

They stood now before his bedroom door. What transpired this night marked the beginning of both their lives. Laurette didn't need to know she'd be a mistress for much less than six months if he had anything to say about it. Con was looking at the future Marchioness of Conover. He'd done everything, would do anything in his power, to make it so. Laurette had refused him once. She would not do so again. He couldn't permit it.

He swept her up into his arms and carried her through the doorway.

"Put me down at once!"

Con grinned. She all but beat her fists upon him. However, that would have required more energy on her part, and his Laurette seemed intent on playing the rigid doll. He was looking forward to loosening each limb, and plying her with his fingers and his tongue, until she was enslaved . . . ensorcelled. He hoped he'd not lost his knack to satisfy her. It had been over a decade since he'd touched her—touched any woman—and longer than that since he'd slept with his relieved wife as he'd done his reluctant duty. Their son was proof that at least something of value had come out of the ill-fated union.

Con laid Laurette on his bed gently, as if she were precious porcelain that might shatter at any moment, and stepped back to light more lamps. Soon the room was ablaze, as bright as daylight.

"Open your eyes, Laurette."

He watched the mulish set of her mouth. He could kiss the difficulty away, but ground rules were to be set. He watched as she gaped in wonder at the furnishings—the richly tented bed, the intricate carvings casting shadows on the gilded walls.

"It's like a seraglio." She didn't sound pleased.

"Just the effect I was going for, my dear. You will find your new abode decorated in a similar style."

"I trust there will be just one concubine at a time."

If she only knew. "As my mistress, you will see to all my pleasures. Should I require an additional companion to join us, I will of course inform you."

He supposed he shouldn't delight in the angry flush that spread up from the cleft of her breasts to her cheeks. She really was too thin and too pale. Worry and genteel poverty were apt to steal youth away, Con knew first-hand, but he was determined to reinstate some of hers, if possible. He had failed badly last year, but would not do so now.

"How does it feel to be worth over ten thousand pounds?" he asked, tearing his tie off. "I expect to get my money's worth, you know. It was once very good between us, Laurette. I have fond memories."

Laurette sat up, pulling up the bodice of her dress, much to Con's disappointment. "What is that scent?"

"Incense, my dear. Do you like it? It burns in the brazier on the hearth."

The fire was roaring, just as he liked it. England was a cold and colorless place after his time in the Orient. While he had abstained from many of the delights of the East, he had been enamored by the smells and tastes, the vibrant hues and decorative patterns. He knew people muttered "Mad Marquess" behind his back, but he was damned if he would return to the half-life he'd had when he was first married. Every blandly fashionable thing that Marianna had purchased to decorate his houses had been carted off as soon as he stepped foot on English soil. The only trace of her lay in the color of his son's eyes.

"I do. It smells like a gentleman's cologne."

Con experienced a twinge of jealousy. From what he knew, Laurette had lived like a nun. He did not care to think of her nose buried in the crook of some gentleman's neck as she inhaled the vapors from his body.

"I prefer it to all others. I'm glad you approve. I shall need help with my boots." He sat down on a crewel-work chair.

He had shed everything save his shirt, breeches and boots. Once Laurette was at his feet, she couldn't possibly miss his nearly painful arousal. Now it was Con's turn to close his eyes to banish the sinful vision of her on her knees from his fevered brain. He was intent on her pleasure tonight as well as his own.

He heard the rustle of her silk skirts as she slid from the satin and velvet bedcovers. He would dress—and undress— undress to perfection, jewel-like colors to showcase the gold of her hair and blue of her eyes. If anything, she was more beautiful to him than she had been before, not that society would count her amongst its diamonds. Her brow was too fierce, her mouth too wide, her nose and cheeks and décolletage spangled with freckles that she still, he could see, took pains to hide. He had once seen the freckles everywhere, had traced them with his fingers and tongue as she writhed beneath him.

He laughed as she tugged off his second boot, landing ingloriously on her rump. He extended a hand to her.

"Now it's my turn to help you undress, but I expect to find you completely naked and willing when I come to you in the future."

Laurette turned her back to him, ramrod straight. "I trust you'll set a schedule for me. I'm not going to prance around nude all day."

Con set to unfasten the tiny row of pearl-like buttons. There were far too many of them for his liking. "Perhaps I will permit you a robe, then. Something sheer and easily removed. One never knows when I will wish to slake my hunger for you."

Laurette turned around angrily, causing a button to come off between his fingers.

"You are joking!"

"I am not, madam. Oh, rest assured, your wardrobe will be full of dresses to wear if we go out, but behind the door of your new house you are to be absolutely available to me at any time of the night or day."

"But—but what about the servants? Or aren't I to have any?"

"I've hired a completely discreet couple. They are aware of my predilections."

"You are inhuman! I will not consent to such a thing!"

"Let me refresh your memory. Ten thousand pounds is at stake, Laurette. And Vincent Lodge. I believe it requires extensive renovation. I shall see to it."

"It's flat-out blackmail. And the lodge belongs to Charlie, the utter worm. I don't care if it falls down around his ears."

Con smiled and put the loose button on the bedside table. "There. That's more like the old you. I see you haven't lost all your temper."

"You've not begun to see it!"

He watched as Laurette looked around the room rather wildly. Con believed she was very close to finding something to throw. His possessions were valuable, his servants extraordinarily light sleepers and quite devoted to him. He pulled her close.

"You are my mistress, Laurette. I have my requirements, and you have your duties to fill. You may not always like them, but you will bow to my will in this and all things."

She looked up at him, her blue eyes now gray with tears. "And if I don't? Shall you send Charlie to the Fleet and me along with him? I don't believe you will, Con. Not even you could be so heartless."

"Don't tempt me, Laurette. You have forgotten about the child."

"Beatrix!" she hissed. "Leave her alone as you left the rest of us!"

Con clamped his mouth shut in fury. In her eyes, he would always be the one who walked away from his vows. All of them. She cut him to the core because she was right.

This evening was a shambles. He was a cur for using Beatrix Isabella Vincent, the one pure thing between them, to manipulate her into his bed. A desperate fool, as well, because he would get her there any way that worked. His need was so strong his honor was but a distant memory.

"Let's not put my resolve to the test. I don't think either of us would care for the results," Con said at last, releasing her. He watched as she tore into the rest of her clothes, tossing them to the floor.

"There!" she spat. "I am naked. Use me as you will."

Despite the danger, Con laughed. "My little martyr, Saint Laurette. I believe there is a special place in hell for the both of us, but I intend to take you to heaven first."

He chuckled again as she snorted, turning his back to shuck the rest of his clothes. He was embarrassed by the evidence of his eagerness. "Get in bed," he ground out. He had not dared to look at her long in her defiant fury, her white skin speckled with gold in the lamplight, her eyes more brilliant in their scorn.

No, this evening was turning into a disaster of the very first order.

He heard her flip back the covers, tumbling the embroidered pillows to the floor. One came very near him. At least she was throwing things not apt to attract the attention of his staff. Tomorrow night would be better, as they would be in their own haven. He must remember to present the key to her new house to her before he sent her back to her brother's lodgings.

The key. That reminded him. His desk drawer key was still in the pocket of his waistcoat, as well as a tiny yellowed sheer muslin bag stitched full of tarnished beads, and a flat pinkish rock. It would not do for Laurette to find any of them in the night and for him to lose some of his advantages. She need not know about the other weapons in his arsenal yet. He swung a picture from a wall and opened his safe. He heard another snort as he placed the items safely atop some papers and bank notes.

"You don't trust me?"

Con shrugged. "Perhaps I don't trust myself. One night with you might drive all sensible thought out of my head, and I might release you from your obligations."

"A man like you can surely find other female company."

"One would think so." He joined her under the covers, covers which she had drawn up to her stubborn Vincent chin. He'd seen quite a bit of that chin lately as he watched Charlie dig an ever deeper hole for himself. But the nights with the young idiot were more than worth it now that he had achieved Laurette's concession. She was where she belonged, even if she didn't know it.

"What do you mean to have me do, my lord?" she asked, a look of clear indifference upon her face.

"I want you to lie absolutely still."

Laurette looked at him, frowning now. No doubt that was what she planned to do in a hopeless attempt to depress his ardor. "Is this a trick? Don't gentlemen expect some sort of response from their whores?"

"You are not a whore! You are my lover, and my wish is for you to lie quietly. I want to reacquaint myself with your body. It has been too long."

"Not long enough," she muttered.

"Hush. Not a sound." Con peeled the coverlet away. Her own scent of rosewater and woman entranced him. Her breasts were fuller than he remembered, although the rest of her seemed too lean. He must fatten her up. With another child soon, he hoped. He brushed the powder from her chest with a linen handkerchief. "No more *maquillage*, Laurette. You are fine as you are." He didn't want to taste the bitterness of her rouge and powder, but wanted to see every inch he had worked so tirelessly to buy into his bed.

Every cell inside him screamed to fuck her, and fuck her fast. Yet he needed to ration his touch or everything he'd planned would be ruined. With one fingertip he lightly tapped the tip of her freckled nose, then slid down the gentle indentation over her mouth. He rested on the artificial color of her upper lip for a moment before he blotted it away with the handkerchief. Her lips parted as he removed the rest and then his finger returned to stroke the moist edge of her lower lip. She snapped her lips shut, inadvertently trapping him inside. Her tongue retreated, so he settled for a quick sweep of her teeth before he extricated himself.

"Are you buying a horse, my lord?"

"You are not to move *or* speak, remember?"

He continued to draw his invisible line upon the bone of her stubborn chin, its soft underside and down the column of her throat. He paused between the V of her collar bone, which was far too visible for his liking. The gap between her breasts was warm, her heartbeat faint. Her nipples had stiffened with the tickling sensation, but he resolutely stuck to his path. He dipped straight down her flat stomach to her navel and swirled a bit, just for a change of pace. Glancing up, he saw her golden eyebrows were contracted. They needed plucking, but that could wait for Nadia. Laurette's eyes were closed but she was paying close attention. He angled his finger slightly until his nail joined the procession down her belly to the golden curls at the juncture of her thighs.

Her hair there was unbearably fine and soft. But he had other plans for it. He combed through, still with just one very fortunate finger.

"The concubines remove this. You will also. To make it easier for me."

The shock on her face was comical. "You are mad."

He only smiled. "So they say. Mad enough to bind and gag you if you not hold your tongue and obey me." She went silent beneath him. Soon he would make it impossible for her to stay silent.

He hovered over her bud. Was it his imagination, or did Laurette strain up a fraction of an inch to give him access? No matter. It was far too soon. He leaned back, observing his handiwork. It seemed to him she was not quite so sacrificial. There was the slightest gap between her thighs and she no longer clenched her hands into the bedcovers. His fingertip slowly retraced its assault back up to her nose, omitting the sidetrip into the warm haven of her mouth.

When his tongue replaced his finger, he felt her quiver beneath him. He licked her lips but didn't try to kiss her yet, being mindful of her strong white teeth. He valued his tongue and had further use of it. She swallowed hard as he laved her throat. When it came to the hollow between her breasts, he decided it was time to make a quick departure from his previous route. Gently pinching the bud of one breast, he lazily suckled the other. He felt her hand tentative on his shoulder and shook it off.

"Be still or I will stop." He could tell she longed to tear a strip off his hide, but subsided into silence as his tongue trailed from her breasts to the sweet indentation of her navel.

Now it was time. His tongue nearly skipped as he headed south, his hands parting her folds, smoothing the gold from the pink. Her sharp intake of breath was as gratifying as the moisture slicking his fingers and tongue. He settled between her ivory thighs, hoping she wouldn't decide to use them as a vise on his poor, addled head. He was where he'd dreamed of being so long he could scarcely believe this night was true. But he wasn't here to gawp in wonder as he inhaled the drugging rose scent of her body, or to question his sanity or his luck.

No. Luck had little to do with it. He'd planned everything, fought his own better angels for this night with her. For the nights that were to come.

Time was wasting. His tongue and hands explored. She tasted clean, so sweetly familiar to him that the years might not have passed. Her honey proved the miracle of her desire. For him. Still. Deserter that he was. He had left as a weary boy and returned a weary man. But Laurette was the elixir he needed.

Con feasted on her plump flesh with exquisite precision, suckling and seducing *her* better angels. He sensed her unraveling before her cries left no doubt that this, at least, was the same as it had ever been between them. He didn't mind her fingers in his hair now, her nails raking his shoulders, her ragged sobs as he brought her to completion twice more before he rose up to sheath himself within her.

Tight heaven. Or perhaps it was his hell. He only knew this was where he was meant to be.

The blaze of light revealed the flush on her cheeks, the torrent of golden hair on his pillow. Her eyes were shut, her beautiful lips bitten from the stubborn resistance she'd clung to. There was no point to restraint. She was his. They belonged to each other. It had always been so.

Oh God. He had dreamt of this, night after night, had denied himself when he could have had his pick of willing women. But they were not Laurette. It seemed a penance easily paid as he kept to his wedding vows for a vastly different reason—fidelity to a woman who was *not* his wife. The memory of the girl who was his first and only love. A girl he had doubly betrayed, a woman now. Some might say he was betraying her again with his scheme to win her back.

He made himself slow down, savoring each touchpoint between them. The glorious heat of her around his cock. Her hesitant fingertips on his jaw. Her long legs clenched helplessly around him.

She couldn't be unaware of the spell she had cast on him.

"Look at me, Laurie."

He wanted her to see into his soul, black and shriveled though it was. See the love in his eyes, too. But she had other ideas. She pulled him down, covering his mouth with hers, her hands well-nigh strangling him.

What an ass he was. She needed to be kissed. It was an inexcusable omission from their earlier play. An intimacy so perfect that had always been almost too transcendent to trust. They'd had years of practice before the kissing led to complications.

She was frantic now, nipping, weeping, as though she wanted to devour him. This was more than a kiss. His blood sang as they locked together, each engaged in a sensual battle for dominance, a battle he wanted her to win.

She took him in deeper, her hips angling him to the point of no return. He'd meant this first time to be more orchestrated, more andante than allegro. But he was damned if the last note would be played arpeggio.

"I cannot last, Laurie. Come with me. Please."

He gloried in her rise against him, the soft ivory and gold of her skin lighting the flames of the past.

They were in the field once again beneath the hot sun, his long-discarded hacking jacket tossed beneath them, her skirts rucked carelessly. He smoothed the fabric with impatience, his hands brushing against the warm curve of her belly. The scent of fresh cut hay clouded his senses. The rich dark soil pillowed softly beneath his knees. He heard the insistent buzz of insects spreading life from bramble to berry in the distance. But soon there was nothing in the natural world to divert him but her body, her scent, her cries, the heat of her skin. In their haste there were still too many layers of clothes between them, but nothing had the power to stop this summer storm or bring them down to earth. Not Con's duty, not Laurette's innocence, not even, when it came to it, his marriage.

He had hurt her once so deliberately, so finally, to prevent just what had occurred anyway. Life was full of ironies, but this woman would at last be his, no matter the price he had to pay.

Chapter 3

Con had driven her through the gray light himself, the only sounds the striking bells of church towers and clopping of horses' hooves. And the pummeling of her own heart, which deafened her to anything else. He let her down from the conveyance with a savage hug, the key to her new house, and an envelope full of the most exacting instructions. Con was apparently not one to leave anything to chance anymore. No accidental meetings, no stolen kisses, and no clumsy coupling in fields and outbuildings.

She remembered the day that everything began to end, a beautiful sun-drenched day when thoughts of a new dress had blinded her to the tension at Ryland Grove.

She was off before Sadie could hook her last hook, her hair tumbling down her shoulders, her straw bonnet still hanging on the wall in the back hall. The sun was high in the sky. Con had promised a picnic lunch and she hoped he hadn't started without her. Since he came down from university, he always seemed hungry. For food. For new experiences. But most of all for her.

Breathless, she found him pacing in the little folly. The basket on the bench had been opened. Laurette detected a few crumbs on Con's cravat and brushed them away.

"Is there anything left for me?" she teased, licking her lips.

She knew her mouth drove him to distraction. Why, she couldn't say. The Cobb girls had called her Fishface. Her lips were nothing like a dainty cupid's bow, but a wide slice of pink that showed too many teeth when she laughed. They told her she'd get wrinkles, too, because she laughed quite a lot. She couldn't help herself when she was with Con.

"I only have some bread and cheese. There wasn't much Mrs. Clark could spare me."

Con was not smiling. In fact, he looked horribly grim. Laurette squeezed his hand. "What's wrong?"

"Uncle Ryland wants me to marry an heiress."

Laurette dropped the peach. It bumped along the painted floor until it came to rest against a pillar.

Con turned to her and smiled. "Don't worry. It's nonsense and so I told him. You'll be my marchioness as soon as I reach my majority. We'll have a Christmas wedding, aye?"

Laurette looked at him. Looked closely. His eyes were shadowed and his dark hair hadn't seen a brush lately. He'd shaved himself, had a nick on his cheek to prove it. His valet had found another employer who could pay him more regularly. "Is he hounding you again?" she whispered.

"He's not beating me if that's what you're asking," Con colored. "We've just been going over the books."

"It's his fault!" Laurette cried. "He's had full reign over your finances for ages."

Con put his arm around her and slid her across the bench. "I wish I could blame him. My grandfather, God rest his soul, was a most improvident man. You know how he loved travel and collecting odd things. Studying the world, he called it. It was he who bankrupted the estate. It's been Uncle Ryland who's kept us afloat, although he's used some shady dealings to do it. No doubt he should have been born before his brother and I wouldn't find myself in this sad pickle. I'd be plain Mr. Ryland, orphan, engaged to not-so-plain Miss Vincent, the most wondrous girl in Dorset."

"Kiss me, Con." She needed to be kissed and so did he. Then the worry would go out of his face. She could do that much for him at least. And how she wanted to do more.

He obliged. His lips were warm, his tongue firm. He tasted of peaches. No wonder he hadn't wanted a bite, the rogue. Laurette opened her eyes to see Con's fixed upon her, a hunted, haunted flatness within. She'd bring the spark back to them. Her hands left the breadth of his shoulders, as his tangled in her hair. He was hard for her already, as she was wet for him.

She broke the kiss. "I don't want to wait anymore, Con."

"You have to go while I can still let you." He smoothed her cheek with a blunt fingertip. She caught it and thrust it into her mouth.

"Don't, Laurie, for God's sake. You'll drive me mad."

"Let's be mad together," she pleaded.

"You are too young."

"I'm seventeen! Girls are mothers at my age!"

"Precisely." Con stood up. "I have nothing to offer a wife now. What if I got you with child? How would we manage?"

"There are ways to prevent—"

Con raised a hand. "Don't tell me how you know such things. We'll go on as we have."

But they had not, not for long. Laurette had won, only to lose him forever.

She checked her reticule. Con had given her money, but not enough for her to flee from him. He knew she was completely dependent, probably knew to the penny the extent of her own debts as well. Her role was artfully constructed, paragraph after paragraph in the papers he presented to her. She had not bothered to read every word of her contract, but signed the documents with resignation. Con oversaw the signing ceremony wearing a banyan-style dressing gown and a grave expression. He must have been sure of his success before she even rapped on his door at midnight, just as she had known she had no choice but to agree.

His terms had been remarkably generous, and she trusted him, fool that she was. She would burn her brother's damages in six months' time. It seemed Con was not quite so trusting of her to release her brother's chits just yet. But Laurette felt sure she could persuade him before long. It seemed she was still his elixir of choice.

She slipped up the stairs to her brother's rooms, hoping to avoid Charlie's landlady. Her encounter with the woman yesterday was an unpleasant reminder just how dire things had become. The room was dim, the curtains drawn against the dawn. Laurette smelled Charlie before she saw him. He was still dressed and partially wrapped in a threadbare blanket on the broken divan, sleeping out here to give her the privacy of the single bedroom. No doubt he had lurched in so late, and so drunk, he had not even thought to tap on the door to inquire how she had spent her evening. But perhaps he'd make a fine clergyman eventually, aware of the pitfalls and temptations life presented. At the tender age of twenty, it seemed he'd partaken of more than his share.

Con had said Charlie was to be spirited away today. Laurette noted a portmanteau open on the rug. She knew her brother had sold everything he had of any value. What remained was rubbish. Con had promised to outfit the boy properly for his adventure, furnishing the tutor, an old professor of his, with enough money to see them through any inevitability. Laurette was grateful Charlie wouldn't be entrusted with the pursestrings.

She turned the bedroom door handle gingerly, although judging from the inebriated snores from the sofa, Charlie was dead to this world and the next. She had the foresight to arrange for a basin of water before she left last night, and proceeded to scrub last night's sin from her skin. She stared, unflinching, in the cloudy mirror over the dresser. She was now a kept woman.

Once she had given Con her love freely, even though she knew the consequences. Even after the farce of his marriage, she had made him to come to her. Needed him with a longing that had not dissipated despite her every effort to drive Con from her heart. She stood now as fallen as she'd ever been, fornicator, adulteress, unwed mother, whore. Harsh words for a mostly chaste life. Odd that her reflection simply showed a woman well past her first blush of youth, eyes shadowed from lack of sleep, hair a frightful tangle from her lover's hands. She was no alluring Siren for all that she had sinned.

She might have answered Con's question differently last year and not found herself in this bloody predicament. He could have helped with Charlie. She would have finally been called "Mama." But when Con had proposed to her, no mention was ever made of their daughter, just his son. He hadn't found Marianna's letter yet.

Beatrix had been a secret. Her secret. After years of prevarication, Laurette couldn't seem to tell him that day, fearful of what he'd do once he'd found out. And she had been right. He had railed at her once he knew the truth, been nearly unhinged, and she had avoided him ever since.

Beatrix's life was perfectly arranged. She was sent to her expensive school in her expensive clothes. The child's primary affection abided with her foster parents, her Cornish Vincent relatives. Laurette would continue to receive correct, neatly-penned "Dear Cousin Laurette" letters for the rest of her life.

Laurette had been stunned by having Con waltz back into her life, assuming they could pick up where they left off. His wife was not even cold in her grave. And if Laurette agreed to marry him, she would be reminded of the loss of her daughter every single day in a marriage that came far too late. How could she permit herself to be happy? She had refused as a matter of course. No amount of imploring during the hour she spent in Con's study had changed her mind.

Picking up her hairbrush, she worked the vicious knots out

with impatience. She had a few hours in which to sleep before Charlie left and Con's man Aram came to fetch her. Until then, her life, such as it was, was her own. She slipped between the mended sheets she brought with her from the Lodge and fell into a dreamless sleep.

Two hours later she was awoken by a guilty Charlie, still rumpled but wearing a fresh set of clothing.

"Laurie, I'm off. Lord Conover sent word he'd make arrangements to get you back to home. I'm afraid—er, Mrs. Bagshot will want a bit of the ready for the rent."

"I'll take care of it." Conover would.

"Thanks, sis. You're a peach. You'll be all right without me, won't you? I don't know exactly when we'll be back. The old turtle in the parlor won't say."

Laurette smiled. The old turtle must have his itinerary and no doubt she would not be seeing her brother for at least six months. "I shall be perfectly fine, Charlie. Do behave yourself. Lord Conover is incredibly generous, giving you this opportunity."

Charlie sat down at the edge of her bed. "I shouldn't like it, though," he said, a worried look upon his freckled face. If his eyes weren't so bloodshot, he'd look like a child with his hand caught in the cookie jar. His tie was askew and Laurette sat up to straighten it.

She'd given up much for the boy he'd been, too much. But there had been no other way.

Charlie had been sent away to school thanks to her silence, discretion that had come too late to save her or her own child. One night when her parents were off gambling, Con's uncle had come to her. Nothing, certainly not a little trollop like Laurie Vincent, would upset his plan to tie Con to Marianna Berryman. He had threatened her, but sweetened his sour words with the offer to educate her brother. So Charlie received his education—not that enough had sunk in—and she had weaned herself away from Con. But not before she came up with a plan of her own.

It was that night that she began to plot her secret, entirely illegal wedding.

And now she had another secret she must keep from her brother. Charlie *did* love her, even if he'd been a fool.

"Conover has concern for the inhabitants of Vincent Lodge, you know. We are neighbors, after all," Laurette said, soothing her brother's bruised pride.

"He won't—won't bother you when I'm gone?"

Perhaps her brother wasn't as naïve as she thought.

"Whatever was between us is long over," she lied. "We were practically children. It was only calf-love. He married, and I have my charitable interests." Charity that she could ill-afford, but now Con's allowance would enable her to be far more beneficent. Her family was really costing him quite a lot, but he had just begun to pay.

Her brother sighed dramatically. "I've mucked it up, haven't I, Laurie? I meant to win, y'know. But I'll do better in the future, I swear. When I get back, I'll be prepared to study. Put my nose to the grindstone."

"Indeed you will." She pecked him on the cheek. "Now, don't keep the turtle waiting. What is his name?"

"Dr. Griffin. Old as the hills, he is. Hope he doesn't keel over in some temple."

"You'll just have to brush up on the last rites, then," Laurette teased. "Go! All will be well."

With a foolishly deep bow, her brother left the bedroom and Laurette sagged back into the pillows. Sunlight slanted into the shabby room, revealing every mote of dust. Mrs. Bagshot was certainly not a good housekeeper, for all she gouged her lodgers out of their coin. London was ridiculously dear.

But now Laurette had enough money for a hot bath and a decent breakfast. She made the arrangements with the disdainful Mrs. Bagshot, who was unimpressed with the Vincents' suspiciously sudden wealth. Laurette had come to town without her maid Sadie, another mark against her. The woman had probably seen her with Con in the wee hours. Couldn't have missed the fierce embrace. Laurette smiled to herself. She was a wicked woman. And determined to be more wicked still.

Once she was grudgingly fed and freshened, she packed her few belongings and paced the squalid little parlor until Con's man Aram knocked politely on the door. Laurette had already heard his quiet but firm argument below with Mrs. Bagshot, who had let out a horrified shriek when she opened her door to the dark-skinned man. Laurette was more fascinated than shocked. Con had described his factotum, who was much more than a servant to him. He and his wife Nadia would see to her every need in her new abode. Nadia was to be her lady's maid and companion as she waited, apparently naked, for her lover to visit.

Aram was tall, dressed in a long embroidered vest over a linen shirt, and loose pants. The metallic threads gleamed in the morning sun, even though Mrs. Bagshot's windows were dusted with soot. When he bowed, Laurette was dazzled by the movement.

"I'm afraid you'll have to settle the rent with that woman before she lets us leave," Laurette said. "I don't think she'll be satisfied with my promises."

"A trifling sum," he replied in nearly unaccented English, pulling a fat purse from his trouser pocket. "I shall see to it immediately." He eyed her bandbox and battered trunk dubiously. "These are your things?"

Laurette felt a flash of shame. Even if he was Con's servant, this man in his exotic finery far outshone her. Well, she was now Con's servant too, and expected the marquess would remedy the poverty of her possessions. "Yes. These are not heavy. I can help you."

"Do not think to do so. You are my master's beloved. He would have my head if you should lift a finger. I shall return." Aram went to seek Mrs. Bagshot, who would probably tack a pound or three to their bill.

"My master's beloved," Laurette whispered. Once it had been so. But it would be too much to hope that it would ever be true again.

Chapter 4

Laurette spent the entire carriage ride composing a letter to Sadie in her head. There was no point Laurette's trying to conceal her circumstances—Sadie was and always had been much more than Laurette's maid-of-all-work. Sadie was the one who told *her*, for goodness' sake, that she was expecting Con's child. Laurette had been too numb from losing him to pay attention to sleep or food or her courses. Once Con was travelling on his honeymoon, Laurette had been too sick to get out of bed, but her illness was not mere heartbreak.

Laurette pushed that unhappy time from her mind. Her parents had been disappointed and disgusted with her, but had at least benefitted from Mr. Berryman's bribery. She had managed to sort her life out since, and would have been fine had her idiot brother not become Conover's mark.

Aram sat opposite, his dark eyes closed. Laurette supposed he had seen a great many odd things travelling and working for Con. For all she knew, she was just one of many women Aram escorted into Con's harem.

She cleared her throat. "How much farther, sir?" How ridiculous that she did not know her own address.

He looked at her then, his eyes nearly as dark as Con's, but kinder. "It is but a few minutes more, my lady."

There was no point in correcting him and pointing out she was plain Miss Vincent. Con's house must be far from the squalid neighborhood of Charlie's boarding house. She would be glad to get the scent of sweat and cabbage out of her nostrils.

"Have you seen the house?"

"Indeed, my lady. My wife and I have been making it ready for you these past weeks. It is our fervent wish, and my master's also, that you will find everything to your liking."

Weeks! How sure Con had been of her desperation. She had only written to him five days ago. She swallowed her irritation. It was not Aram's fault he was employed by a ruthless bastard.

"I am sure I will like it as well as I can under the circumstances." She bit her lip. "I am to be the only resident, am I not?" How humiliating it would be to discover some other poor woman—or women—in the Marquess of Conover's debt.

Rumors had swirled around Con the moment he stepped upon British soil.

It was whispered he had gone completely native during his exile. His inky hair fell to his shoulders, and his skin was still bronzed though he'd been under the gray skies of England for more than a year. She had seen a tattoo of the Jerusalem Cross on his shoulder in the flickering firelight last night, however, so perhaps it was not true that he was a Musselman with a penchant for multiple wives.

"Indeed, yes. Apart from the staff, who will do all they can in their power to serve you."

"Are you a Christian, Mr. Aram?" she blurted.

He inclined his head. "My Lord Conover was most ashamed to discover I have more knowledge of the Bible than he does. My wife Nadia is a Christian also." He smiled. "She would not tolerate sharing my affection, I can assure you. Nadia is a gentle creature, but most intemperate when provoked."

"I'll do my best to be unprovoking." Laurette sighed. It would be difficult. She felt jailed already.

The carriage came to a gradual stop in front of a narrow

house with a simple façade. It resembled its neighbors in the short street, distinguished only by its deep blue door and fanciful crescent moon and stars doorknocker. For a moment Laurette was reminded of her spangled dress, but surely Con had forgotten about it long ago. Aram helped her alight and escorted her to the door. It was opened at once by a slender dark-skinned woman. Her sober dress was enlivened by a fichu threaded with beads and golden strands.

"You see, my lady, my beautiful wife. Can you imagine she is mother to six sons? Nadia, may I present Miss Vincent."

Nadia curtseyed. "Do not worry, mistress. My boys are not within. We would have not a moment's peace. The marquess has been so good to find them all employment at his estates."

"Don't you miss them?" The words escaped. She was already being too familiar. Laurette wanted to bite her tongue.

Nadia waved a slender hand. "They are busy. Two have family of own now. The marquess is generous and gives time for us to be together several times a year. Is not just any man who would have sponsored so many of us to come to your country. We owe great deal. Come, let me show through house." She turned to Aram and spoke hurriedly in a language Laurette did not understand.

Nadia's mastery of English was not as accomplished as her husband's. Laurette stood uncertainly in the hall while they conversed. Its walls were hung with dark red figured paper. Gleaming brass sconces were set at intervals. A porcelain bowl of feathered tulips stood on a round table in the center of the marble floor. A long corridor to the right of the stairs led to the back of the house, with a door that was open to a walled garden. She could see a profusion of greenery and flowers, and watched as a yellow bird flew by with a chirrup.

"Please," she said to Nadia, "may I see the garden first?"

"Of course. It is only just finished. My lord moved heaven and earth for it to be so." The woman grinned at her own joke.

Once outside, Laurette could see that the plants had been selected for their vibrant colors and glossy leaves. Young trees had been placed where someday they might provide shade. Laurette would no longer be here, of course. The path beneath her feet was laid in blue and white ceramic tile, swept clean of any debris. A fountain gurgled at the end, a group of yellow birds frisking on its lip. A low stone bench ran along the back wall. The bricks were stacked high and tipped with ornate metal spikes, guaranteeing peace and privacy. But the upper windows of the neighboring houses had a perfectly good view of Laurette standing in her threadbare dress, a sparrow amongst the exotic trappings of the marquess's pocket garden.

"It's very beautiful."

"My lord designed it himself, you know. For you. So you will not miss country."

The sound of the water splashing was lulling, much as the ripple of the River Piddle at home had been. Con was very clever.

"How long has the marquess owned this property?"

Nadia's eyes darted away to the busy birds.

"Please tell me," Laurette said softly.

"It has been not quite a year."

Laurette had refused Con a year ago. He'd had almost a year to create this love nest and bring her brother to ruin. Perhaps she was not even its first occupant.

Laurette chewed the inside of her cheek to keep from exploding in anger in front of this woman. It was clear Con could do no wrong in her eyes. He'd imported her family and provided them all with opportunities. It was not always easy to be a Christian in the Holy Land.

"My lord has excellent taste. Before we came to England, he refurbished villa in Greece. His many friends visited. Sir William Bankes? The famous Lord Byron? But should anything displease you, my lord will have it changed." Nadia snapped her fingers.

"Just like that."

Laurette wondered where Con had picked up his aesthetic sense. Ryland Grove had been a comfortable shambles until Marianna redecorated. Laurette followed Nadia back into the house and the ground floor parlor. While not as ornate as Conover House, the room was nevertheless filled with beautiful objects and lush color. The walls were midnight blue silk, the carved woodwork dark. Landscapes of distinctly un-English places hung between the long windows. Laurette examined them and looked out into the street. Con's carriage had disappeared.

"The dining room." Nadia slid the mahogany pocket doors open. The table was already set for one, silver and crystal shining in the bright morning light. "You must give me list of favorite foods to guide Cook. My master most anxious that your palate be pleased."

Laurette had not eaten really well since Marianna died. Their weekly luncheons had been enjoyed for both the fare and the company. Laurette's stomach flipped at the thought of rich food and sauces. She and Sadie had subsisted on very little and her loose gown was proof.

They climbed the carpeted stairs to the first story. Another reception room faced the street. It was a bold emerald green, the wood floors polished and covered with several shimmering rugs. The furniture was velvet, tufted and low. Embroidered pillows were scattered on the sofas and floor. The hammered brass lamps and vases might have come from some Eastern bazaar. Whereas the parlor downstairs was colorful yet conventional, this space was more foreign. Laurette wondered that Con had not tented the walls and was not surprised to find a palm tree growing in a painted pot.

"Your bedchamber is down hall. Three more rooms above. Aram and I and your maid occupy two of them. Cook and her helper are below near kitchen. Is small staff, but you will not lift finger."

Laurette needed to contact her own small staff. Convincing Sadie to stay put in Dorset would require every ounce of Laurette's persuasive ability.

"Is there writing paper in my room? I need to write home."

"But of course. The maid Martine is unpacking your things, but all else in readiness."

The door to her new bedroom was open. Within a very young maid was looking comically dismayed at Laurette's belongings. She quickly curtseyed and plastered a smile on her pretty face.

"Martine, this is your mistress, Miss Vincent."

"Bonjour, Mademoiselle." Martine twisted her hands. "Milord has ordered you the new clothes. Should I perhaps place these things in storage?"

Laurette did not speak. Could not. Her room literally took her breath away. All was gold within, from the ornate posts on the bed to the satin coverlet to the fringe and braid on the pillows. The walls were pale yellow stippled with a darker abstract design. An enormous mirror framed in gilt hung on the ceiling over the bed, with matching mirrors lining the walls. Laurette felt a blush from the tips of her toes to her ears, imagining her body—and Con's—reflected in the dazzling glass. An intricately carved wooden screen stood a few feet in front of the single French window, allowing sunlight to filter through. Laurette slipped behind a panel and gazed through sheer drapes to the garden below. She turned the curved brass handle and stepped onto the iron-railed balcony. It was just large enough for a pot of flowers and a delicate chair. She saw a dark-haired woman in the garden beyond the wall and darted back indoors.

"There's someone next door."

"Do not worry, Miss Vincent. You are safe here. Jane Street is famously exclusive. The neighborhood is most discreet."

In other words, the woman she had seen was another man's mistress. Each little jewel box of a house in this area sheltered a woman just like herself, fallen from grace. No wonder the street was deserted in daylight. There were no nurses with children in prams or morning callers, just women inside, waiting. Even buried in the country, she'd heard about Jane Street. Con must have a fortune indeed to afford a house on it.

"Mademoiselle, your baggages? What do you desire for me to do?"

"I don't care." Laurette walked past the marble fireplace. Vases of yellow roses and lilies were lined up against yet another mirror. "The dressing room is through this door?"

"A bathing room," Nadia said proudly. They entered a room almost half the size of the bedroom. A bank of cupboards was open to display an enormous number of gowns. A tall dresser, a tub, and a screened commode were tucked into corners. A small fireplace, equally bedecked with roses and lilies, was burning brightly despite the spring sunshine. There was a thick Oriental carpet here as well, and a divan with a pile of books stacked neatly at one end.

"He's thought of everything, hasn't he?" Laurette would be lying if she said she was not impressed, but the house did not make her like her position any better. Con of all people should know how it felt to be bought and bullied.

She remembered what he looked like the first time she saw him after he came back from London. After he'd been bought and bullied himself.

She'd set off at the back of her garden along the river path and crossed the little stone footbridge to Conover land. She hadn't gone far when she caught sight of Con striding across the field. He was shirtless, his chest and hair damp with sweat.

He was beautiful. Like a statue in a museum. Not that she'd ever been to a museum, but she occasionally read her father's outdated London papers. No Greek statue could compete with Con.

"Con!" *She smiled and waved gaily.*

There was no return smile, but he walked steadily toward her.

"What are you doing here, Laurette?" *He pulled a kerchief from his back pocket and mopped his face and neck. He then quickly untied the shirt from his waist and pulled it over his head as though she hadn't seen him stripped bare a hundred times.*

"I hoped to see you. At our tree. Is that where you were going?"

Con shook his head. "No. I was walking the fields. It's time for the first cut hay. Past time, really. I don't know why my Uncle Ryland hasn't thought to do so."

Laurette grinned and waved away a bee. "You've gone from scholar to farmer! How was your trip?"

"Beastly." *Con eased himself down in the tall grass. He shaded his eyes with an arm.* "Go home, Laurie. I'm not fit for company."

"Pooh." *She settled down next to him.* "I hope you're not too tired to dance with me tonight."

"I made you a promise."

His voice sounded odd. His eyes were closed against the high sun. Laurette pulled the rose from her hair, peeled a petal off and dropped it onto his face. He batted it away impatiently.

"Really. Just leave me alone. I've got to think."

She plucked at his damp shirt, wishing she could pull it off again. "I can help you think!"

"Not this time." *He sat up.* "Laurette, the estate is in ruins. Mr. Berryman owns me lock, stock and barrel. I've got to find a way to turn a bit of a profit this summer, or—" *He clamped his mouth shut.*

"Or what?" *Hesitantly, Laurette traced his lips with a fin-*

gertip, but he made no move to open them. Instead, he seized her hand and pulled her up from the ground with him.

"I've got to go. Talk to my bailiff if he's not too drunk to listen. I'll see you tonight."

He squeezed her hand and dropped it. She watched him stride away, shirttails flapping. Something was terribly wrong, something her beautiful blue dress might not be enough to fix tonight. Laurette scattered the rest of the rose petals in the flattened grass and waited until Con was gone from sight before heading back. Feeling deflated, she went to gather more rosebuds for her bath.

How far she'd come since then. Now she had a little army to wait on her, and there were enough rosebuds for a week's worth of baths on the mantel alone.

"Martine, leave us please." Nadia spoke a few instructions in French. Laurette recognized "hot water." She'd had a bath just this morning, a tepid, grudging one to be sure, but she was perfectly clean. She raised an eyebrow to Nadia. Hard what to think of her as. More than a maid. Housekeeper, perhaps. Minder.

"My lord wishes you to be prepared for him tonight. I shall assist you with that," Nadia said vaguely. "You find everything you need to write letter in escritoire in bedroom. Aram will have my lord frank it."

And read it, too, I'll wager, Laurette thought.

She reentered her golden bower and made for the delicate desk. Its legs were gilt in the French style, its writing surface elaborate marquetry, little cubbies holding fine weight paper, ivory and silver pens. Several silver-topped crystal pots of ink stood at the ready. Laurette sat in the spindly chair, which was more comfortable than it appeared. Taking a deep breath, she penned a few lines to Sadie, enclosing some of the money Con had given her this morning. She would speak to him later about repairs to Vincent Lodge. Sadie could oversee all of that, and put about that Laurette was remaining in London with friends until the renovations were complete.

Con had mentioned taking her about in society. Surely he didn't mean it. People would know at once she was his mistress. He could not expect her to forfeit the reputation she'd worked a dozen years to reclaim. Her friendship with Marianna had done much to squelch the rumors that she and Con had been young lovers before his marriage. Talk had died down when she was seen frequently in the company of his son James. Surely the marchioness would not permit such a thing from a rival.

And Laurette was known in London. Of course she did not move in the highest circles of the ton, but her brief time with her grandmother after Beatrix was born had won her a few acquaintances.

England was a very small country with very big gossips. If she was seen on Con's arm—if her residence in this house was revealed—on the most notorious street in London—all would know that the virtuous Miss Vincent was nothing but a courtesan on "Courtesan Court."

Six months of confinement. Six months of staying indoors, or in the perfect little patch of garden, spied upon by other ladybirds. She would go mad.

"My lady." Nadia stood at the door to the dressing room. Laurette had been aware of the quiet commotion next door as Nadia and Martine arranged for her bath. "All is in readiness. If you will please to follow me."

There was steel behind the woman's subservient words, as if she expected Laurette to balk. There was no point in taking out her animosity toward Con on his servant. Laurette left her letter and went into the dressing room. Fragrant water was steaming in the bathtub, but it was not quite full. The divan had been draped with several large towels. A bowl and pestle were on the low brass table, along with shears, a razor, powder and other instruments Laurette didn't recognize. A small brazier with a copper pot atop it had been set before the now-roaring fireplace. The room was close and warm, too warm for a fine spring day. Laurette felt slightly faint.

"My lord wishes you to be removed of your hair."

Involuntarily, Laurette's hand shot up to the messy coiled knot on her head.

"No, no. Not there. My English is perhaps not so good."

"You speak better French than I do," Laurette smiled, willing her nervousness to go away. She had only the most cursory acquaintance with the language. Her education, such as it was, had been provided tuition-free by the eccentric Trumbull sisters in Lower Conover. The spinsters ran a sort of haphazard dame school in their parlor, something that Laurette was now doing in their stead for the village girls. The Trumbulls had a dislike of all things French, even the Empire style of clothing. They gave up their wide skirts and hoops only when they were buried in their narrow coffins.

Nadia blushed beneath her brown cheeks. "I speak French, Arabic and English. A smattering now of Greek. Some Turkish, too. It was necessary to get on. Come, I will help you remove your gown."

Laurette stood still as a doll as Nadia divested her of her clothing. She was glad her unmentionables were of the finest quality at least. And yet to be paid for, Con would know she had made a concerted effort for last night's meeting when he marked the date on her tradesman's bill. Had she known he'd already purchased her a complete wardrobe, she might have spared herself the trouble of the fitting with the rigorous Madame Lamarche. Laurette had not needed a new corset to complete their business deal.

She was down to her threadbare old shift. "Raise your arms, my lady."

She was blushing now.

"You must remove all your clothing. My lord was specific. The hair under your arms, on your legs, your nether curls—

all must disappear. I shall pluck your eyebrows a little, too. Should you wish privacy in your bath later, I will of course oblige."

Laurette untied her shift and pulled it off over her head, disarranging her bundle of hair. Nadia plucked the pins out and ran her fingers through the waves. "A sultan would have paid a high price for you, my lady. Such lovely, thick yellow hair. Please to lie down."

Laurette would not have to be in Arabia to know *purdah*. She was locked up right here in London, under the thumb of a wicked Englishman. But she obeyed, closing her eyes. Nadia covered her with a sheet. She heard the stirring of the pot, smelled lemon and sugar boiling. Con had been startling bare himself last night in the shadows. His member had seemed somehow larger now that it was not nestled in black thatch.

She smiled. It was, she supposed, every man's dream to be bigger. She had no comparisons, but it seemed Con was big enough to begin with without resorting to this peculiar foreign custom.

"While the halawa cools, we shall begin to trim, my lady."

Nadia attacked her eyebrows first, then lifted the lower portion of the sheet and began to clip bits of golden fluff. Laurette soon felt a sticky warm ball rubbed onto her skin. She bit her lip from crying out in mortification. No one save Con, Sadie and the midwife who delivered Beatrix had ever touched her *there*.

No, that wasn't quite true. There had been times over her long years of celibacy when her tension was so great she had tried to replicate Con's touches. But her fantasies had brought her only frustration when the waves crested and she found herself alone in her childhood bedroom. A spinster. A mother with no child.

Nadia applied the same substance to her legs and beneath her arms as Laurette willed herself to be still.

"Now it must dry." The woman covered Laurette with another sheet that had been warmed by the fire. "You are comfortable, yes? Not chilled?"

Laurette nodded, much too embarrassed to speak. She had never been especially miss-ish, and had once flaunted her body. No more, apparently.

"Good. Martine and I can bring in the rest of the water. Do excuse us."

Laurette was alone, feeling an odd sensation everywhere the paste touched. But soon the warmth of the room and her exhaustion conspired to slip her into a light sleep.

"My lady," Nadia whispered.

Laurette opened her eyes.

"I am afraid the rest will not be so pleasant," Nadia apologized. She proceeded to gently scrape Laurette's skin, discarding the resin into a paper sack. Laurette felt like her body was being combed. Some areas required a razor, some stubborn hairs were tied with thread and pulled. She had half a mind to pull Con's long hair out by the roots tonight in retribution.

"There. It is done." Nadia helped her off the sofa and brought her to the standing mirror. Laurette's skin was flushed and rosy, and apparently freckled *everywhere*. "Beautiful, yes? Islam requires this purification, but even Christian women in the East practice the habit. It will become less difficult once your body adjusts to it. Do you wish me to stay and wash you?"

Laurette shook her head. Poor Nadia had seen quite enough of her every nook and cranny already. She would do the rest herself.

The water was deliciously hot. The round hammered brass table had been cleared of the implements of torture, and moved next to the tub, and now held pitchers of rinsing water and soap, creams and lotions. Laurette dipped her head back and relaxed.

This was one aspect of a mistress's life she could get used

to. To be pampered. For a time. It wouldn't do to become used to the luxury, but she would enjoy it while she could.

It helped to know that it was not Berryman money that funded her position. Con had done well for himself abroad and Marianna had tied up all her funds for her son. Con's estates had prospered in his absence and he had earned enough somewhere to assure they continued to do so.

He had returned to Lower Conover several times since he came back to England, but Laurette had managed to mostly avoid him. She knew he was still angry that she had not told him immediately about Beatrix.

It was not even dawn when he turned up at the Lodge. The wild knocking at the front door roused her from a deep sleep. Charlie! What else could he have gotten himself into?

But it was Con. He'd ridden all night from London, and the stink of horse and sweat was overwhelming. He clutched a crumpled letter in his fist, and his face was frightening.

"I understand we have a daughter, madam."

His voice was cold. Beyond cold. Arctic.

Laurette nodded stupidly, too surprised to speak.

"You didn't think to tell me? I've been back two months!"

"It's none of your concern."

Con towered over her in fury."None of my concern! I am her father!"

"No, you aren't. And I am not her mother. Go away, Con. There is nothing you can do. She's well-provided for, and happy. Think of one of your children, for once, instead of your own selfish needs. I absolutely forbid you to see her."

She shut the door in his face and threw the bolt, waiting for the banging.

But it did not come.

He had his revenge now. She had vastly underestimated his determination to bring her low, using Charlie's stupidity to bind her to him in this wretched bargain.

Her body might belong to Con, but she would not let him into her heart again.

She washed and rinsed her hair with the rose-spiced soap, then slathered herself with suds, scrubbing away the leftovers of her treatment. Once she was clean, she wrapped herself in a bath sheet and padded to the closets.

Con had outdone himself, despite his wicked threat to keep her unclothed. Each dress was more elegant than the next, the fabrics bright yet tasteful. The contents of the dresser revealed exquisite underthings. She was relieved she was not to be dressed as a harem girl, veiled and belly bared. But the nightgowns were so sheer she might as well be naked. There was not a virtuous white muslin night rail in sight.

Brushing the tangles from her hair, she sat on the divan and stared into the fire. Her stomach rumbled, and she was reminded of the place setting in the dining room. Six months was not so very long. It was time to dress and begin her new life.

Chapter 5

She had lunched alone. She had dined alone. Some of the food had been unfamiliar but delicious, course after course. Laurette couldn't possibly do justice to all of it by herself, and so had gone downstairs to the kitchens after the evening meal to compliment Cook and request modifications to her menu.

Cook was Qalhata, an extraordinary Nubian woman with a golden hoop in her nose. Laurette faltered at first, disconcerted by both the nose ring and the glacial stare the woman gave her when she invaded the kitchen. The kitchen boy, perhaps Qalhata's son, scampered off at once, not a good sign. Laurette explained she didn't eat everything, not because it wasn't tasty, but that she simply didn't have so big an appetite.

The woman had looked her up and down, then broke into a wide white smile. "Master says to fatten you up. You'll eat. Real men don't like skinny women."

Qalhata herself was very shapely, wrapped in a brown garment that tied at the shoulder, exposing a bare arm adorned with a stack of gold bangles. Over her costume she had tied a spotless white apron. Her hair was ruthlessly braided but uncovered. Having spoken her piece, she continued to lay out the food for the staff and called out to the boy in what Laurette presumed to be the Nubian language. Laurette did not wish to delay their meal and hurried back upstairs.

What an odd household she lived in. So many languages, so many skin colors. Martine helped her undress and she dismissed her for the night. She had no idea when Con would turn up, but inserted one of the vinegar-soaked sponges she had brought with her to London. There was a limited supply. She had not expected to find herself installed as Con's mistress, although she had been prepared for one night in his arms. She would have to ask Nadia to help her with further preventative measures.

Laurette had donned the most modest of the nightgowns folded into her drawer, but modest was a relative term. The garment was a sheer cap-sleeved violet-blue silk, scooped low. The matching robe was frivolously pointless, as it was cut even lower in front and tied with a grosgrain ribbon, easily untied. Con would have her out of it all in seconds flat.

She had time this afternoon to review their contract. Laurette knew the document itself was worthless. It had not been witnessed, and could, if it came to it, prove to be signed under coercion. Blackmail was such an ugly word, but Laurette had been its victim before. Threats from Con's uncle and his father-in-law had kept her silent and her family fed. She doubted Con would use her shaky signature to expose her to the world, but she could not be sure. He had changed in the dozen years they'd been apart. She wasn't sure if she knew him at all.

Sitting at her dressing table, she picked up a silver-backed brush and ran it through her hair. She saw Con in the mirror before she ever heard him enter. He had removed his boots somewhere and was barefoot on the golden carpet.

She willed herself to be cool. "Good evening, my lord."

"Laurette."

His voice was raspy, as though he had spoken to no one all day. Laurette wondered how he had spent his day now that his plans for her had come to fruition. He needn't dwell on ruining her feckless brother any longer—that must free up the hours. It was clear how he would spend his night—he was already untying his cravat.

"I trust your accommodations are satisfactory?"

"Everything is very nice."

Con made a face at her bland choice of words. Too bad. She was not going to sing the praises of her gilded cage.

"Here. Let me."

Con was behind her, still in his shirt and breeches. He took the hairbrush from her hand. She leaned back as he drew it through her waves. An involuntary sigh escaped her. The bristles of the brush caressed her scalp as one large warm hand rested on her shoulder.

There was silence in the room save for the crackle of the fire in the hearth Martine had lit. Although it was spring, it seemed Con was always cold. Laurette had been overwarm all last night, and it was not due solely to the searing heat of Con's passion. Nadia had explained on the tour of the house that the marquess insisted upon a fire in all the rooms of his townhouse. In this house, Laurette was to do as she pleased during the day, but her bedchamber would be prepared for Con's comfort at night.

She met his eyes in the mirror. They were black with need. Odd how the nakedness of his desire stirred her fury. Laurette should be gratified he still found her attractive after all these years, but instead she was resentful. Why couldn't he find some other woman to torment? He was free now, and they never would be able to mend the rift between them. He should find some innocent girl fresh from the schoolroom to lighten his heart.

A girl like she used to be.

She watched his hand leave her shoulder and dip into the bodice of her gown, palming her left breast and brushing her nipple with his roughened thumb. He continued to watch her face for signs of her arousal, but Laurette was determined to disappoint him. She had been foolish last night, foolish several times, but she had a tighter rein upon her senses now.

He placed the brush back on the dressing table and sought her other breast. Laurette closed her eyes as she felt the pressure of his fingertips.

"No. Watch me. Watch us."

He had freed her breasts from the twilight silk, lifting them, peaking her nipples between his thumb and forefinger. He rolled his finger on the tips, turning her nipples wine-dark. He bent, his breath hot against her throat, and bit her, never stopping the caressing of her breasts.

"Attempting vampirism, my lord?"

Con chuckled. "I shall taste every inch of you tonight. Last night, I was far too hasty."

It was true. He had fallen upon her like a starved man, and she, God help her, had been just as greedy. She watched as he pulled the ribbon on the robe and pushed down both garments, until she was exposed from the waist up, her arms bound against her. Despite the warmth of the room, a wave of gooseflesh warred with her freckles. She held her hands tight in her lap as he traced a pattern into her skin with a fingertip.

"Rise." There was a pause. "Please." He must have heard how imperious he sounded.

Laurette stumbled up from the bench, her knees traitorously weak. He tugged the silk away until she stood in a purple puddle.

"Turn so I may see you."

He expelled a breath, and Laurette fought the urge to cover herself. His eyes were fastened on her perfumed, pink-skinned mound. His hand cupped her and she was branded by his heat.

"I trust this did not cause you any discomfort?"

Laurette shook her head, unable to speak. Once she had

been so at ease with him, had been brazen enough to tear her clothes off in the sunshine. Now this shadowed room was still not dark enough to conceal her hesitation.

"What are you thinking, Laurie?"

"You have gotten what you wanted."

"Have I?" He slipped a long finger into her passage and drew her closer. There had been no resistance. She was shamefully wet for him. Her nipples grazed against the fine linen of his shirt. She steadied herself, putting her hands on his shoulders.

He kissed her, his finger meanwhile working a slow, slippery glide inside her. His thumb left the surface of her newly-shorn skin and slid down to her swollen clitoris. She buckled but he held her fast against him, his left hand splayed across her back. She could feel his touch everywhere, little licks of fire on his tongue, his palm, his fingers. Even the silk at her feet added to the sensation. She had meant not to kiss him back, not make it easy for him, not fist the cambric of his shirt, not cry into his mouth as the first rapturous wave stiffened her spine and loosened her tears. She would never last six months with him. And worse, when the six months were up, how could she last the rest of her life without him?

She shook in his arms as he held her. "Don't cry. I cannot bear to see you unhappy." He kissed the top of her head as though she were a child, picked her up, and carried her to the golden bed. She kept her eyes shut as he moved about the room. When she opened them, he was gone.

Con cursed his boots in the hallway. What he'd give for a pair of sandals to slip on so he might disappear into the night. He stuffed his tie in his pocket and shrugged into his coat, closing the blue door behind him with a soft thud. All along the short street, houses were alight with candles and muffled laughter. Other men were enjoying the perfumed mystery of their mistresses, while he strode along with a raging hard-on and his walking stick at the ready. He had dismissed his driver, planning to spend the night in Laurette's arms, so was destined to walk home if he could not summon a hack.

It was not so very late. He had delayed going to her as long as he could. She had not been asleep, after all, just brushing her glorious gilt hair. If only he'd come an hour or two later, he might have slipped into her from behind as she was curled up in her bed. It might have seemed a dream.

Instead, he had made her cry.

He'd been a fool to think the finery of her new household could make up for the dozen years they had lost. But she had looked undeniably exquisite in the golden room.

As exquisite as their first time.

Every word of good-bye he had prepared himself to say to her vanished. Sunlight filtered through the leaves onto Laurette's pale skin so she gleamed like polished ivory. Her eyes were huge, imploring. They had been careful so far, bringing each other to welcome madness, but Con had dreamed of sinking within her and losing himself for years. His nights at university had not been spent with maids or whores, but in his solitary bed, his hand working feverishly as he imagined Laurette beneath him. He watched her fingers play with the pink ribbon at the end of her pigtail. When her wavy hair cascaded down her back, he reached for her face.

She turned to kiss his palm. He brushed the tears away and set his mouth to hers. Her hands tugged at the fabric of his shirt, the placket of his breeches. He had no time to strip himself bare but fell back with her on the quilt, stroking down her body to her center. She was drenched for him. He was undeniably hard for her. He tucked her under him and plunged into her heat, catching her sob with a kiss.

He was clumsy. Selfish. But the barrier seemed easily broken. He stilled with difficulty so she could adjust to the size of him, but he thought he would never adjust to the glory of her. She was hot and tight around him, so tight. He had never felt such exquisite agony. He curbed his need to spill instantly, placing a hand between them to her apex. He thought of the taste of her there, a mistake, as he felt himself lose control. He kissed her, their tongues dancing in concert with his fingers. She raised her hips and he thrust deeper.

He couldn't last, awkward ox that he was. He wanted to make the first time good for her. It had to be their last; he couldn't allow her to hope for a future with him. And he was robbing her of hers. Bad enough they'd spent the past year wrapped in a haze of lust. He'd now taken her virginity. There would be consequences. There could even be a child. . . .

He felt his seed begin to erupt and tried mightily to withdraw from her honeyed walls. Her long white legs were locked around him as she lifted her body in response, trapping him within. Her inner spasms imprinted their joy along his shaft as he emptied himself in a series of mindless spurts. He was swept clean of any thought but the purity of Laurette, her thousand freckles, the smile on her well-kissed lips, the gilt of her eyelashes as they fluttered on her flushed cheeks. He buried his face in her amber hair and breathed roses. The press of his shirt button on her bare breast had left an imperfect circle and he sealed the mark with his tongue. She moaned beneath him as he slipped reluctantly away.

He buttoned himself, wrestled a handkerchief out of his pocket and wiped the evidence of their lovemaking from Laurette's glistening cleft. There wasn't so much blood as he'd feared. She lay still as he stroked her tenderly.

"I'm sorry if I hurt you," he said, his voice tight. He couldn't promise it would be better next time. There could not be a next time.

"It was perfect."

"Liar."

"I did not please you?" She looked up at him, hesitant. She resembled a chastened child, just missing the braids he used to tease.

He had used her like an untried youth, he thought in disgust. Which he was, but now he had injured her feelings as well.

"You are perfect. I will always love you. Thank you for this gift." He brought her up to him and kissed her forehead.

Laurette reached for her shift. "I have been trying to give it to you for ages." For a moment she disappeared under the wrinkled muslin. "And you have given me a present, too. I am a woman now, Con!" she cried, leaping up off the blanket and spinning in her bare feet in the grass, "Do I look different? Can you tell?" She bent over him, her blue eyes dancing, her breasts brushing against him.

He closed his eyes to the blaze of her innocence. He felt his cock shift and stiffen. The church bells rang in the distance. Service had not even started yet.

They had an hour. Con, who had meant to be honorable and honest, cupped both her covered breasts. Her pink nipples peaked under the thin fabric.

"I'm not sure," he said slowly. "Perhaps the first time didn't take, Laurie. You look much the same."

She fell to her knees in front of him. "We will do better this time."

"I will do better." He tore at his clothes, kicking off his boots. He would touch her everywhere, so her skin would remember him when they parted. But he would withdraw before he climaxed. He could do that much at least.

But he had not. Con's anger at himself for the past and the present pushed his steps, and he was home before Aram's son Nicolas could open the front door.

"My lord, we did not expect you back tonight."

"Change of plans. Go on to bed, Nico. Or wherever you want." Nico was engaging in a mild flirtation with a parlormaid next door. Now that his parents were not on the property to oversee his courtship, the boy had a new swagger to his step. Con only hoped the girl would not lose her position.

He already had quite enough of Aram's dependents on his hands.

He was too restless for bed, and could not go out again to face anyone at his club. Con belonged simply because his grandfather had. He had never sought to be part of London society, but he had a child—children—to think of now. Most of the men he knew had seen and done nothing to merit their blithe confidence.

He entered his library and poured himself a brandy, even after the year home still not entirely acclimated to its taste. As a youth, he'd been too poor to drink it; as a young man travelling where liquor was forbidden, he had not missed it. As a peer of the realm, it was nearly his duty to imbibe. It was the only thing that had gotten him through his interview last night with Laurette. When he touched the cut glass of the decanter, he had really wanted to touch her.

He settled himself in his plush leather chair, pulling open the bottom drawer of his desk. Ironic that as a student he'd been loath to write anything at all, and now he was in the middle of his memoirs detailing the ten years he'd spent abroad. He wrote not for himself but for his son, to whom he owed an explanation for having been absent during his young life. Although Con had written faithfully to the child even when pen and paper were hard to come by and delivery was uncertain at best, his letters were not enough. He was still a stranger to James and James was an enigma to him.

Oh, the boy was polite; Marianna had raised him to have beautiful manners. There was no whiff of the City to Viscount James Horace Ryland. Con knew James was capable of a great deal of mischief, if the reports of his schoolmasters were anything to go by, but their encounters as father and son thus far had been punctiliously correct, bland if not downright dull. James held himself aloof, his cool blue eyes assessing Con's every good intention.

Con was already on his way back to England from his self-imposed exile when news reached him of his wife's death. It was very clear that James thought this effort was too little too late. But how could Con have imagined that Marianna would die before her fortieth birthday? She had not been ill—and then she was, suddenly.

He had found all the letters he had written to James amongst her papers. It was these bundles of parchment that jogged his memory for the book. Marianna had saved each one, and from the looks of them they had been read and reread. He owed his wife something for keeping him alive to James.

By the time he arrived on English soil, Marianna had been buried at All Saints next to her father for weeks, and he had mostly managed his confusion and anger. He set the renovation of Ryland Grove in train, arranging for his warehouse to be emptied of some of its treasures, and went to London to be nearer to his son, and to transform Conover House to his taste as well. It was hypocritical for him to observe a year of mourning, so he had summoned Laurette and asked her to marry him. Stunned when she said no, he couldn't imagine why she refused. He hadn't known about Beatrix then.

When Berryman's business associate Foster finally gave him Marianna's letter revealing that he'd not only abandoned a son but a daughter, Con had made a hash of it all and confronted Laurette. All the years of repressed emotion blossomed to the surface again—his feelings of being impotent, betrayed, manipulated. For every mile he rode, his fury mounted. He had been so angry, mostly at himself. But then he began to see a way to get Laurette to change her mind.

The fact that he knew neither of his children well shamed him. He'd had no choice with Beatrix; that was all Berryman business. But he'd walked away—no, *run* away from his son and heir. The book was his feeble attempt to rectify part of the past.

He assembled the manuscript and letters on the desktop.

He once found school a bore and the papers his uncle waved before his face baffling. Who could imagine the Mad Marquess working on his memoirs when he could be making merry with his mistress? He almost chuckled. It would do to keep his sense of humor, rusty as it was.

One day she'd not be crying in his arms but laughing with joy. In the meantime, he'd continue his celibacy, and revisit his journey to Tunis and the ruins of Carthage nearby. Not in person, of course. He'd not leave England again without Laurette and his son and daughter. But tonight he would reread the letter he had written to James describing the walled seventeenth-century medina.

He turned up the lamp and held the worn letter in his hand, ruefully realizing that the little boy he'd written to probably had no interest in the shadowed winding streets scented with incense and spices, the multilingual merchants hawking everything from live chickens to exquisite silver that he'd described so vividly. James was not much more than five or six when Con had written the letter.

But Con could almost taste the strong bitter coffee he had shared with his traveling companions, or hear the mournful call to prayer at the Great Mosque. In his mind's eye he saw the blue-and-white hillside houses of Sidi Bou Said perched over the Gulf of Tunis outside the city. The shore had reminded him of the water that surrounded his own island and connected him to so many different countries. These reflections would be meaningless for James even now. But surely his son would be interested in the exploits of the Phoenicians, and Dido, and Hannibal as he invaded Italy with his elephants, so Con set to describing Carthage and inserting a bit of a history lesson in his manuscript. After some consideration, he decided it would be ghoulish to mention the hundreds of graves where small children had been sacrificed to the gods and then buried. That horror would be best left to the real history books.

Con worked late into the night, pausing only to toss more

fuel into the fire. When his hand was tired and his mind empty, he put himself to bed. He'd try his luck with Laurette again tomorrow. He was probably the only man in London who kept a mistress for her own pleasure, not his. But like his memoirs for James, the little house was a temple to his love for Laurette, and it was just the beginning.

Chapter 6

Laurette heard the front door close and shot out of bed. Con had *left* her? She gazed down at her flushed freckled body, then went to the dresser. Martine had reluctantly folded Laurette's ancient nightgown amongst the newer fripperies. Laurette pulled it over her head and paced her room. Con had *left* her, left her with an aching inside so deep even he would not be able to fill it. It wasn't just his body she craved, but the friendship they'd shared so long ago.

But they were different people now. He'd had experiences that were completely alien to her. Laurette imagined him a pasha indolently sprawled on pillows, surrounded by skilled seductresses who fulfilled his every erotic need.

She would never sleep tonight; she was too enervated. Con had brought her to intense orgasm as she stood pliant to his probing tongue and fingers. She had wanted more. Last night had been a revelation—she was still a woman and Con was still the man who completed her.

Laurette wanted to slap some sense into her idiotically romantic head. What rubbish. She was independent, had been even when her poor parents were alive. She knew how to take care of herself. With Sadie's help, of course. They had made a quiet and satisfying life in Lower Conover, raising vegetables and ornery chickens, doing what they could for their neighbors. Laurette had found a vocation replacing the

Trumbull sisters, her parlor filled in the afternoons with village girls looking to improve their education. Her teaching methods were unorthodox but reasonably successful. And in each grubby little face she looked for a glimpse of what her daughter might be like, off in her fancy school.

Laurette sighed. She would write to Beatrix tonight, and James, too. She'd somehow explain her temporary new address. She was less than twenty-five miles from Eton College now—perhaps she could arrange a day to see James. She'd got just a glimpse of him in December, when Con was doing his damnedest to be Father Christmas and Lord Bountiful wrapped in one. It wasn't presents James needed from his father, and someday Laurette would tell Con so.

He seemed unaware that Laurette even knew James. And what would he say if she told him his wife had been her best friend?

She would not have believed such a thing possible twelve years ago.

On first meeting, Marianna reminded Laurette of an expensive porcelain doll, but there was something about her which looked sturdy, unbreakable. She would not break easily. A woman of lesser strength would never have befriended her husband's mistress.

It would be awkward to reveal the truth now, and disastrous if James guessed what was happening between his father and favorite honorary aunt. James would view it all as betrayal of the first order. He'd loved his mum and loathed his dad.

Laurette braided her hair over her shoulder and sat at the pretty desk, lighting another branch of candles. The letter to James flowed in fun. She was more careful with Beatrix, parsing each word to perfection. Tomorrow she'd send them off with Martine with some of her coins, avoiding Con's franking privileges.

She blew out the candles and padded over the thick carpet to her golden bed. The day had been both exhausting and exciting. She would have to find a balance for the next six months if she were not to expire at the end of it. Exit. Exhumation. Exhibit. Exhilaration. She removed the sponge and let it fall to the carpet. Exploration. Explanation. Extinction.

It was in this fashion she finally fell asleep.

Laurette had written her letters yesterday. Nothing much had transpired to fill up any other pages or any more hours to her day. She had awakened early as was her custom, although Caesar the rooster was not responsible, just the sound of a merry whistle somewhere in one of the back gardens. She doubted any of them were as lavishly appointed as hers. She had stretched on her little balcony and spied over the high walls. Martine had brought her breakfast and seemed to think she should be eating it in bed. Laurette disappointed her by sitting in a chair near the window screen, letting the morning breeze waft over her and the coddled eggs.

She bathed and dressed. She made the tour again of the house without Nadia, poking into every chest and under every fat cushion, admiring the art work and selecting a book. She settled for some hours in her green upstairs sitting room, unable to make sense of the words before her. Her mind kept wandering, wondering what Sadie would do when she got Laurette's letter. Wondering when Con would come. Feeling Con's skillful hands slide over her skin when he did.

When Nadia found her, she discovered she was now expected to come downstairs for lunch. Still full of breakfast, Laurette was tempted to decline. She thought of Qalhata's fierce face and set the book aside. The cook had evidently taken her words to heart, for the portions were fewer but the dishes more than delectable. She ate until she thought she'd burst.

The afternoon now stretched before her. There would be no afternoon callers or jaunts to the shops. There was no basket of mending she could muck up with her crooked stitches or vegetable plot to weed. But the day was fine, so she walked about in the garden, watching the bright yellow birds flit from branch to bush. The fountain burbled, the flowers exuded their fragrance, the sun braved the haze of the city to shine on her bench. Laurette sat in the square of warmth and gazed up at the windows next door, all discreetly laced and swagged in curtains. She wondered if the other mistresses were as bored as she. Perhaps she could form a kind of Mistresses' Union, where they might take tea together—or something stronger—and complain about their ennui. She let out a laugh.

"What is so amusing?"

Con walked toward her, looking every inch the marquess this afternoon. His bottle-green coat and buff breeches showed every muscle, the stock at his neck was blindingly white. A large emerald held it in place, glittering in the sunlight. If he wasn't careful, he'd invite every ambitious footpad in London to rob him. The stone alone could feed her and Sadie for years.

"Good afternoon, my lord. I was not expecting you until this evening."

"I wanted to see how you are getting on." Con sat down next to her. His thigh brushed hers and she resisted the impulse to push closer.

"I am, if you must know, dead bored."

Con raised an eyebrow.

"I'm used to activity, you know. Vincent Lodge takes a great deal of work, and then there are my pupils."

Both eyebrows were raised now.

"You, a teacher?"

"I am not stupid!" Laurette said hotly.

"No, of course you're not." Con took a hand and kissed her fingertips. Laurette sat up straighter even though Con kept hold of her hand.

"The Trumbull sisters passed away, you know. A few afternoons a week some of the village girls come to visit. We—we discuss things." She trembled as Con rubbed her palm, each circle tingling to her toes.

"So." Con's face was dark. "You are now the genteel impoverished spinster the children seek for improvement."

"It is not so bad," Laurette whispered.

"I can give you more."

Laurette tugged her hand away. "You cannot make me feel useful here. I imagine Qalhata would slice my throat if I invaded her kitchen."

"My dear, I imagine any cook worth his or her salt would absolutely forbid you from ever entering their domain," Con drawled.

Laurette's cheeks grew hot. She had once been fairly hopeless in domestic matters. "I've improved. I had to." She thought of the scores of burnt meals that she and Sadie had eaten stoically until Sadie had taken her very firmly in hand. With a few simple ingredients and subdued ambition, one could manage well enough.

"No doubt." Con stood up abruptly. "If you wish to feel useful, let us go upstairs."

"*Now?*" Laurette gulped.

"Now."

She rose from the bench, smoothing her skirts. Any hope of flattering candlelight was burned away by the steady sunshine. Years ago she had eagerly exposed every inch of herself to him in daylight, but she had been a foolish girl. Now it seemed she was equally foolish, for her heart raced with anticipation. Her pale lashes fluttered to her cheeks.

"As you wish."

She could feel his eyes upon her as he followed her through the tiled garden path and into the house. He caught her when she tripped on the stairs, then wound his arm around her as they climbed up together, his hand firm upon her waist. He said nothing, but the pressure of his fingertips implied control. She belonged to him, and he would not let her fall.

Or get away.

Her bed was already turned down and a fire crackled in the hearth. Nadia or Martine must have had instructions upon his arrival. The house was silent. Laurette wondered if the servants had been dismissed for the afternoon, or imprisoned in their rooms. It was mortifying to know they were aware of her role as Con's mistress. She was determined to be very quiet in Con's arms, as silent as the house itself.

She stood still as he unhooked and unlaced her down to her rosette-ribboned garters and stockings. Despite the fire, gooseflesh washed over her. Con held her shoulders and stepped back, as though eyeing his purchase. She raised her chin.

Years ago she would have teased and asked if he liked what he saw. She might have spun about the room unpinning her hair and darting beyond his reach. He would have caught her—she would have made sure of it—and they would have collapsed on the bed in a burst of laughter. They would have fallen over each other in a frenzy, hasty with their kisses and awkward embraces. Judging from Con's performance two nights ago, he'd acquired considerably more finesse.

Con had been her first and only lover. Anything she'd attempted in her lonely spinster's bed to recapture their summer had been a pale imitation at best. This man stood before her now, dark and distant, although they were separated by the mere length of his arms. She had no idea what was going through his mind apart from the fact his buff breeches revealed a rampant erection. But a man didn't have to think to feel lust. Any naked woman clad in silk stockings might produce the same effect.

Con expelled a breath. "It's your turn to undress me."

Laurette nodded. She went directly for the emerald pin in his cravat, tugging it out of the starched fabric with some difficulty. It was heavy in her hand. "This is rather vulgar for daylight, isn't it, my lord?"

"They expect it of me. The Mad Marquess, you know. You should see the ruby." Con's face twisted in a smile. "I am allowed eccentricity."

"You have grown like your grandfather." Laurette placed the stickpin on her dressing table. How odd that she did not feel self-conscious walking about bare as a baby, or nearly so.

"I suppose I have, save I've learned to make money rather than just spend it." He started to pull the tie from his throat but she stopped him.

"I am to undress you, remember?"

"Get on with it, then."

She looked up at him. "Am I going too slowly?" She touched a silver button on his waistcoat with the tip of one finger.

"Yes, damn it."

He'd growled at her. Interesting. She removed the length of stock, wrapping the fabric around one hand, then laid it next to his emerald.

His jacket was next, molded to his muscular torso. She unpeeled it and padded on her stocking feet over to a chair, draping it neatly on the back. Con clenched his jaw, looking as if he wanted her to toss each garment to kingdom come, but said nothing.

Beautiful silver buttons, each embossed with the Conover crest. They were worth something, too. She bent down and pushed them through the buttonholes, watching as Con's manhood twitched below.

He had much less mastery of himself today than he did when she had so ignominiously fallen on her bottom removing his boots. That slow torture with his fingertip must have nearly killed him. As it had almost killed her. She licked her lips and heard him groan.

"Enough." He pushed her away and tore off the rest of his clothes, kicking off his boots with near violence. His vest, his shirt, his breeches, his boots were now strewn around the room. She tried to pick up his billowing white linen shirt from the floor and was rewarded by a smart tap to her backside.

"Leave it. Come to bed."

Laurette rubbed her bottom. "You are spanking me?"

"I shall do worse, unless—"

He must have heard how he sounded, seen Laurette's shock at his words and actions.

He enveloped her in his arms. "Forgive me, Laurie. I would never hurt you," he whispered. She rested against his chest, puzzled at the change in his mood. His hands fumbled with her hairpins and she felt the mass of amber fall down her back.

No. He would never raise a hand to her. His hurt was of a different nature, and one she had been battering against for a dozen years. But Con had been as much a victim as she, she supposed.

She shook her head, impatient with herself. It was time to stop making excuses for him. He had married and fathered a child, then left to indulge his senses in all manner of foreign debauchment. She had seen the brass hookah in his bedchamber, after all. Whether he used flavored tobacco or hashish, it was still a disturbing habit. Even an English gentleman's cheroot was a nasty thing to her way of thinking.

She sat at the edge of the bed, untied the garter and turned her stocking down with deliberate precision. She imagined she could hear Con's heart thudding in his chest as he stood naked just inches from her. She took her time with the other leg, enjoying his apparent torture. But then, he resorted to his earlier roughness. Pushing her backward on the bed, he covered her with his weight, his kiss feral and demanding, his hands whirling through her hair and over her skin, his thumb grazing her nipples, his cock with one abrupt thrust embedded within her. It wasn't rape. Her body had been ready from the moment he entered the garden, even if her mind had not been.

But she had inserted no sponge. There had been no time. She tried to scramble back but he held her in an iron grip, gloving himself within her so completely that she soon ceased thinking of consequences, and only felt each quicksilver connection between their flesh. He pushed deeper, she rose to meet him, tumbling together atop the fine linens in a sensual dance that made her dizzy. At the start, it was a country dance with little finesse but much enthusiasm. But he had found his rhythm, and she followed where he led.

Con had taught her to dance, had been her first partner. In everything. She had given him her heart as a child and he still held it. She opened her eyes to watch Con's exquisitely agonized face over her. His teeth bit into the fullness of his lower lip, his eyes crinkled shut, his brow beaded with drops of perspiration. His wild dark hair hung damp at his shoulders. His arms were corded with muscle and braced on either side of her. The cross tattoo leaped before her eyes. Con was *working*. She was the center of all his attention and glad of it.

He owned her. Bought her for ten thousand pounds. She should be fighting him off, but couldn't. He possessed her body without the house on Jane Street or the clothes or the servants. She had given up trying to keep him at bay. A time would come when their arrangement was over, so she'd best let him have his way. It was as good for her as it was for him. Maybe better. She'd lived in solitary confinement. While he'd spent his seed all across Europe and Asia like some pagan god, she was on her knees praying for redemption. Release. But she might as well have her own tattoo of *Conover* inked upon her breast.

She gazed down her body where they joined. They were waltzing now, his thick cock gliding out of her slowly and just as slowly reentering. She ached when he withdrew, but the anticipation of his return caused her skin to prickle.

Laurette breathed in the air around them, vestiges of sex

and sweat, his sandalwood cologne, her rosewater, the fragrant wood burning too hot in the hearth, the beeswax applied so earnestly by one of the servants, the exotic garden through the open window all blending in a heady single scent.

She was in a haze of languid sensation. It was as if she had been shut off for years in grayness, and suddenly the world was in bloom inside her, bursting through her pores and straight into Con. As if he knew, he opened his eyes and watched her as she came apart. He smiled down at her, triumphant.

But he was not done, and neither, it seemed, was she. When she thought he could not coax one more frisson of joy from her, he amazed and exhausted her, his hips grinding and rolling her to welcome oblivion. She was spinning from his dance, lightheaded, love struck. He bent to kiss her sobs away, swallow up her soul. She felt him stiffen and flood her. She couldn't be sorry.

They lay in each other's arms, the heat of the room and their exertions coating them in slippery sweat. Con took a corner of the sheet and wiped her face, throat and under each tender breast. Laurette stared at the mirror over the bed, wondering who the flushed and foolish wanton was who smiled back at her.

"I went blind, you know." Con's voice was still ragged. "I thought I'd never see you again."

Laurette looked at him in alarm. He hadn't meant to tell her. It was old news. He and his school friend William John Bankes had traveled a hazardous, indeed deadly, journey to see the sites of ancient civilization, and he had been struck with blindness. Ophthalmia was the medical term, but whatever one called it, it was devilishly painful and could cause permanent loss of sight if he was unlucky.

Of course, Con had felt unlucky for some time. Perhaps it was his failure to fully appreciate the wonders he had seen these past eight years that Allah decided he needed a lesson in humility. The fact that Con thought now in terms of Allah might have been an additional reason his Christian God had punished him, but Con had found it more convenient to pay lip service to the god of the people surrounding him.

William had clung to his English gentleman's mode of dress, but Con had succumbed to the robes of the natives. With his black hair and eyes and skin tanned from hours under the scorching sun, it had not been so very difficult to assimilate. He had even grown a most ferocious mustache and beard worthy of any self-respecting bey. His appearance, and the Arabic in which he was now nearly fluent, had been useful. Any way he could avoid getting his throat slit was worth pursuing. He was one Frank who did not feel his time on earth was quite up. He planned to return to England and meet his son. If he could not see him, it would be a pity. He remembered one of the last days of his darkness, but would not bore Laurette with the story.

He lay in his tent, his man Aram alternately soaking cloths in strong tea and honey to combat the infection. Bankes had suffered the same affliction before Con had joined him in his journey, and had made a complete recovery, taking notes and sketching the magnificent ruins in meticulous detail. Con was hopeful he would do the same. He was expected to be a guide of sorts in the Holy Land at the end of Bankes' expedition, having landed there early in his own exile. There had been too many idle Englishmen in southern Europe when he first ran away, and then the forces of war had made life distinctly uncomfortable. Con had left behind his own idleness and served England in a very unofficial capacity. For a boy who had difficulty declining Latin verbs, he suddenly discovered he had a facility for spoken languages and the ability to blend in to indigenous populations. He was not a blond, blue-eyed Englishman afraid to get dirty or be devious.

But he found he had a distaste for death. His trek east had been meant to find some meaning in his life, some peace, but he could not say that he had been successful except under the influence of a bubbling hookah.

He knew some might wonder about his manhood. His association with William would raise some knowing eyebrows in Britain, although William was being most discreet in lands where his bisexuality would condemn him to death. But Con had touched no woman—or man—since that last day with Laurette, despite frequent opportunities. His celibacy had not prevented him from being an observer, however, and he was privy now to all manner of ways humans intoxicated themselves with desire.

He heard a rustling and the thud of boots on the hard-packed mud. Con pulled off the linen strips over his eyes and sat up.

"Don't disturb yourself. It is only I."

Con heard William's drawling voice and smiled. "Have you come to feed me roasted locusts again?"

"Lord, no! Although I've had worse. Some think they taste like shrimp. I'll not forget the first time I saw them swarm, like a storm of black snow. I wish you had come with us today. I stood on the roof of the most magnificent temple. Climbed all the way to the top."

"Buried in sand, was it? Did Finati give you a leg up, or did you hop?"

William snorted. "Sharp as ever. Wish we'd had time to do a bit of digging, but it's time to move on. We'll make for the boat tomorrow. Will you be up to it?"

"I suppose I'll have to be. Just lash me to the camel."

"We'll stay at the convent in Cairo until you're well again."

"If I ever am." Con disliked the complaint in his voice, but his hours of solitude in camp while the party explored had given him too much time to feel sorry for himself.

"It could be worse—you could be covered with buboes. Although they might be an improvement over the beard. You are quite horrifying, you know."

Con laughed. "It is just that you are so pretty." He ran a hand through his beard, wondering if Laurette would even recognize him. Whether he would recognize himself in the mirror, should his sight be restored.

Laurette still looked stricken. But he could see her, praise Allah, Jesus and Venus. "What happened?"

Con flipped on his back and held her hand. He watched their reflection above in the mirror on the ceiling. They looked as if they were the original sinners, Adam and Eve, fresh from a romp in the Garden. But somewhere the serpent was sure to be lurking.

"Ophthalmia. I was in Egypt with William. It's quite a common disease there, but some never recover. I got lucky."

"Indeed. I imagine you had more than your share of adventures."

Con shrugged. "I had to make something of my life." He turned to her. "Be *useful*, if you will. I even dabbled a bit for King and country until I got shot."

"*What?*"

"It was when I first ran off. To Spain first, and then Portugal."

"You were in the army?"

"Not officially. William was there and knew Wellington. One thing led to another."

"I see," said Laurette, who looked as if she didn't see at all.

"It wasn't for very long. Just long enough." He rubbed a shoulder. The puckering beneath his tattoo reminded him of those times on a daily basis. "It's just a scratch. I'm no hero, believe me."

"You should tell James," she blurted. She had a point—it might go some way explaining to his son why he had deserted him.

Con laughed. "He wouldn't stay in the room long enough to listen."

"Then write."

"You have found me out. I'm actually writing a book for him."

Laurette sat up, covering herself with the damp sheet. "A book! You?"

"Now who thinks who is stupid?"

"Who thinks *whom*," Laurette corrected.

"I'm not sure about that. We shall have to find a grammarian to settle the issue." He teased her back with a fingertip.

"But you were never bookish."

"True. The tutors my uncle hired saw to that," Con said, kissing the pulse at her wrist.

For a second Con thought Laurette was softening, and then the serpent slithered into the Garden. *Stop now,* the serpent warned her. *He is trying to charm you again as he did when he first sucked a thorn out of your finger when you were seven. You are seven no longer, my girl, you're not even seven and twenty.*

She withdrew, wrapping the sheet more decisively around herself. "If we are done, my lord? I am sure you have important matters to attend to."

Con frowned. "I cannot think of one more important than you. Than us."

Laurette slid off the bed, fashioning the sheet like a Roman toga. "I must bathe. We were careless just now. I shouldn't want to provide you with another bastard child."

Con bit his tongue. There was nothing he would like better than to have Laurette filled with his child, watch them both grow round in domestic bliss. But the possibility of marriage to him was obviously not on her mind. He had led her to believe the very impossibility of it when he maneuvered her into his bed two nights ago.

He would not spend on the sheets or wear anything that was a barrier between her honeyed heat and his rod. He had waited too long. "You are right, of course," he said carelessly. "I assume you know how to prevent such an occurrence? I will not deny my own pleasure as I once did."

"For all the good it did," Laurette said shortly. "I shall speak to Nadia. You'll have nothing to worry about."

Damn. So it was to be sponges like last night. If she had not wept in his arms, he would have pulled at the string and flooded her with seed. He did not think she had been protected when she came to him two nights ago. He had not been certain she would agree to this hellish bargain himself. He got up and gathered his clothes.

He was in the middle of tying his neckcloth when she asked, "I will be safe, will I not? You have not got one of those gentleman's diseases that will affect me in any way? Something else you picked up on your travels?"

He turned to her, his lips twitching. "I assure you, Laurette, I am as pure as the driven snow."

She snorted. For a moment he thought he'd tell her everything—that he'd been celibate over a decade and found it to be no hardship—but she'd think him a fool. But no one could think he was a greater fool than he himself.

"I shall dine with you tomorrow night. At nine. Tell Qalhata. She knows what I like."

"Yes, my lord. We all do."

She didn't have a clue, but someday—someday, she would know everything.

Chapter 7

Nine o'clock was hours and hours away. Laurette hardly knew how she was going to pass the time until then.

It was not that she was so desperate to see Con again. Or take him into her bed and into her body. Certainly not. She didn't care that he'd sit opposite from her eating fish in a sauce seasoned with an herbal medley she had never heard of—*zaatar*—peas, beans, rice, mixed green salad, and the strange flat bread that Qalhata baked daily. The meal was, Qalhata and Nadia assured her, his favorite. Laurette had been hoping for lamb with mint sauce but would be presented that tomorrow at luncheon as a consolation offering. She was still too full of breakfast and lunch to even dream of dinner, whatever it might taste like. In fact, it was clear to her that she needed to go upstairs and unlace her stays, perhaps remove them altogether. She might undress. Take a nap, although she was too enervated to be sleepy.

This was now the third full day of her mistressness. Was that even a word? Mistressship? Too many of the letter 's'. Mistresshood? Whatever it was, it was not agreeing with her. She was not used to idleness or isolation. She could not fault Con for the appointments in the house or the well-stocked bookshelves. But there was simply not a thing for her to do besides read and stare at her freckled reflection in the mirrors positioned throughout the house. Even the garden was immaculately weed-free, each dying petal plucked by unseen hands so all was tidy and serene.

She paced her room in irritation, finally summoning Martine to help her change from her new day dress to one she had brought with her. Laurette had not thought it too shabby when she packed it, but in comparison to the clothes in her dressing room, it was a horror. . . . Good. She felt horrible. At least the old blue gown was hers, sewn by Sadie too many years ago to recollect. Laurette would wear it as she paced the upstairs parlor, paced the downstairs parlor, paced the garden. Con had given her no instructions about leaving the house, but with her luck she was likely to bump into an acquaintance and all would be lost.

It was one thing to lie by letter, quite another to look into someone's face and dissemble. Laurette had never been good at telling fibs, although she had left out a great deal of narration growing up. And look where that had gotten her. At one time she had thought it fortunate that her parents were so distracted with drink and gambling that she was able to slip off with Con. Now she saw the error of that. She had a secret child and a wastrel brother, and she was waiting for her Machiavellian lover.

If she had been a young lady properly brought-up by proper parents, she would know how to occupy the useless hours that stretched ahead of her. She might be tatting or playing the pianoforte that was below. Embroidering a slipper or arranging flowers.

Well. Perhaps she could arrange flowers. The ones on the mantle were a bit droopy. At home she would gather up buds and put them in clean jars. Here she had crystal vases. The garden was in riotous bloom.

She stopped in the kitchen for shears, drawn by the rapid chatter. Both Nadia and Qalhata were engrossed in tonight's supper preparations, the scrubbed table laden with all manner of foodstuffs. They seemed alarmed to see her. After a lengthy discussion as to why she didn't ring for someone,

Nadia needed to be convinced that Laurette was capable of cutting her own flowers and being entrusted with a pair of scissors. As if, Laurette thought grumpily, wielding scissors could cut her way out of her current predicament and get her back home.

"I shan't stab you with them," Laurette mumbled, exasperated. "I shan't stab myself, I swear. It hasn't come to that."

"Oh! My lady!" Nadia rubbed her hands nervously on her pinafore. "Are you not happy here?"

"No. Yes," she said, catching the dismay on Nadia's face. Laurette sat down on a kitchen chair. She reached across the table for a green bean and snapped it in half, tossing it into the earthenware bowl. "You are all very kind. It's just that—" Laurette looked at the women. They would think her fit for Bedlam if she complained she wanted to work. They were both up before dawn and until well after dark creating this blissful artificial life for her. To them just one day of utter idleness would seem like a dream. Even though the house was small, Laurette knew how much effort it involved. She snapped another bean.

"I live in the country, you see. I keep chickens and a garden. I'm just not used to inactivity. Waiting."

"Ah." Nadia sliced a cucumber for the salad, so thin it was transparent. "You are lonely. I have neglected you."

"No, no. I don't expect you to entertain me. I'll get used to this. It's not for so very long."

Nadia and Qalhata exchanged a look.

"I'm sorry. I'm keeping you from your tasks. If you will just tell me where the shears are?"

Qalhata rose from the table and went to the Welsh dresser. "You may keep these for your flowers. I have other pairs."

Laurette took the shiny scissors. They were as new as the rest of the furnishings of the house. "Thank you. I won't trouble you again."

"Is no trouble. We are here for you, my lady."

The long kitchen opened to both the street and the garden

by way of stone steps. Laurette shut the door behind her, because she was certain she did not want to hear the women's comments on her spoiled behavior, if they even discussed her in a language she could understand. Everyone in this house was far more capable linguistically than she. Perhaps she could get them to teach her to speak something other than English and very fractured French.

Ah, how ridiculous. As if they would have time for that. She was the only one with time on her hands. Laurette had seen even the young kitchen boy doing chores upstairs. Aram seemed to divide his job between Con's townhouse and hers, but he was here in the evening to sleep beside his wife.

Laurette glanced at the little timepiece she had pinned to the bodice of her dress. The watch had been her mother's, and it told her she was but fifteen minutes closer to Con's arrival since the last time she looked. She sat down on the stone bench. The back wall of the garden was bathed in sunlight, its bricks warm against her back. Deep blue and white tiles that matched the footpath were set at random intervals into the brick. Con must have rebuilt the rear wall, for it seemed twice as thick as her neighbors', which she spied from her balcony. Thick glossy ivy climbed along the side walls, too well-established to have been created for her benefit.

She closed her eyes, listening to the water splash. She should rise and cut some flowers. Roses, or perhaps something unfamiliar. The garden was full of plants she could not identify, all growing miraculously in the city in their square beds. Her garden-mad mother would have loved it, but would have been shocked to find her daughter installed as Con's mistress.

And then she heard the groan.

It was actually more of a growl, coming from the next garden. There was a yip, a shriek, and the thud and crash of objects being thrown to the ground. Breakable objects from the sound of them splattering on the hard surface.

"There!" came a satisfied feminine voice. "That will show the bastard!"

Laurette moved to the ivy-covered wall, her curiosity quite overcoming her lassitude. "I say, is something wrong? Are you all right?"

"I am now. Who's there?"

"Your neighbor." She thought about giving a false name, but she never had been a happy liar. She'd lied too much. "I'm Laurette."

"How do you do? I'm called Charlotte. When he remembers my name," the woman mumbled darkly.

How very odd this was to talk to a disembodied voice. It was like something out of a play. A farce, for certain. "Are you going as mad as I am?" Laurette asked, throwing all caution to the wind. What did it matter if a courtesan thought she was crazy?

"It depends how mad you are. I have always thought of myself as being the steady and sensible one, but lately I have reason to doubt. This is rather absurd, talking through the wall. There's a wooden door, you know. I imagine it's covered over on your side, but I'll rattle the knob."

"There is?" Laurette stuck her hand through the ivy, searching at the sound. She found the door handle and pulled, but it wouldn't budge. "I'll have to cut back some of the ivy. Hold on." She hacked away with Qalhata's shears until she saw the seam in the wall. She then pulled on the door with all her might. The hinges creaked, and the door opened, but not wide enough for her neighbor to pass through.

"Bother. Can you push?"

"I can try." Charlotte giggled. "If this doesn't work, I suppose I could always come round and ring your doorbell."

"That would take all the adventure out of the endeavor. Here, I'll pull, you push."

The rusted hinges cried out as if they were in dire pain, but at last Charlotte squeezed through the space. Laurette gave her a wide grin, the kind of smile the Cobb sisters had said showed far too many teeth.

This Charlotte did not look like anybody's mistress. She was pretty enough—quite beautiful, really—but could have passed as a governess. For one thing she was old, at least Laurette's age. Her dark hair was covered by a little starched cap, something Laurette wouldn't have worn in a thousand years no matter how firmly on the shelf she was. Charlotte's ugly gray dress was buttoned up to her chin and she wore a fussy fichu around her neck. The woman might as well have "Virgin Spinster" tattooed to her brow.

But of course, that couldn't be.

"Oh! How absolutely lovely this is!" Charlotte gazed around the garden. "I watched them put it in from my bedroom window, you know. They all worked like fiends. Even Lord Conover dug right in." She lowered her voice. "He removed his shirt. You are a lucky woman indeed."

Laurette snorted. "He *is* a fiend."

"Oh, my dear, you've no idea of a true fiend. Sir Michael Xavier Bayard's portrait is penciled in right next to the word in Dr. Johnson's Dictionary."

"Then why—" Laurette stopped herself. "Forgive me. It's none of my business." She certainly would not want to divulge her own particular history with Con.

Charlotte sat on the stone bench and sunned herself. "It's rather a long, sordid story. Let's just say that one's family obligates one to do things that are distasteful if not downright repugnant."

"Exactly so," Laurette agreed, wondering how her scapegrace brother was fairing with the old turtle Dr. Griffin. "How long have you been in residence?"

"Long enough. It seems like I've been here forever. An eternity. But at least I won't have to look at the damn cherubs any longer."

"Pardon?"

"You heard my little fit. The smashing and the screaming. I just broke what are no doubt valuable but entirely vulgar little naked statues that belonged to my predecessor. There are still more in my bedchamber. Would you like to help me finish off the rest?"

Perhaps Charlotte *was* mad, and it had taken her very little time to get there. What would Laurette be like in a month? She shuddered to think.

"Truly, I am not usually so bloodthirsty, not that there's any blood in gilded plaster, mind you. But when you see them, you'll understand. Come." Charlotte stood up and extended a hand.

"I'm not sure—they might miss me," Laurette said lamely, tilting her head toward the house. For all she knew, this Charlotte would take it into her head to smash *her*.

"Oh, you poor dear. I've heard all about the strange and mysterious Conover. I saw the *tattoo*. Is he keeping you a prisoner, then?"

"No! Not really."

"Well then. Come along."

Laurette swallowed. This prim and proper courtesan was exactly like a governess who brooked no dissent. After one longing look at her kitchen door for a last-minute rescue, Laurette slipped through the ivy covered door and into the next garden. It too was pretty in its way, but nothing as magical as the garden Con had created for her. And he *had* created it. Charlotte said she watched him do so in his half-naked state.

Charlotte looped an arm through Laurette's. "Is he stingy, your Lord Conover? Your dress looks seasons old."

Laurette laughed. "That's because it is. It's my own. I assure you, Conover has filled my closets. I just chose not to be tempted today."

"Very wise. I myself will not wear what Sir Michael has bought. It drives him to distraction." They ducked into the kitchen entryway. The room was clean and empty. "My servants are out, otherwise I would not have had the courage to kill all the little angels. Follow me."

They moved through the house. The layout was identical to Laurette's, although the furnishings were far more traditional. Except for the paintings. Laurette felt her face go hot to see so much exposed canvas flesh. There were naked women on every single wall, doing everything a naked woman could think to do and other things besides. Still, the brushwork was very fine, and Laurette said so.

"None of them are my doing. Sir Michael is quite the connoisseur. He has excellent taste in all things, except mistresses. What that Helena did to the bedroom—well, you shall see for yourself."

They mounted the stairs and entered Charlotte's bedroom. Laurette stopped in her tracks, speechless.

"You understand, don't you. How can one possibly live in a room where so many plaster eyes are on one? And they look far from innocent. See their leering little faces?" Charlotte poked a dimpled cheek and shivered.

"I'll help you. A pity we cannot borrow a wheelbarrow and roll them down the stairs."

"I daresay the exercise will do us good, but I'm grateful you're here. We'll have the job done in half the time." Charlotte gathered up her skirt and started depositing the little Cupids in the fold. Laurette thought her new friend had lovely legs.

It was a heady experience, dropping the plaster angels on their heads and shattering them. Laurette could not remember when she had more fun. After she was covered in dust and a healthy sheen of perspiration, she left Charlotte wielding a broom to push the evidence under the bushes, and returned home. They would take tea together tomorrow.

She ordered a necessary bath and killed off another hour waiting for Con. Tomorrow she would entertain the rather entertaining Charlotte Fallon and kill more time. Six months was not so very long. She could—she must—do this.

Hours later she sat opposite Con, who had fallen upon his plate as though he were a starving man and now was biting into a flaky, honey-laced pastry. He had dispensed with English clothing for the evening and arrived in a long embroidered jacket and loose trousers. His black hair was unbound, falling past his shoulders. Laurette thought he looked as a pirate might, if pirates washed and played at dress-up. No wonder her neighbor thought he was mad; he looked the part tonight. The gangly boy from Dorset was gone, and a thorough rogue was in his place. She took judicious sips of wine and passed up dessert, too nervous about what was to come.

It had taken all her resolve not to weep with happiness after they had sex. She must continue to remind herself that their relationship was based on lust alone, that their friendship—and love—had ended long ago. She was simply a woman whose animal nature, long dormant, responded to a male of the species. It was not a sin or a failure of principal, but a simple fact of life.

"A penny for your thoughts." Con gazed across the table, his eyes so very dark.

She was not going to flatter him telling him her thoughts had been about sex.

With him. Over him. Under him. Con moving lazily behind her, pressing her against his clean, warm body, his fingers tracing down her belly to the apex of her womanhood.

His fingers were amazing appendages. All ten of them had impressed her with their amorous indecency. Laurette looked at her own ordinary hands that had never managed to be skillful at much of anything. "I do not wish to bore you, my lord."

He sighed and dropped his fork to the plate with an ungentlemanly clatter. "Please, I beg of you. This 'my lord' business is offensive to me. We have known each other twenty-five years. You once called me by my given name."

Desmond. Des, most of the time, as they explored his estate, gorging on early strawberries and dropping half-dressed into the Piddle from their tree to swim and wash away their berry-stained mouths.

But one day an eleven-year-old Desmond Ryland had come to her door, a black armband pinned to the sleeve of his best jacket. His grandfather had died on one of his endless trips, leaving Des in the care of his horrible uncle. How she had wanted to giggle when he'd looked at her so earnestly and said, "You must call me Conover now."

Her maid Sadie had said then that her old friend had risen in consequence and that Laurette should behave when next she saw him. "A marquess won't have time for the likes of you," Sadie had sniffed in a vain attempt to make her charge see the light of ladylike ways.

Sadie had been wrong.

"Twenty-four. My great-aunt invited us to live at the Lodge with her when I was five. But I shall do just as you say, call you what you will. I am yours to command for the next five months and twenty-seven days."

Con's lips quirked. "I have a mathematical prodigy on my hands, I see. I don't remember you being so precise, Laurie."

"I never had reason to be before." In fact, she'd been so careless with numbers she'd been two months gone with child before she realized. It was Sadie who reminded her. This time, the maid was right.

"I suppose you teach maths to your little girls."

For a moment her breath hitched. Then she realized Con was talking about her informal lessons with the village children at the Lodge. She nodded. "I do. A woman needs to have useful skills to get on. I learned that the hard way."

Laurette had been thoroughly undomestic and undereducated as a girl. Why would she want to sit indoors with a stuffy book when Con was home from school and waiting for her at the riverbank? She'd had plenty of time over the years to correct those flaws, living with Sadie in the country, and tallying up Charlie's expenses and excesses. She knew quite a lot now, and one thing she knew was that the man opposite was trouble.

"I am so very sorry, Laurie," he said quietly. "If I could change the past, I would."

She rolled her eyes. "What's done is done. Let us not become maudlin, my lord. Conover," she corrected.

"Con."

It was she who'd shortened his name, because Conover clearly belonged to his dead grandfather. "As you wish." She placed her linen napkin on the table and rose. "Enjoy your brandy, and smoke a cheroot if you must. I shall await you upstairs."

Almost six months more of waiting upstairs. What would her pupils do without her? Run wild, like she did.

She was wild no more. Now it seemed she was a tamed pet, fed, brushed, dressed in finery, and at the mercy of her owner. She was Con's mistress, in the same unequal position as every other poor girl on Jane Street. Laurette wished she had a cherub to smash, right on Con's dark head.

Con watched her walk away from the table, her back stiff with pride. She was no doubt on her way to insert one of those dratted sponges—and he couldn't stop her. Ah, well. He had time. Five months and twenty-seven days, if she was counting correctly. He pictured her calendar with a big black X through each day.

Con sat in isolated splendor in the dining room. He raised a brow when Aram entered.

"Is all well?"

"I believe so. But Nadia tells me my lady met the woman next door today."

Con frowned. It wouldn't do to have Laurette revealed as his mistress before he made her his wife. The next Marchioness of Conover would have trouble enough getting on in society being married to the Mad Marquess. "Who is she?"

Aram shrugged. "You know the house belongs to Sir Michael Bayard. He has kept several women there. This latest is the sister of the woman who was there before."

Con wrinkled his nose in distaste.

"It is not what you think," Aram continued hurriedly. "There was a mix-up of some sort. A mistake. Martine has the story from the maid Irene, but as her English is not perfect—" He shrugged again.

"Keep an eye on the situation for me. I cannot have Miss Vincent's reputation jeopardized by some jade."

"Very good, my lord." Aram bowed and slipped from the room as silently as he had entered.

Damn. He didn't want Laurette to feel imprisoned, but surely she couldn't befriend a whore on this street.

Whore was probably far too strong a word. This little enclave catered to the most exclusive courtesans in London. One did not reach the pinnacle of that profession without having exceptional beauty, skill and intelligence. A man would pay only so much for an ordinary fuck. The costly women here were beneath no one except in the strictest sense. Assorted government ministers, lords whose patents dated to the Conquest, and captains of industry owned the dozen houses on the cul-de-sac, nicknamed "Courtesan Court."

It was a coup to remark casually that you were off to Jane Street. It meant you had the blunt for the house and the stunning woman within. Con had a devil of a time negotiating the price for his, long before his plan for Laurette had become clear. At the time he was so gripped with despair by her refusal to marry him that he'd talked himself into setting up a mistress. If he couldn't marry Laurette, he'd marry no one. Surely a decade of celibacy was enough to atone for his youthful mistakes.

But in the end, the house remained empty. He'd interviewed likely candidates and come away cold to the bone. His hand and his memories would serve as well until he found a way to win Laurette back.

And then her idiot brother came to town and provided the key to his conquest. Con drank the last of his port, brushing his long hair behind his ear. He was unfashionably shaggy but the style lent credence to his dangerous reputation. He wouldn't want it known that within, he was still a poor boy who had been stripped of his honor and forced into a marriage of convenience. Emasculated.

Heartbroken.

Ah. The melodrama was at full ebb. Con grimaced. Too much wine and too little women and song of late. That would be remedied in perhaps ten minutes, as soon as he stoppered the brandy and sought comfort in Laurette's arms. Of course the Greeks translated the concept of "wine, women and song" to "fire, women and the sea," a most worthy, if dangerous, substitute. The Turks called for "horse, woman and weapon," revealing their bloodthirsty side. Con wanted nothing less but peace between his mistress and himself. He was not likely to get it tonight, but the effort would be amusing.

He unhooked his coat as he climbed the stairs. He'd dispensed with a throat-clutching cravat, much to Nico's disgust. His young servant was becoming more English than King George IV. Con hoped soon to be far from the London heat of the summer, where cravats would be unnecessary. He had several plans in motion. None were ideal, but he would not let a few bumps in the road deter him from uniting his family.

Laurette had lit the lamps and sat up in the center of the bed, sinfully, gloriously naked. Her hair rippled down her back and over her breasts in a gilt river. A book remained between her hands and she did not look up at him as he entered the room. Her eyebrows were drawn into a V of concentration and she gave every impression that Con's arrival meant absolutely nothing to her.

Two could play at that game. He tossed his coat and shirt on a chair, yawning conspicuously. "Push over."

Laurette wiggled over an inch or two. Con dropped his trousers, sat on the edge of the mattress, and kicked off his soft shoes. He was in Turkish garb tonight, perhaps an affectation, but he was comfortable for the first time in an age. He slid under the covers and closed his eyes, wondering how soon he could commence snoring. He heard the turn of a page, then another. Either she was a fast reader or the book was deadly dull. Or she wasn't reading at all, but using the book as a prop to keep him at bay. He gave an experimental wuffle, then something between a deep breath and a frog in his throat.

Soon he was pacing the noises in a steady cadence. The book snapped shut and fell to the floor with a thud.

He felt Laurette leave the bed and soon the room was in total darkness. She got back in with more than necessary vigor and he snorked. It seemed he had quite a repertoire of sounds he could conjure. He sniffed, he sniffled, he snuffled. He was exceptionally proud of a drilling sound at the back of his throat that was bear-worthy. Laurette bounced on the bed as she turned, kicking him—quite deliberately, he thought— as she did so. He remained on his back, mouth open, nose whistling a snoring symphony.

"This is intolerable," Laurette muttered. Con replied with a great gasping breath and a flourishing twitch for good measure. He hoped it was too dark for her to see him smile.

He waited as long as he could, until her body ceased its impatient rolling and her breathing was even. To Con's way of thinking, it took an eternity. His cock was so stiff it might have passed for marble. If only she'd looked at him, she would have seen his ruse for what it was.

But he had dreamed of waking her from her own dreams, to find her warm in his bed. In his arms. He placed a hand upon a breast and felt her tingle of awareness.

He thumbed the nipple, feeling her peak and pucker. His lips suckled and his fingertips stroked below to her newly bare skin. She lay still at first, as if to deny that she was complicit in her seduction, but then his tongue traced the path of his hands until she shivered and touched his shoulder. He laved the center of her pleasure, the plump bit of flesh encircled by his mouth tasting like rose soap and sweetest sin. It was child's play to send her up far beyond any thought of sleep, her breathless cries and writhing body only increasing his desire.

He needed her, worshipped her now more than ever. Not a word was exchanged as he entered her tight, hot passage. Tonight time was suspended, each glide slow and thorough, each kiss deeper and more determined. Laurette seemed to melt into him, to yield, no trace of her stubborn pride left. She belonged to him.

They belonged to each other.

When it was over, he tucked her against him and fell into peace. His light snores this time were real, and were joined in a duet with the woman who was by his side at last.

Chapter 8

Laurette examined the tea table in the downstairs parlor. Despite the destructive streak of Miss Charlotte Fallon, she seemed to be a conventional woman who would be more comfortable here than the exotic emerald green reception room above. It was hard to picture buttoned-up Charlotte flopping down on the tufted divan or arranging her gray skirts on a shimmering floor pillow.

Everything Laurette saw before her was just as it should be at the finest homes and more—the white linen was bleached to blinding perfection and the silver service twinkled brightly against the deep blue of the walls. Qalhata and Nadia had filled the crystal cake stand with tiny, fragrant sweet morsels filled with dates, raisins and citrus peel. There were simpler bread-and-butter sandwiches and jam tarts. It looked as if there were enough to feed all the mistresses on the street and their protectors besides.

Which proved to be a good thing, for when Aram announced Miss Fallon she was not alone.

"Lady Christie, Miss Fallon," he said in his most stentorian tone.

Laurette swallowed. She had not expected Lady Anybody, and certainly not the bosomy cool-eyed redhead who entered the room on Charlotte's arm.

"Do forgive Charlie," she said immediately, sensing Laurette's discomfort. "I invited myself. Your arrival on the street in the Mad Marquess's house has caused quite the commotion, and when Charlie said she was coming to tea, I couldn't resist. I am Caroline Christie." She extended a gloved hand and pumped Laurette's with energy. Her gray eyes were bright with mischief and her round cheeks dimpled.

"How do you do, Lady Christie?" Laurette murmured.

"Please call me Caroline. The less we hear of my husband's name, the better." She settled herself on the settee and patted a pillow. Laurette didn't dare to sit anywhere else, while Charlotte smoothed down another dull gray dress's folds on a chair opposite.

Her neighbor really had the most dreadful clothes, and once again a spinster's cap was peeking out beneath an ugly straw bonnet. It was hard to fathom how anyone could mistake Charlotte Fallon for a woman of easy virtue—this Sir Michael must be a blind man.

There could not have been a greater contrast between the two arrivals. Charlotte looked ready to pass out temperance tracts or succor orphans to her tightly-laced bosom. Lady Christie was dressed at the height of fashion in a bronze silk dress, with a naughty feathered confection perched in her russet curls and a thick topaz-and-gold bracelet clasped around each gloved wrist. Bits of topaz winked from pins at her shoulders. Lady Christie was a dazzling, shiny creature.

"Stop gawking, Laurette. See, I told you you'd scare her, Caroline," Charlotte said, grinning. "Would you like me to pour? I'm quite used to Caroline by now. She's been a lifesaver."

Laurette bit a lip. Could it be Lady Christie was one of those reformers who took in fallen women? The woman didn't look the part, what with half her chest exposed, but appearances could be deceiving. Laurette herself did not credit that her aging, freckled self still attracted Con in the way his actions last night had certainly proved.

But he would not permit any more tea parties if wind of their situation breezed all around London. Con had not made good his threats to take her out in society. She was almost in purdah here on Jane Street.

As if she were a mind reader, Caroline patted her hand. "Don't worry, I shan't reveal a thing to any of our other neighbors. I can be discreet if I care to be."

Laurette was floored. "You *live* here on Jane Street?"

"Indeed I do. My husband bought my house five years ago when we separated. He thought to make a point, you see, to let me—and the world—know what he thought of me. But I find the street suits me very well."

"Caroline lives next door to me. One morning she heard me in my garden. I seem to be a noisy neighbor." Charlotte winked a blue eye at Laurette and passed a cup to Caroline.

"All men are beasts. I am sorry I missed the demolition of those deviant little angels. I should have enjoyed getting my hands around their scrawny golden necks."

"It *was* fun," Laurette bit into a pastry and waited to see where else this bizarre conversation would lead. For the next hour she was regaled with the history of each house on the street and the two women before her. Lady Christie was appallingly frank, and Laurette's head swam. She contributed very little to the conversation, but it was quite lively without her.

It seemed they both had sad tales to tell, but in her opinion, Laurette's was much more dismal. Neither one of them had been compelled to give up a child. A cold husband and an absent and absent-minded lover did not seem so very bad. It seemed that Charlotte was to be turned out of her house, but Caroline would still be reigning on the street, solving problems and writing about them in her naughty romance books. If Laurette was bored during her tenure as Con's mistress, Caroline had offered to loan her a complete set.

When her guests took their leave, the platters held just crumbs and crusts, and the thought of dinner was unwelcome. Con had told her this morning that he had business to attend to tonight and not to expect him until very late. Laurette would have to find something to do with her time, if only to digest her tea. She had learned, though, that Sophie Rydell at Number 4 hosted a card party for the neighbors every Wednesday afternoon, that Victorina Castellano at Number 12 was always good for full-bodied Spanish wine and a weep, and that Mignon Boucher at Number 7 had a green thumb and was most anxious to inspect Laurette's garden. She should avoid Lucy Dellamar in Number 9 because jewels, and small objets d'art had been known to disappear after her visits. Laurette had said, unthinking, that she had no jewels, and both Caroline and Charlotte had been shocked speechless.

It was, all in all, one of the oddest afternoons she had ever spent, but also one of the funniest. She had missed Marianna's clever chatter. Now she had two new friends, strange as they might be.

When Con roused her from sleep, she didn't think to protest but gave herself up to his wicked, wonderful ways.

Con looked at the dispatches on his desk. The plan to take Laurette and the children to his villa in Greece would have to be postponed. His contacts had promised war with the Turks was imminent, if not this year, then next. His best-laid plans once again stymied, he thought wryly. He had longed to take his family to Cliff's Edge, his whitewashed house perched over the brilliant blue of the Mediterranean. He had imagined the children scrambling up the stone steps that were cut into the rockface, and plucking the purple flowers that stubbornly sprouted between the cracks. He had wanted to share the air, the light, the food, the *life* with the woman he loved. Every effort he made to entice Laurette here in London was met with feigned indifference. He *knew* she still cared for him. Her body could not lie as well as her lips did.

He had discovered she was more willing when he roused her from slumber, as if she made no waking decision to join with him. She lost her stiffness and distance between her warm rumpled sheets and was a perfect physical match for him in every way. But he missed her conversation. Things were not easy between them when they were not entangled on the bed.

He leaned back in his leather chair, shifting in his seat. Just the thought of her made him hard. Laurette, on the other hand, had softened in the few weeks she had been his mistress. She had obediently eaten all the dishes Qalhata prepared and now was sleek and plumper, her sharp angles, if not her sharp tongue, a thing of the past. Enforced idleness had done her good, although she never ceased to rail at him that she was bored in her confinement. He had sent books, several of which had been thrown at his head. Her aim was nowhere near as accurate as it had been when she was a girl.

He remembered her long-ago offer, but she seemed to have forgotten it.

The July sun was blazing and brutal. Some said it was a sign from God at His displeasure at the sins of man. Even holy Gloucester Cathedral was struck by a fireball. Farmers dropped faint in their fields. Animals, babies and old people died. Thatch caught on fire and the River Piddle dried up to a trickle. What wasn't burnt brown first was pelted by hail and torrential rain afterward. Con's struggling crops were ruined, his tenants—and he himself—doomed to go hungry this winter. What was to become known as the Heat Wave of 1808 had far-reaching implications, the principal one for Con being that he had to marry. There was no point to de-

laying the inevitable. The notes were due, and only his title would pay them.

He couldn't avoid it any longer. His measures had proved hopeless. Pathetic. He was no farmer. If anything, finding fossils and broken shards of pottery on his land as he plowed and planted made him want to replicate the steps of his grandfather, off on a quest around the world. To be free of obligation and the baleful glances of his people.

And Laurette. She knew without his saying a word that their chance was turning to smoky mist. It had made her more desperate. Reckless. She had denied him nothing, had cried when he withdrew and spilled into a linen handkerchief. She was not thinking.

Someone had to think. There were times when Con thought his head would explode from thinking. His uncle was like a terrier, Mr. Berryman worse. Not a day went by without a veiled threat from one or the other. Miss Berryman was due any day and Con had yet to tell Laurette. He didn't know how he was going to.

He was a coward. A coward with a conscience. If he had none, he'd take his own life and skip the family plot at All Saints, crooked gravestones of Conovers and Rylands be damned. They'd done nothing for him but sink him into this pit of penury.

Con clapped a ragged hat on his head, to shade him from the inexorable sun, and set out for a walk to the ring of standing stones. That was certainly a misnomer; most of the stones remaining had toppled or sunk into the earth. He and Laurette had gone there as children, chanted silly spells, and waited for a Druidic presence to scare them away. Nothing had happened, but the spot still felt powerful. He had worn a trail across the fields lately, seeking he knew not what.

She was there before him, as if she knew he was in need. Naked as a pagan sacrifice, her clothes abandoned on the dry grasses, her skin flushed pink in the heat. Wordlessly, she *knelt on a blanket, her eyes as blue as the scorching sky above.*

He couldn't refuse her. Her lips circled his cock, drawing him deep into her own warmth. He leaned against a stone and let her take him, take everything. Watched as her rosy cheeks worked, sucking, her hands stroking his balls. Heard her groan in pleasure as if he were offering her a banquet.

He was a selfish bastard who was all but engaged to another woman. Con half expected another round of lightning to pierce him through the groin. But he was spared long enough to bring her to completion with his own tongue. He tipped her back on the old patchwork blanket, spread her long white legs and feasted. The sun beat down on his back, but he would stop only when he'd given her the only pleasure he could. It was too hot to couple—even limiting the contact between their bodies, they glistened with sweat. He buried his face in her rose-scented curls until she shook him free with the violence of her contractions. He wanted to keep the flavor of her in his mouth forever, hold her, soothe her, but knew what he had to say required distance.

He sat up, nearly dizzy from loving her. "Laurette, we must talk."

She lay splayed next to him, the rise of her chest hypnotic. She nodded sleepily.

"Get dressed. You'll be red as a beet. We'll find some shade."

She scrambled into her dress and followed him barefoot over the field to a withered stand of trees. He spread the blanket again and pulled her down.

She folded her hands on her lap tightly, as if she wished to squeeze them still. "What's wrong, Con?"

"You know why I went to London in the spring."

She nodded, puzzled. "Yes, before my party." She nervously braided her hair back up, securing it with pins from her pocket. Con watched her turn from pagan goddess to prim miss in the twist of her wrist.

"Mr. Berryman. You've met him."

"Yes, of course. Your uncle's friend."

"He's no friend to anyone," Con said in disgust. "He owns my debts. And my uncle's. I've been working like a slave this summer, but it's come to nothing now. The weather—" He smiled crookedly. "I'll not bore you with the topic of conversation on every Englishman's tongue. My people won't survive until next year. I have to do something. Something I don't want to do."

"You'll marry," she said softly, surprising his words away. Her hands reached for his, but couldn't catch them before he stood.

"Oh God, Laurie! You know I love you. I couldn't love anyone else, ever."

"I know. Mr. Berryman has a daughter. Is she to be your wife?"

The meadow was as silent as a tomb. Con felt his tongue and throat swell, making it impossible for him to utter any words. Laurette blurred before his eyes.

She sprang up. "Don't cry. It will be all right."

"How can it be?" he asked bitterly.

"I'll be—I'll be your mistress!" Laurette said, her voice wobbling. "We can go on as we have. I won't give you up."

"Oh, Laurie." He held her damp body close to his, feeling the fervor of her heart. "I can't do that to you. I can't do that to Miss Berryman."

"What is she like?" she whispered.

"I don't know. I haven't met her. She's not you. I wish—I wish—"

"Shh. Love me again. Love me properly this time."

And he did, because he wanted to love her properly forever. They had a month to make last a lifetime.

Laurette had changed a great deal from that heedless seventeen-year-old who had desperately offered everything she was to him. He had learned too late—just this past year—that she had carried a great secret, a secret he had been stunned to discover in the rather touching letter Marianna had written to him on her deathbed.

He had been so shocked it had taken him two months to perfect the plan to become acquainted with his daughter. The distinguished, stiff-necked spinsters who ran Beatrix's school had been naturally suspicious when he turned up, money and sweets in hand. They had made him feel like a pervert until he reluctantly disclosed his relationship to their pupil. When he had taken them into his confidence about his scheme to win the child's mother, they both were in transports, as only spinster virgins could be at such romantic audacity. Con had left out the mistress part entirely so as not to sully their illusions.

He was beginning to wonder if he should have just courted Laurette in the conventional way, after a year of mourning he didn't feel had passed. She had spurned him when he returned, most thoroughly, but she had been stunned by his clumsy, distasteful haste. Marianna had not been dead for any decent length of time before he proposed, and he'd had no idea Beatrix even existed then.

When he did—after the horrible, endless ride to confront her about their secret daughter, things had only grown worse. The few times they'd crossed each other's path in Lower Conover had not been conducive to seduction. Laurette had been frostily polite and he could hardly have spirited her off during church service. Now with the coming unrest in Greece, it seemed he would have to spirit her away to his Yorkshire estate.

Estate was too grand a word for it. He'd seen the place, once, last fall. Time and Uncle Ryland had not been kind. Somehow it had fallen out of the Berrymans' purview and was in a shocking state, worse even than Ryland Grove had been at its lowest point. The farmland grew nothing but rocks and the house was home to living creatures who did not walk upright. Con had arranged for a caretaker and drawn up renovations, which were proceeding, as far as he could tell, at a snail's pace. First there had been torrential rain. Then snow. Then more rain. He wondered if he should not instead look to rent a suitable stranger's property for this family reunion. Perhaps he was foolish to want to start again on his own land, even if the property was less than ideal. Ryland Grove was out of the question for the moment. He felt cloistered there, smothered in memories, and Laurette could never return in any way other than his wife.

James and Beatrix would soon be on school holiday. He had arranged to have them both rounded up and sent north with Nico and Sadie. Nico would have to abandon his maid next door and Sadie her deep-seated doubt. The Vincent guardians had been heavily bribed to extend Beatrix's usual week-long summer visit with Laurette. They were rather rigid, God-fearing people who seemed concerned more for Beatrix's immortal soul than a summer of sunshine, and reluctant to turn over her welfare to the wicked man even they in their Cornish isolation had heard called "the Mad Marquess." Con felt as if he were mending fences throughout Britain, not just the fallen walls in Yorkshire.

But his most important convert had yet to be won. He hoped his surprise would not result in disaster. He was willing to install Laurette in a separate bedchamber no matter how much it would pain him. He looked forward to time with his son in neutral territory, and wished to learn more of his daughter than what was possible at supervised outings in the local tearoom near her school.

Con wondered from the occasional glint in her forest-green eyes, if the child suspected who he really was to her. She looked very like his mother, from what he could remember. The same red-gold hair, the same straight narrow nose. Bea was a beautiful child, and it broke his heart that Laurette was denied the joy of raising her. Of course if she had, he doubted his daughter would sit so still or fold her little gloved hands with such self-possession, not a hair out of place or a spot to be found on her school uniform. Laurette was still delightfully rumpled, although her new friend Lady Christie seemed to be taking her in hand.

Con finished the last of his letters. He'd done what he could. The rest was up to Providence and Laurette.

Chapter 9

Laurette squinted at the pristine linen encased tightly in the new embroidery hoop. There was no design, no clue as to what she should create, no pretty pattern to follow. She could not draw to save her life anyway.

What was simple enough for someone with her limited skills to execute? A leaf? A chain-stitch monogram? She picked up a sea-green skein of silk thread, licked one end and poked it through the tiny eye of the needle. She would be blind by the end of the afternoon.

It had come to this.

Sewing.

She had sewn only under duress or necessity a missing button to be reattached, a stocking to be mended, a seam repaired. Just once she had tried her hand at fancywork, helping Sadie with the beautiful blue gown that became her come-out dress. *Her wedding dress.* There had been hundreds of sparkling stars and moons and crystal bits that had come loose and Laurette had done a creditable job affixing them back on the stiff satin. The dress had been a marvel, designed to lure Con from his self-imposed celibacy.

And it had worked.

The miracle dress was a substitute for a most unsatisfactory, decidedly unmiraculous dress. Punching the needle through the cloth, she remembered the early summer day Sadie had tried to fit it to her. She had been imagining dancing with Con at her ball, and had promptly ripped the gown beyond repair when she raised her arms. Not that she minded much. She hadn't really wanted to wear the white dress anyway, but Sadie had insisted that ladies wore white at their come-out.

Poor Sadie. She'd tried hard to turn Laurette into a lady, with lemons and milk baths when they could afford them. Laurette still had every original "spot" and more besides. They were graced now by faint wrinkles at the corner of her eyes and lines bracketing her mouth. She believed, if she looked hard enough, there might be a strand or two of silver mixed in with her golden hair. And she was apt to lose her wits long before she grew much older—she was hopelessly bored. She was *sewing*.

And thinking of days best forgotten.

She'd had her triumphant night all those years ago, and the morning that came after it. But one had to be careful what one wished for. She had never expected to turn into Con's mistress, waiting impatiently for him to show up and take her to bed.

There was little else she could do on Jane Street. Con's lips had thinned when she explained the various mistresses' weekly amusements. It was clear he did not want her traipsing up and down the street for tea or card games. So she had to be satisfied with back-garden chat with Caro and Charlotte.

And sewing.

Ugh! She tossed the hoop aside. There was no hope of anyone seeing a leaf in her crooked stitches—her handiwork looked more like a garden slug. Laurette wondered how her own Dorset patch and its slugs were faring—gardening was one of her few domestic accomplishments. When her mother died, Laurette had turned the flower beds on the grounds of Vincent Lodge to rows of vegetables. Flowers were all very well, but Laurette and her little family had to be practical— and eat. She had forced Charlie to help her build a henhouse, its walls approximating plumb, and bought chickens. Sadie had a thriving sideline selling eggs and produce from the garden, and Laurette had labor to take her mind off the fact that she only saw her daughter for a few weeks every summer.

But not this summer. This summer, Laurette was in a gilt cage on Jane Street, discouraged from venturing out, forbidden to pull so much as a weed up in the lush walled garden. One of Aram's sons did that, stopping by every afternoon. That was the reason Laurette was shut up inside with a rainbow of thread—the boy was bent over a flower bed right this minute, making everything falsely perfect.

Laurette was not meant to be indoors or indolent for any stretch of time—she questioned how all the Jane Street mistresses managed to make it through their idle hours without shrieking in frustration. And Con was much more attentive than most of the gentlemen who owned property here—fully half his day was spent with her. He arrived promptly every evening for dinner, slept in her bed once he had exhausted himself between her thighs, and ate a hearty breakfast in the dining room. He then left to attend to his duties, and Laurette had an idea he'd just as soon not be dutiful—he seemed reluctant to leave every morning, luring her over toast crumbs to one last ravishing kiss.

She would go back in the garden when Tomas—or Nico, she wasn't sure which—left, feel the sun on her face, listen to the birds and gentle burble of the fountain, check to see if the boy missed anything. Her hands were too smooth now. Useless.

She was becoming spoilt in the truest sense—she felt "off," as though she were mouldering within. Resentment and regret were braiding inside her, twisting like the hopeless pile of thread in her silken lap.

She bunched up the thread and set it back in the brand-new sewing basket that had been purchased for her. Nadia had thought of everything, tiny silver scissors meant to look like a bird, every color of thread in the spectrum, a packet of mother-of-pearl buttons, a painted china thimble. Sadie would snort at the sight of all of it.

Laurette snorted herself. How foolish she was to feel sorry for herself for living in such luxury, with concerned servants and a forceful lover who spared no expense. But what Laurette needed couldn't be bought for any price.

She left the chair by her bedroom fireplace—lit even on this seasonable day—went to her little balcony door and threw it open to the fresh air. There was no sign of her gardener, although a bucket of weeds and a garden fork lay on the tiled path. Laurette took a deep breath and was rewarded by the perfume of London—coal smoke overlaying the flowers below, nothing like the scent of her cottage garden in Dorset. What exotic spices did her brother smell on his trip? Probably nothing so unusual as she could find in her own kitchen on Jane Street.

It was certainly as hot as a kitchen in her bedroom. Of course! The fire—it could only mean one thing. Con was on his way for a daytime dalliance. How stupid of her not to realize.

She crossed the room to the mirror. Her hair had as usual escaped its knot, but the rest of her was presentable. Despite Martine's pleas, Laurette did not paint her face or resort to any artifice to appear to be anything than what she was—a woman nearing middle age who had spent a great deal of time in the sun. And after Con left, she would go right out to the garden and catch the last fading rays of light.

Laurette frowned, oblivious to the wrinkles forming on her brow. What if he stayed all afternoon and all night? She would have to put up with him—that's what mistresses did.

In all honesty, she could not object to what Con did night after night to her body—whatever he had learned in the East was put to very good use. But he still wanted to talk to her, either before or afterward—not during, as he concentrated far too hard on their pleasure to make any sense at all, his mouth busy with kissing her pretty much everywhere. And although Laurette was lonely, she did not want to talk to Con.

There were some things best left unsaid.

She focused on the house across the way. How vexing those people must find it to share a garden wall with "the Janes"—that was the name given by the ton to the women of the exclusive courtesans' cul-de-sac. But perhaps they looked for shocking activity in the pocket gardens to entertain them. Laurette had reason to love al fresco, and knew that it could be very entertaining indeed.

But today she would shock Con. Laurette struggled with the fastenings of her dress and laces of her corset, stripping down to the sheer shift and stockings. She was immediately more comfortable, and would tempt Con from talking. She inserted a sponge and arranged herself against the mass of golden pillows, pulling the pins from her hair. As an after thought, she pushed one lace sleeve down over her shoulder.

And then she waited. Book-less. Embroidery-less. She gazed up at her reflection in the mirror on the ceiling—she looked as decadent as was possible for a freckled woman past her prime. Her lids drooped in the heat and soothing crackle of the fire. In minutes, her tedium put her to sleep sitting up.

Con had wanted to catch Laurette unawares, but not so literally. He'd asked Nadia when he left this morning to prepare the room for him this afternoon, but it was obvious Laurette had cottoned onto his plan and had beaten him into bed. Her cobwebby shift, finely wrought and almost translucent, revealed her every curve. But the effect was somewhat spoiled by her open mouth and the not-so-gentle snores competing with the birdsong outside and the roar of the fire within.

He moved stealthily toward the bed, shedding his proper English gentleman's clothes. He'd spent the morning with his man of business, arranging for a sort of sabbatical from his life again. This time, however, he would not be fleeing from his family.

It seemed a shame to wake her, but his needs were not satisfied only in the dark hours. The summer would give him the opportunity to live with Laurette, away from the filth and pressures of London. They would have a mock marriage, although precious little sex.

Then again, according to many of his friends, that's what most marriages evolved to anyway—a lack of physical intimacy was almost de rigueur amongst most peers and peeresses once their heirs were secured. That's not what he ultimately wanted, but he would take Laurette in the daytime any way he could have her. He was that desperate.

She was his weakness. His flaw. In all these years, he'd not been able to uproot her from his heart, and he *had* tried. A little. Others were disappointed in love through separation and circumstance—lovers even died and people marched on with their lives, one step at a time. Laurette had been his lodestar since he'd outgrown short pants, and he didn't want to be anywhere but on a path to her.

They used to make each other laugh. Now they were separated by silence, united only when skin brushed skin.

That was better than nothing.

He cupped a silk-covered breast in possession and she stirred.

"Wake up," he whispered. "I want you to know I am here."

"As if I could miss you," she muttered, half-opening her eyes. "You've taken off your clothes already. Lord, you could have murdered me in my sleep!"

Con eased himself down beside her, slipping her shift up over her thighs. She wore no drawers and he was treated to the sight of her bare, smooth skin, lightly dusted with gold flecks. It was as if she'd been dipped in gilt from head to toe. He'd designed her golden bedroom to showcase what she considered her affliction. He would never forget when he fought through her layer of clothes so many years ago and discovered her tiny scattered secrets. It had been his mission to kiss each one.

No, he hadn't fought. Laurette had gladly shed those clothes, making it impossible for him to ignore his pent-up desire, even when he knew he was pledged to another woman.

Even after he was married.

"As if I've gone to all this trouble just to remove you from this earth."

"You've removed me from my home. That's almost as bad."

"Ah." He traced a line from navel to slit. She was, as expected, wet, just as he was hard. They seemed to have this instantaneous reaction to each other, even if Con was fairly sure she wanted to box his ears. He followed his finger with his lips, pausing to look up when he scented the disappointing whiff of vinegar blending with her rose perfume.

Damn. He had meant to surprise her, but she had prepared for his visit.

"When you go back, you'll find everything tidy and fresh." He tugged the string but decided to leave it in place. One less thing to fight over.

"I don't care." The Vincent chin thrust out.

Yes, she was in a martial mood. This conversation was not going as planned. The Lodge belonged to foolish Charlie in any case. Laurette deserved to live at Ryland Grove, now that it was truly his home.

The time for talk was over. Con parted her folds and proceeded to make love to her with his mouth until she was liquid beneath his touch. He focused his senses on the rose oil on her skin, and kept the string carefully to the side unless it tangle with his tongue and impede his progress. She was sweet, tart, Laurette.

There was no more arguing, or sound of any kind as she kept strict control over her reaction to his attentions. There was no one to hear her anyway—Con had given everyone the afternoon off. He wanted her to himself, every inch of her. Qalhata had prepared a basket for their supper later, which he intended to share with Laurette in their private garden. It wasn't the green Dorset downs, nor were there standing stones or the steady trickle of the Piddle—just a frothing marble fountain. Tomas had carted a rug and pillows out of doors to place in the shade of the red maple tree Con had planted himself.

He broke through her barrier of silence quickly as she arched beneath him. "Oh! God, Con, I need you."

Blessed words. He needed her too, to be inside her, to lose himself. To stop thinking of the past and concentrate on their future. Everything was in place. With luck—and continued lust—she'd be his marchioness at summer's end.

"Take off your shift." His words had a harsh edge—she would know he was as anxious as she. But he didn't care that his every action revealed how deeply he was enthralled with her. Did not every woman want a man to master?

No, that wasn't right—they mastered each other, were complimentary halves of the same whole. But she wouldn't acknowledge that yet, had resisted all his blandishments beyond the bedroom. He would prevail, or die trying.

But no death yet, just hot friction surrounding his cock. He watched impatiently as she struggled with the ties, then helped her tear the garment over her head. Her breasts begged for kisses, so he complied. Her skin was flushed, dewy. Her pale lashes fluttered as he suckled and stroked, her lips set in the tiniest of smiles.

He took a nipple gently between his teeth and released it. "Tell me what you want again."

"You know."

"I want to hear it. I *live* to hear it."

"If I don't say it, will you go away?"

"Not a chance. I'll never leave you again."

"*I'll* leave *you*. In four months and eighteen days."

Con was just as aware of the finite nature of their bargain.

"Don't forget to add the eight and a half hours until midnight. When I opened the door to you, you were mine again."

He remembered her as she had been in his shadowed hallway, pale and careworn, her clothes—except for the extraordinary undergarments he saw shortly afterward—pitiful. She had dressed to seduce him, but there was no need. He was hers even if she didn't want him. He could see every lost, lonely year between them in the gaslight, so sharp in the angles of her face and collarbone. At least by now she had lost that pinched look under his protection, even if she fought against his loving restraints.

Laurette shook her head. "Don't be tiresome, Con. I am yours only through your blackmail. A piece of paper signed under duress can mean nothing."

She was right, of course, but he had used every means at his disposal, legal or otherwise. And he would do it again.

He cupped her cheek. "Tell me."

"I've changed my mind. I want nothing."

He should have plunged in when she first asked. When her need was so great that she forgot she meant to be a forbidding stranger to him.

"Say it."

"Damn you, Con! I've had my pleasure. More or less. I don't care if you have yours."

He raised a brow. "Selfish, are you?"

"Completely."

"I don't believe you. If anything, you've always cared too much." For her rackety drunken parents. For her little brother. For him that summer when he was so miserable he simply fucked her instead of made love.

"Well, I don't care now! Do whatever you like! I misspoke before."

"You don't need me then?"

"Of course not."

"You don't need this?" He thumbed an erect nipple. "Or this?" His lips returned to their earlier task. She lay stiff beneath him, furious. Her mouth was frozen in a grim line, her eyes filling with tears.

This would never do. Even he was not so heartless to take a woman against her will.

He pulled back and covered her with a sheet.

She was not content with this reprieve, but felt compelled to hurt him further. "Anybody could touch me in such a way as you do. It makes no difference. What you do is nothing to me. Less than nothing. It's something to be borne until my servitude is over."

Con felt an unholy flare of jealousy, but he knew she had never betrayed him. Not once. Sadie had been more than clear on the subject when she rained threats upon his head when he told her what he meant to do to win Laurette back.

"I will not release you from your obligation no matter how cold you are to me, Laurette. It seems pointless to argue when we could be enjoying ourselves. And you cannot tell me you have not enjoyed yourself this past month."

"One month and thirteen days."

Lord, but she was stubborn. "Don't forget the next eight and a half hours."

"As if I could forget any of it, you horrible man! And yes, wipe that smug smirk off your face! My body is a traitor. I cannot help it if when you touch me—" She broke off, blushing scarlet. "But as I said, my body would respond to anyone with a modicum of skill and hygiene."

"You once loved me in my dirt. Remember the afternoon you found me after haying? You didn't care that I was covered in sweat and smelled like a goat. You knocked me up against the hayrick and had your wicked way with me."

"I was young and very stupid."

Con sighed. "We both were, my love. But we're older now, and have more choices. Fucking in a bed is much more comfortable, is it not? And we won't be vexed by scratchy straw and those tiny insects that bit our arses. I trust you're completely cured now?"

"I was cured a dozen years ago. Of you and everything you did to me."

"Are you certain? Let me have a look."

Laurette gaped at him. "You want to inspect my bottom?"

"I can't think of anything more delightful."

"You truly *are* mad. But I must do as you request, mustn't I, since you are my keeper. *Temporarily*." She made a great show of sighing and rolling over, "accidentally" elbowing him in the process.

Con peeled the linen sheet from her, admiring her pale pink stockings and the lacy garters still holding them up. He might have preferred black had he been consulted, but Laurette was really not the black stocking type. Her narrow back and bum were just as freckled as the rest of her. He smoothed a fingertip down her spine, bumping to her waist. She was very tense, no doubt from being sexually thwarted. She *did* need him, no matter what she said, or how she distanced herself from him.

"Oh! What's this?"

She turned her face from the pillows. "What?"

"This right here." He circled a square of skin on her left buttock.

Curious now, her hand came around to touch the spot. "I don't feel anything."

"I need a closer look at the thing. Lie still."

"What does it look like?"

Ah, the old Laurette would have known he was playing a trick on her, and play along with him. This Laurette seemed genuinely alarmed. He didn't want her to worry. About anything. Certainly not about a tiny heart-shaped freckle on her beautiful white arse that he was going to bite in about six seconds.

"You bloody bastard!"

"Lie still, Laurette." This way he wouldn't have to see her ruthless indifference, because Con had decided he was taking her, against her will or not. She could pretend all she wanted that she didn't care, but he knew differently.

He pulled her up on her knees and stuffed some of the golden pillows under her. And then, with no preamble or discussion, he gripped her hips and entered her. She shrieked, forgetful now to hide her response, and continued to scream as he drove deeper. He was quite sure she screamed with pleasure tinged with some surprise, and as she didn't reach behind her to squeeze his balls off, he took it all for noisy submission.

Her bottom was luscious split by his cock. He watched as he slid into her pink. He could see her consume him, and reluctantly release him. He was gasping, rocking, rough hot sensation rippling through him. Her fingernails dug and clawed into the bedding, her cries muffled now by the mattress. One more thrust and he bent to nip her shoulder. Mark her as his.

Make her mine. Mine. Mine.

Fill her with seed. Get her with child—no, the damn sponge. But soon. Soon. She belonged to him and always would.

His release shook him to his core, blinded him again. She had to know—had to. He'd paid. Suffered. They both had—she more than he, really. Con would make it up to her. Over a picnic dinner tonight. In the carriage tomorrow, and all the days afterward as they journeyed to Yorkshire. And then hopefully, for the rest of their lives.

Chapter 10

Madness. But what could one expect from the Mad Marquess? The carriage pitched despite the well-sprung wheels and skill of Tomas, one of Aram's sons. Laurette had been thrown against the doors, against Con, and once tumbled to an undignified heap upon the floor. Con had ceased being amused some miles back and was now sitting opposite, grim, his fist firmly wrapped around the carriage strap. He had cautioned her to do the same, and Laurette had lost the feeling in her fingertips as she held her arm up in a death grip.

"How much farther?" she ground out.

"We are on my land now. The road was not nearly as bad last fall."

"It's b-bad now." She slid to the side and clung to the leather for dear life.

"Perhaps we should walk the rest of the way." Con tapped the roof and the carriage swayed to a shuddery standstill.

Tomas clambered down and opened the door. "Aye, my lord?"

"I believe we'll walk the rest of the way. Over the field. It cannot possibly be more rutted than my road."

"Aye, my lord." Tomas grinned. "Do you care to wager who will arrive first, my lord?"

"I'm not much of a betting man anymore, Tom. Let's just hope none of us winds up in a ditch. You've done well so far."

"Thank you, my lord. I thought of the lady."

Laurette tried to smile. If she had truly been in the young man's thoughts he would have put her out at the last signpost.

This trip was most ill-advised. Just when she was getting used to her little house and garden and making the acquaintance of her neighbors, Con had informed her they were leaving London. He spouted nonsense about the city heat and the crowds, but she had been comfortable in the shady corner of her garden, tucked away in her exclusive street. People were hardly going to seek her out and disturb her peace. Only Con did that, the devil.

Laurette looked down at her rumpled travelling costume and thin-soled half-boots. Just this morning at the inn she had been the picture of perfection, or at least Con's version of it. Nadia had told her weeks ago that he had selected every stitch of her wardrobe himself. She and Aram were some miles behind in the larger conveyance with all the trunks.

It had suited Con down to the ground to torture her alone over the miles in the confined space. They had done everything they ever thought to do in a bedroom and a few things more. Laurette blushed to think of the day before yesterday in particular. It was as though Con was trying to cram a life's worth of sexual adventure into the journey to Yorkshire. When she reminded him he'd surely find a bed in which to slake his lust once they finally reached his misbegotten property, he had smiled, and continued his amorous assault.

Laurette simply could not understand why, when he'd gone to all the trouble and expense of Jane Street, he was so all-fired up to see the West Yorkshire dales.

Con steadied her elbow as she nearly tripped over a rock. Certainly now that they were off that dreadful lane, and her stomach had settled, the countryside was quite beautiful. The

Pennines were in the distance, wispy clouds obscuring their peaks. White drystone walls crisscrossed the landscape and a few artistically twisted trees broke up the undulating ridges. She heard the water before she saw it and looked questioningly at Con.

"Nothing like Aysgarth, of course, but our own little waterfall, just over the hillock. And if I'm not mistaken, a cave behind it. I've been told the limestone hills are riddled with caves and caverns. We should have liked this place when we were children."

They climbed over the hill, Laurette firmly encased in Con's grip. She failed to see her young self roaming the fells or anywhere else, until they came upon the waterfall. It was not much, as waterfalls went, just a jumble of rocks and a vibrant splash of silver water eddying below the hill where they stood. The stream cut into the green and disappeared behind a giant boulder. But she was enchanted.

Con led her down the steep bank and to the quicksilver stream.

The air was instantly cooler here. The waterfall and stream it fell into were quite lovely—noisy, too. Good. It would spare her more conversation with Con. It had not been easy keeping her distance from him in the carriage when they were not engaged in lust. She might allow him—welcome—the liberties he took with her body, but each word she spoke was rationed. He was not her friend.

Once he was—her best and only. Laurette had loved her Dorset village home well, mostly because Con was her neighbor.

He had promised to marry her, to love her forever.

He had not.

"It empties into a small lake not far from the house," Con shouted. "We're not more than a mile away as the crow flies." Con picked up a stone and skipped it. He'd not lost his technique. She thought of the pink skipping rock he'd given her all those years ago, easy for him to find amidst the gray and black rocks of the Piddle. She'd left it in the crook of their tree for him to find before she lost Con and it for good.

"How did you come by the property? You never spoke of it at home," she shouted back, forgetting her vow of silence.

Con grimaced and pointed upstream. They walked away from the rushing water until they could speak in normal tones. "It was left to my mother. Of course when my parents died, my grandfather had no interest in it. He couldn't manage Ryland Grove as it was. There were tenants for a while. Then the house was more or less abandoned until my uncle was banished here, and I've had to spend a fortune on it since. I hope it's in better condition than the road."

It was his wife who had solved the problem of his uncle. He had wanted to be revolted when they first met, but he was not. Marianna Berryman was pretty, and far more genteel than he had expected a daughter of her father to be. She played the out-of-tune piano more than passably after their first supper together, and sang a duet with her dour chaperone, who had a surprisingly sweet voice. Her conversation was lively and intelligent.

But he felt managed, and so was mulish. For every prod of his uncle's he became unresponsive, then finally mute. Even Miss Berryman gave up and turned her charm on his uncle, who puffed and swelled like a sun-bloated fish. There had been plenty of dead fish in the chalk beds of the River Piddle this summer, and hungry people who dared to eat them. Miss Berryman's money would put finer fare on their tables.

Duty. An empty word compared with losing himself in Laurette. He had to—he must—

"Don't you agree, my lord?"

Con roused himself. He had paid no attention to the conversation. "I beg your pardon?"

"I have just told Lord Robert that Papa will set him to manage one of your lesser properties—the one in Yorkshire. Some farm, I believe."

His uncle looked stricken. The farm in Yorkshire was so

unproductive and negligible Con had been unable to sell it off. The barn was in better condition than the house, and that was not saying much.

Con looked at his fiancée with new appreciation. The Berrymans must be fully aware of the state of all Con's holdings. They had made their investment in him with open eyes.

"See here,"said his uncle, "I've given almost ten years of my life to Ryland Grove. Raising my nephew. I'll not be turned out like some—some—"

"Mad dog?" Marianna asked sweetly. Con noted she had one dimple in her rounded cheek.

"The nerve! I say, Conover, tell these people you'll not stand for it!"

Con allowed himself a swallow of weak tea. Soon, that would change, too. There would be strong tea, and coffee, and port, brandy and wine, thanks to "these people." He'd have oceans of liquid to drown in as he became Mr Berryman's son-in-law. Marianna's husband.

"I don't know, Uncle. The open dales. The bracing cold air. You might like it."

"Damn you! It's through my offices you've got as far as you have. You'd never be marrying without my say so! You need my signature."

Con looked at his uncle but said nothing. He hoped it was perfectly clear what he thought of his uncle's efforts and his signature. He might be forced to marry, but he was not going to like it.

"I think that's a brilliant plan, Miss Berryman."

His uncle rose up in anger, spilling his glass of whiskey on the carpet. Berryman's whiskey. They had had no spirits in the house until Berryman moved in, bringing half of Fortnum and Mason's Food Emporium with him. Con had choked on the fancy jam on his toast just this morning.

Lord Robert must have thought the better of his outburst, and sat down abruptly. Things must be worse for his uncle than even Con knew. He returned to his reverie, imagining

Laurette as his marchioness, wearing the Conover tiara. It was paste now, of course, had been since his grandfather financed a trip to the Sinai. But Laurette didn't need diamonds and rubies when her love blazed so brightly. Love that Con had to find a way to extinguish once and for all.

The tiara had been restored, every diamond and ruby, and waited for her in a vault at Berryman and Sons Bank. The bank would be James's, should he care to run it. If not, Con would see that it was managed well.

Breathless, Laurette stopped and shook a stone out of her shoe. "You've not been here before?"

"I came up last fall for a few days." Con took his hat off and shook his mane of black hair in the sunlight. "That water looks refreshing."

"We are *not* about to go for a swim," Laurette said, firmly. "The sooner I get out of these dusty clothes, the happier I'll be." She hooked an arm in his and tugged him over the grass, guiding him for once.

"In a hurry to find a bed?" he teased.

"In a hurry to settle in. Travel does not seem to agree with me."

She *had* looked a bit green around the gills the last few days, and had been silent as a clam. "Pity. I'd hoped to take you to some of my favorite spots in the world."

"We only have four months left, my lord. I hardly think there will be time." At least she'd given up tacking on the exact number of days. She took a long stride forward. A golden plover rose up from its nest and fluffed its feathers practically in her face. Laurette gave a little shriek.

"There now. You'd think you were a city girl," Con said, laughing, catching a swirling feather and tucking it into the brim of her bonnet. "Last I was here, there were birds in the *house*. I do hope my caretaker has managed to evict them."

Laurette glared at him. "Just exactly why did you bring me all this way? From everything you've said, I'm surprised you can give up all your luxuries to camp out in the back of beyond."

"It's true the house was so dilapidated we couldn't even sell it when we had most need to do so. The best of the acreage went long ago. But what's left is family land. My mother was born here and I wanted to show it to—you," he said quickly.

That had been a near thing. He knew he had to tell her the truth soon, but not when she might clout him with one of the rocks she kept tripping over.

They climbed up another hill and she was too out of breath to pepper him with more questions. Con was right. The weeks in London had turned her into a city girl, sequestered in her harem, and stuffed with pastries. If she wasn't careful, she'd outgrow her new wardrobe.

Below her was Con's "farm." Only a man who lived with the remnant of Conover Castle on his front lawn could consider the substantial stone manor house with such modesty. It was a large gray rectangle with four chimneys and a swath of ivy growing up near the arched doorway. Pots of blooming flowers flanked the recessed door. The slate roof looked new and the odd-sized windows gleamed. Behind it was a collection of outbuildings in various stages of repair, but some new work had been done to them, too. Neat stone walls enclosed a large pasture. The overall impression cheered Laurette up considerably. A glimmer of blue through the trees must be the lake Con talked about. There was no sign of Tomas and the carriage in the crushed stone courtyard, nor, in fact, any signs of life.

"Welcome to Stanbury Hill Farm. I believe there must be chickens, but I'm afraid there is no other livestock at present."

Laurette grinned. "They do not reside in the house, do they?"

"Not to my knowledge. There have been a few improvements since my last visit, and I hope that is among them. And rest assured, my great-uncle is gone as well."

Laurette knew Lord Robert had been exiled quite against his will to Yorkshire. Both Marianna and her father had held him in the utmost contempt, although he had been useful to them in acquiring Con. Marianna had been surprised when his letters of endless complaint stopped arriving a few years ago. After investigation, she discovered that he had wandered off one winter day and never returned. It was presumed he had gotten himself lost in the moorlands and died, although his body was never found, even after a search in the spring. There were icy fells and water aplenty for an old man to have slipped from and into. The local woman employed as his housekeeper reported that Lord Robert had become increasingly difficult and irascible.

In Laurette's opinion, he'd always been horrible. The man had made Con suffer growing up in a thousand little ways, from hiring vicious tutors who beat Con when he didn't decline verbs properly, to bankrupting him through the Berrymans. She, like the rest of the villagers of Lower Conover, attended his brief memorial service, but none of them shed any tears.

"He let the house go, as you might expect, not that it was in good shape to begin with. The man would do anything to cause me trouble. It should be livable now after all I've spent on it, but the first order of tomorrow's business is to get a crew together to repair that road. I can't believe they didn't tell me—" Con closed his mouth abruptly.

This was the second time he'd stopped himself from saying what he was thinking. "Who is they?"

Con took her hand and squeezed it. They both still wore their gloves, but she could feel the heat of his palm. Suddenly he looked so serious that she thought he might say his uncle was still a danger, walking the moors as a wraith.

"I had wanted this to be a surprise, but perhaps I should prepare you before we go further and enter the house. Maybe we should sit down."

A gust of wind caught her skirts, and she struggled to hold them fast. Her last wish was to tempt Con with a sight of her legs right now. She dropped to the grass and arranged herself in her most forbidding manner. "This sounds ominous. Get on with it."

"It's not meant to be." He pulled off a glove and ran his fingers through a thatch of bright green grass. "We will be spending the summer here."

Laurette shrugged. "As you wish. As long as I'm home before Christmas." She had already prepared herself not to see her daughter this summer. Thanks to Marianna's generosity—and guilt—she had been able to see Beatrix for a week every year.

Ten years ago, after Con had been missing for months, Marianna had invited Laurette to tea, and she had reluctantly consented. They were neighbors in the country—it would have looked odd to avoid each other. When she had been presented to Viscount James Horace Ryland, Laurette knew she held a piece of Con's heart in her arms. The handsome child, so different from her delicate Beatrix, won her over immediately. From there, one cup of tea had led to several years of ironic friendship.

Marianna had been her blunt self that first day.

"I know my husband loves you," she began, once the nursemaid took James away.

Laurette had the choice of feigning shock or being honest. She had lived a lie too long already. "He married you," Laurette said, equally blunt.

Marianna dropped a lump of sugar into her teacup, paused, then shrugged and added another. "So he did. I tried my best, but he was very unhappy. I came to love him a little, you know." She gave a brittle laugh. "Foolish of me. I was much older and wiser, or so I thought. I'm used to getting my own way. Papa spoiled me dreadfully. I'm afraid I simply expected Conover to fall prey to my charms."

"You are very pretty. Elegant." Everything about Marianna and her house was perfection.

"Yes, well, I am finding it ever more difficult to slim since the baby was born. I see your figure has returned to you."

Laurette felt a hot blush sweep across her face. It seemed like hours before she found her voice. "You knew?"

Marianna pushed a pale curl from her forehead. "Not until after James was born and Conover disappeared. Papa didn't want to worry me. But he always tells me everything. Eventually. The business may be called Berryman and Sons, but there are none, you know. Just me. I am his partner in all things. I would have married Conover even if I knew you were increasing, though. It had been planned for years. Conover just didn't know it."

Laurette put her cup down. The rattle of cup to saucer seemed very loud.

"You think me an evil witch, I'm sure, but I'm only telling you the truth. Papa had selected Conover for me before he started to grow whiskers. Even sent him to Cambridge so I wouldn't marry some country dolt. Once he got his hooks into Lord Robert, it was only a matter of time. Of course, there were a few other candidates, but none of them suited me so well."

"Didn't you care?" cried Laurette.

Marianna waved a small white hand. "Of course I did. I wanted to be a marchioness, and so I am. My position in society is assured. I have lovely homes and a beautiful son. If Conover had been unattached, I'm sure we would have got on splendidly." She paused, looking directly into Laurette's eyes. "I didn't repulse him, you know. Our honeymoon was everything it should have been."

Laurette felt ill. Surely she wasn't going to be miss-ish and faint before her enemy.

"But he was attached." Marianna extended the same hand she had waved so dismissively. Laurette stared at it stupidly until Marianna took hers and shook it. "I congratulate you. Once he knew I was with child, he never touched me again. Not once." Her voice sounded wistful. "Despite all my father's machinations, Conover did exactly what he was required by the terms of their agreement—but no more. When I was safely delivered of James, he disappeared within the week. Didn't even collect the sum my father was prepared to release to him. I don't expect to see him again. He may have been young, but he outsmarted us all."

But Con had been left himself, let down by every adult he had ever known. *"I'm sure Con knows you are a good mother."*

Marianna smiled. Her small perfect teeth were whiter than her earbobs. *"He thought me a most managing female. And I am. Which is why I invited you here today."*

Laurette's brows rose in question.

"We can do nothing about the disposition of your daughter, but I can arrange for funds so you can visit her every year. I know if James were taken from me I could not bear it."

Laurette swallowed, not trusting her voice. Her cousins had not forbidden her contact, and were scrupulous reporting Bea's every milestone by letter. Laurette sometimes wished they wouldn't write. Every post reminded her of her emptiness.

"But I shouldn't like Con to know about Beatrix just yet. Not that I have any way to contact him, he moves about so. I imagine he'd be so angry at my father's deception that he'd take my son away. And he could. Children belong to their fathers, no matter that it's Berryman coin that puts the food into Jamie's mouth."

For one instant Laurette saw Con striding into the house to take James. It would be what the Berrymans deserved, after plotting to ruin his life. Her life.

But no. They hadn't ruined anything. Con's uncle had been the treacherous one. They had just seen a bargain. Mar-

ianna Berryman had restored Ryland Grove and the prosperity of the Conover villages and was raising Con's son to merit his title.

"Why are you telling me this?"

"Because, my dear Laurette, we have a great deal in common. And I could use a friend. Those Cobb twins are simply hideous."

It was not Lord Robert's wraith but Marianna Berryman who sat beside Laurette on the hillside. Her old enemy-turned-friend. Marianna's long-estranged husband sat across from her. What would Marianna say to her refusing Con's offer of marriage and settling for being Con's mistress? Laurette imagined a sharp-tongued lecture from an entirely practical point of view.

But she could not marry Con. They could never acknowledge Beatrix. Her delayed happiness could not paper over such a hole in her heart.

Chapter 11

Con kept his dark eyes focused on the grass. He had been silent so long she wondered what this difficult subject could be. At last he cleared his throat. "We will not be alone."

"Of course not. Aram and Nadia will be with us. I know you think you would die if I did the cooking. I have told you over and over I am much more proficient in the kitchen than I was."

"Stop interrupting!"

"Yes, my lord. I've forgotten my place as your mistress once again. I am completely at your mercy. Wherever you wish to spend the time for the duration of our contract makes no difference to me." She gave him her haughtiest look.

"Damn it! You are making this difficult." Con ran a hand through his glossy, shoulder-length hair. Good. She liked to discompose him when she could. It seemed only fair when his every touch drove her to complete distraction.

"The children are here." Only half of his mouth turned up in a smile, revealing his anxiety.

Another blast of wind took his words away, but she was afraid she'd heard them clear enough. "I beg your pardon?"

"James and Beatrix. They're here. Nico and Sadie brought them last week."

"What have you done?" she whispered.

"Something that should have been done long ago." He edged away as if he knew she wanted to get her hands around his neck. "I want us to spend time together. As a family."

A family! Something that could never, ever be. The man was indeed the "Mad Marquess" if he thought to throw them together like this and erase a dozen years of heartbreak and betrayal. "Does she know? *Did you tell her?*" Laurette asked, not masking the desperation in her voice.

"No, of course not. I would never tell her without you. Though she's very sharp."

"You've *seen* her?" Each of Con's words was worse than the one before. Laurette saw pinpricks of black race across her eyes, felt the bile rise up in her throat—she was going to be sick. Panicked, she thought of cool, rainbowed waterfalls, icy water and fresh snow, but she lost her fight. Despite her efforts to push him away, Con cradled her as she made her mess on the grass, after which he wiped her mouth tenderly with his handkerchief.

He picked her up as if she weighed nothing and carried her some yards away. She was too disconsolate to protest. Con settled her against a small boulder for support and began to pace, making her dizzy all over again. She shut her eyes, but could not shut her ears.

"Last year I asked you to marry me, and you refused. I knew it was too soon after Marianna died—but damn it, Laurie, I'd waited too long to have you. I did not love Marianna—why should I observe a full year of mourning for a woman who was practically a stranger to me?"

"Not such a stranger. She was the mother of your son," Laurette retorted.

"But I loved you. You don't know what—well, it doesn't matter. I asked, and you said no. I was almost, *almost* ready to give up the idea of you—the idea of us—and then I found out about Bea.

"Then your refusal made a kind of sense to me. No wonder you hated me. I hate me too." He drew a breath. "But when you forbade me from ever knowing her, I couldn't bear it. I made it a point to go to her school, meet with her guardians. She's so lovely, Laurie. Different from you. And me. But she is a clever girl. I want to tell her. I want us to tell her together. I think—"

Laurette leaped up. "*You* think! You *think*!" she shrieked. "No! She'll be ruined! Everything I've gone through to give her a respectable life will be for nothing!" She wanted to tear out her hair. She wanted to tear out Con's. How could he do something so very stupid? So very selfish?

He reached out for her but she darted away. "Listen to me. I can make her my ward. In the eyes of society, they'll never know. When we marry—"

"What? We are not going to marry! I will never, ever marry you! I hate you, just as you said!" Laurette tore off her feathered bonnet in frustration, tossing it down the hill. It bounced until it came to rest on a rock. "You have a son. Worry about him. Leave my daughter alone."

"She is *our* daughter, Laurette. I robbed myself of knowing James, but I will not make the same mistake now that I know I have a daughter. I will not abandon two children. I had hoped that by all of us staying here James and I can make peace. That you can help me with him."

"I? Your *mistress*? You are absolutely mad!"

"I know he thinks of you as a kind of aunt, Laurie. He mentioned you to me last Christmas, even if you never once indicated that you and Marianna were friends," he said quietly. "I've known all along that you know him. That you knew *her*."

He expected her to feel guilty. Well, she was not. She kept her past quiet for a reason.

"He admires you. Looks up to you." Con stared off into the distance. "So many secrets. I'm done with secrets, Laurie. Just done. My life has been one long cock-up, but no more. I love you. I love my children. Please give this a chance."

Laurette clenched her fists and paced at the top of the ridge. Nothing would induce her to go down to that silver-gray house now. Nothing. "I am going home. I cannot—I will not—be party to this ridiculous family reunion. Bea is fine as things are. I am her c-cousin. That is all."

"You're afraid, aren't you?"

Laurette glared at him, wishing she could wipe away the calm concern on his face. He looked so—hopeful, so understanding. He knew *nothing*. "Oh, you stupid, stupid man. I had to give her up! *I gave my own child away!* Of course I'm afraid. She'll never forgive me. I can't forgive myself." She broke out in noisy sobs and pushed him away when he tried to comfort her. "You've ruined everything. Everything. I don't care about my brother's debts. Find him and clap him in jail. Toss me out of Vincent Lodge. I'll become some other man's mistress." She hiccupped. "That's all I'm good for anyway. You have wrecked my life once more, Desmond Ryland. I never want to see you again."

She turned and stumbled down the hill they'd climbed, tears blurring the limestone outcroppings.

Con caught her as she twisted her ankle and started to fall. He held her until she had no more tears to cry, his shirt soaked through to his skin. Once again he'd handled everything badly. He had hoped she would be happy to have the whole summer instead of one stingy week with Beatrix. And he'd mentioned marriage. Just because it was always on his mind did not mean Laurette shared his sentiments. She couldn't hate him, though. That would be far too cruel.

"You did plan everything, didn't you?" she asked fiercely. "From bringing down my brother to corrupting Beatrix. You cannot have what you want this time, Conover."

He felt the muscle jump in his cheek. "I've never had what I wanted!"

"You could have said no to Mr. Berryman."

He almost had. He had been given the bare bones in London when he went hat in hand to Mr. Berryman's bank a dozen years ago, learned more as Berryman accompanied him back to Ryland Grove. Like a fool he thought he could perform miracles and avoid the inevitable. But the crops failed, and the vise squeezed, and the details of his future had been written on bank draughts for a decade. Con remembered his despair as if it were yesterday. He'd had to sign his life away that day. A life with Laurette. But at the young age of nineteen, he could see no other way.

He was filled with resolve now, and an urgent need to explain himself, if it were remotely possible. Con dropped his arms from her shoulders. "And then where would my tenants have been? Two whole bloody villages!"

"You picked your poison, my lord." Laurette wiped her face with a shaking hand. He had never seen her so angry And she was right, in her way. They could have run off together all those years ago. But could he have lived with his selfishness? Could she? He pulled her to him again.

"Listen to yourself, Laurette. You've forgotten your part in this. One word from you and I would have left Marianna at the altar. One word. A sigh. I kept hoping you'd say something, do something. But you were silent then. You knew I was doing the only thing I could do. Your strength gave me mine so I could go through with it."

She wouldn't meet his eyes. "I didn't know then about Beatrix."

"Nor did I, my love. And I only know now because of your friend Marianna. You never would have told me." He watched the flame cross her pale cheeks. "She did us both a surprising kindness, writing that letter. She must have hated me for leaving her and James."

Laurette shook her head. "She loved you."

"Impossible. I didn't bed her for much more than a month. I barely spoke to her, escaped every chance I got. I was a very poor husband, I assure you."

"It didn't matter. She told me herself she was quite besotted. She even admired your pride."

"My pride has cost me my son." Con released her and set to do his own pacing. "We cannot, no matter how much we wish to, change the past."

"Nor can we go back to it, Con. I will never marry you."

He stopped. "Why?"

"I am not that heedless girl anymore. You are not that innocent boy. Think what you have done to bring us to this place, Con, and tell me you are not the most ruthless of men."

"What would you have me do, Laurie? Pretend I don't love you?"

"If you loved me, you would not have threatened me with such disgrace. You've made me your mistress."

"Only because you would not have me any other way—"

"I might have. Once a suitable period of mourning had gone by. Once we had come to some agreement about Beatrix."

Con wondered at her. She looked so calm now, her fair hair rippling in the breeze. She'd always been beautifully stubborn. She'd avoided him at every turn this past year, fixing her sea-blue eyes just to the right of his ear when they were thrown face-to-face. Slipping through a doorway once she'd discerned he was present. Embedding herself in a circle of gaggling women as ruffled protection. If he had been patient, could he have won her over? It seemed to him he had been patient too long already. He'd been robbed of her for a dozen years.

He swallowed back his infamous pride and looked into her face. "Tell me what I should do, Laurette."

"I scarcely know. You say the children have been here a week?" She sat down on the hill again, worrying at the creases in her skirt with her gloved hands. Con longed to tear off the gloves, tear off every bit of clothing and take her under the wide sky. This was no time for his lust to overtake him, however. He nodded.

"They were passing friends from Bea's summer visits. Not close, really. They must think this arrangement very odd. What have they been told?"

"Only that their holiday would be spent in Yorkshire rather than Dorset. That construction was being done on both our properties and as neighbors I had invited you and Beatrix to join me here. And it's true. You know Vincent Lodge is at sixes and sevens at the present. There's always something that needs doing at the Grove and I'm doing it." He sat down beside her again and began to uproot long blades of grass.

She suddenly looked horrified. "You didn't imagine we'd share a bed with the children present, did you?"

Con found some humor that had been sorely lacking these past few minutes. "Why do you suppose I've been such a randy devil? I knew the minute we got to Stanbury Hill we would resume the fiction of being childhood friends only. I would never dishonor you before them. I had hoped, actually, to court you."

"And use James and Bea in that endeavor!"

"Why, yes. I think they would welcome our happiness."

Laurette frowned. "I'm not so sure of James. He was sincerely attached to Marianna. She was an excellent mother."

Con sighed. He knew and was glad for it, but part of him still wanted to demonize all things Berryman. "I know. But you would be an excellent mother as well. He already holds you in great affection."

"I have said I will not marry you. I mean it absolutely." She heaved a sigh. "Under the circumstances, I feel justified to break our bargain. You have put me in a dreadful position, Con. And I cannot possibly spend the whole summer up here pretending that all is normal between us."

Con examined the square of earth made visible by his nervous gardening. "No, I suppose not. But give me a week, Laurie. Then you may take Beatrix back to Cornwall if you wish. I only meant well. You cannot know how much I had wanted—" He broke off. No point to belaboring the issue. Her lush lips were drawn in a thin angry line.

When they opened, she said, "Hell is paved with good intentions." Her clouded blue eyes met his. There was a bleakness there he'd hoped never to see again.

"I admit defeat."

No. He could not. Not ever. But it seemed to be what Laurette wanted to hear.

He managed a grin. "We shall be polite, proper old friends, no more. I'll destroy your brother's debts as soon as I return to London, or send them to you if you do not trust me to do the thing properly." He rose and extended a hand. "Come, let's see what mischief the children have gotten into."

"Beatrix is not mischievous." Con thought Laurette sounded a tad disappointed.

"I understand James is mischievous enough for the both of them. The reports I get from school are enough to make my hair curl." He walked down the hill and picked up her hat. "A proper, polite lady would be wearing this." Even if it was a bit squashed from its tumble.

Laurette straightened the brim and tied it back on. "I hate hats."

Con thought of the dozen he had bought for her. "I want you to keep your wardrobe, no matter what, Laurie. It is the very least I can do."

She sniffed but didn't argue with him for once. They plodded down to the house, silent.

Con reassessed how he could have been so wrong—again. It was becoming a bit of a habit, and he couldn't blame it on youthful folly or idealism any longer. He wasn't twenty anymore, pushed to his limit by poverty, desperate to assert himself in the only way available—the desertion of his own life.

Despite her suspicions, he was not the Machiavellian monster she thought him to be. Charlie Vincent had brought on his own ruination with very little assistance from Con. But it had been impossible not to take advantage of the situation. He had felt blackmailing Laurette to be his mistress was the only option, given her haughty dismissal of both his proposal and his person during the past year.

These last weeks had been glorious. To have Laurette in his arms again, to skim her dappled skin, taste her mouth, and seat himself deep in her exquisite heat had been a long-deferred dream. If she was less than enthusiastic when he engaged her in ordinary conversation, she had made better use of her tongue in bed. He had hoped they would recapture their old easiness with each other at Stanbury Hill Farm, but now that ease was permanently shattered. He glanced sidelong at her and noted the defiant Vincent chin. A week with her in this state might be seven days too long.

But damn it. He was going to prevail, no matter what he had to do. While he could not correct the past, he certainly had some influence on the present. He knew—*knew*—she still had feelings for him, no matter what she said. He still had a week. Barring sleep, that was over one-hundred hours to woo her. He was as good with numbers as she was.

Chapter 12

By the time they reached the peastone courtyard, Tomas was jostling the horses at the front door. There was no sign of welcome from the house. Con pushed in the somber black-painted door, squelching his urge to pick up Laurette and carry her over the threshold. This was not their honeymoon, nor would they ever have one if Laurette had her way.

The flagstone hallway was swept clean and a vase of grasses and wildflowers stood on a polished credenza. The house smelled of beeswax and lavender, a sure sign that Sadie was somewhere about. Nothing scurried across the floor or walked on the walls. Quite a change, all in all, from the last time he occupied the farm for a few damp days in the fall.

Tomas brought in the small cases from the carriage and went to see to the horses. Laurette was rigid with nerves, standing close to the open door, as though poised for flight. She looked ill, every freckle dark against her white face.

He wanted to take her in his arms, but he had promised friendship, nothing more. "I expect you will want to see your room before we meet the children, wherever they might be."

The house was far too quiet to think two eleven-year-olds and their minders were within. Laurette nodded and he led her up the center staircase, a massive, sturdy construct of oak. He paused at the oriel window to search the field and outbuildings behind the house, but saw no movement. He knew where he told Sadie to put Laurette—as far from his bedchamber as possible. They turned left at the top of the stairs and walked down a wide newly-carpeted hall to the end of the "Ladies' Wing." He and James were at the opposite end of the hallway, with plenty of bedrooms between.

His maternal grandparents had been blessed with several children, but none had survived save his mother, and she was doomed to die young, too. Con had already outlived both his parents by almost a decade, and he planned to stay alive as long as it took to get Laurette to marry him. One day, they might fill this house with more children of their own. If his plan failed, he would deed the house to Laurette to be held in trust for his daughter. They would both have some independence once the farming operation was in full swing again, and Laurette would never have to be at the mercy of her feckless brother.

And she would be far, far away from Ryland Grove. If she wouldn't marry him, the thought of her next door was much too painful to contemplate.

Laurette said nothing as she took in the blue-and-white sprigged room, so very different from the exotic Jane Street bedchamber. He had attempted to replicate a traditional country manor house for her, and from the looks of everything, his caretaker had followed his instructions to the letter. Chinoiserie ginger jars were lined up on the mantel, some filled with more wildflowers. He hoped that Beatrix had a hand in doing that.

He opened a casement window. "You can see the lake from here. And I believe I see where our children are."

Laurette looked at him with disapproval. "Where *the* children are," she reminded him, walking over to the window. "You will have to take much greater care when you speak."

She squinted into the distance. Con noted the fine lines at

her blue eyes. This morning he had pulled a long silver hair from his own head.

Half their lives were over. So much time wasted. Would he be there to see her amber hair turn to pewter?

"They are swimming! I did not know Beatrix knew how. She was always shy of water, even the Piddle. She heard tales of so many drownings in Cornwall I could never convince her to do more than take her boots off and stick a toe in."

"I imagine Nico taught her. You should have seen him in Greece with his brothers. You'd never know they were almost grown men, splashing about like seal pups. It was very beautiful there."

"I wonder why you came home at all," she said tartly.

Con pushed a frilly cushion away and sat down on the window seat. "A decade of running away was long enough. Too long, as you know. I meant to be a father to James."

Laurette lifted a golden eyebrow. "Not a husband?"

Con shook his head. "Never. Marianna and I would have what so many of the ton have, a convenient marriage. I had my heir."

"She might have seen things differently."

"She had lost her stranglehold over me, Laurette. I made my own fortune. In any event, this conversation is pointless. I did not expect her to die so soon, and I regret our estrangement was a cause for any unhappiness."

He stood up abruptly before he betrayed himself. As shocked as he had been to learn of his wife's death, he had also been glad. Relieved he would not have to spend the rest of his days being polite to Marianna as they led their separate lives. That was not a point in his favor. He was not cold. Not ruthless. At least when it came to Laurette. "You'll want to freshen up before the children come in. I'll leave you to it."

A husband. The words had no meaning to him. On the day of his wedding, there was only one woman he cared about, and she was not standing at his side or lying next to him in his bed.

He saw Laurette at once in the church, her face so pale each freckle stood stark, splashes of mud on snow. She was wearing her best straw bonnet, flowers from the Lodge's overgrown garden wilting on the brim, and a plain black dress. Her little brother shuffled restlessly next to her. Her father was not there to squeeze his shoulders to compliance. Her mother, dressed in unrelieved mourning, did not meet his eye.

But Laurette did. Every thought was visible. Her yearning. Her fear. Her acceptance. His gut wrenched in agony. He would make it up to her somehow, some time. Surely she knew he'd rather be anywhere but here at All Saints, waiting for his unwanted bride.

He shoved his trembling hands in his pockets and examined the stone floor, wishing somehow it would open and swallow him up. Send him down a shaft to another dimension, where tenants weren't starving, and cattle and sheep not dead, and crops not burned in the ground. Where Ryland Grove was not crumbling and collapsing about his head, crushing his dreams. Crushing his life.

He felt his uncle tug his sleeve and looked up. Marianna came toward him, leaning on her father's arm. She was a blur of blue and roses. Con supposed her wedding finery cost more than anything he'd spent on his own clothes in a dozen years. Lord knows the preparations at Ryland Grove were horrifically extravagant. The wedding breakfast would be a triumph, but Con was sure it would all taste like foulest sin to him.

Would Laurette come with her family? Marianna had invited everyone in the area at church last week. Uncle Ryland would have been sure to repeat the invitation when he warned Laurette off.

He couldn't help himself. He turned from the vicar, turned from his vows, and sought Laurette in the little crowd behind him. She stood stiff, her eyes bleak but dry. One word from *her and he would extricate himself from this farce and find himself in her arms again. One word.*

But she knew his duty, better perhaps than he did. Her beautiful lips remained pressed together in an almost-smile. She inclined her head, and he looked down into the face of his wife. Marianna lifted a plucked blonde brow.

"I will," he heard himself say. He barely recognized his own voice.

The rest of the morning passed in equally unrecognizable increments. The wedding party moved without a stumble past the ruined gatehouse up the lime walk to the house, grateful villagers gathered and tossed petals at the bride and groom. Hands were shaken, food eaten, champagne drunk. The Vincents were nowhere to be found, and for that, Con was grateful.

The night came both too slowly and too soon.

In the dark, and near desperate, he just managed to do his duty by his new wife. His wife! He was not so very experienced, but he expected more difficulty getting the deed done. Laurette had been so tight the first time, and there had been a cry of pain despite her desire. Con remembered Laurette in her imperfect perfection. This night was nothing like any other before it.

His guilt was overwhelming. He had made the business a bore for Marianna, and betrayed the woman he loved. And there was tomorrow. And tomorrow after that.

Laurette startled at the distinct slam of the door as he left. Con was angry, but so was she. At least this farce would be over in a week, and she could go back to being plain Miss Vincent of Lower Conover. Her small portmanteau was still below in the flagstone hallway, and her clothing miles behind in the luggage coach. But there was a ewer of water and some crisp linen towels on the dressing table, along with a set of silver-backed brushes and combs. Laurette removed her gloves and her hat, wondering if Sadie could fix the crimp in the brim. She wiped her face and hands with a cool cloth and unpinned her hair. She brushed it mindlessly, too vexed to count the strokes.

Something dreadful had happened to Con to make him think that he could alter all their lives like this. Bad enough that he had manipulated her to become his mistress. She had to admit she truly had no complaints on that score. Never had she felt so cosseted and protected. Never had she felt so sexually satisfied, not even when she was a vibrant girl in the first throes of passion. Con's travels had taught him much and her body was the beneficiary of his knowledge. But to involve the children in this scheme—

He *was* the Mad Marquess.

Laurette knew she was being unreasonable. She told herself that she had wanted to be more a part of Beatrix's life, and now here Con was handing her the perfect opportunity. But she had never truly faced what confession might mean—total rejection. She couldn't bear for Bea to look at her the way she had seen James look at Con this Christmas in church. It was a wonder God didn't smite the boy down and remind him of the Fifth Commandment.

She braided her hair and pinned it into a neat coronet. She shook her skirts free of dust and went down the worn oak steps. Con was nowhere to be seen, thank goodness. She passed through the hall, peering into tastefully furnished rooms. There was not a great deal of furniture, but what was there was sturdy and handsome, if a bit old-fashioned.

After a few wrong turns, she found the kitchens in an ell which had not been visible from the hall. The room was whitewashed and empty, the fire out in the enormous black stove. She lifted a blue-striped cloth on the sideboard and found a loaf of bread, already missing several slices. A drawer below it yielded a knife, and Laurette cut her own slice. It was delicious, Sadie's familiar recipe. She didn't realize how much she missed the simple taste as she ate the exotic fare of Jane Street.

She was swallowing crust when she heard laughter. Hastily she brushed her hands of crumbs and plastered a smile on her face.

The little party entering by the kitchen door was merry and very wet. A handsome dark-skinned young man—Nico, if she remembered correctly—broke into a white smile.

"Look! The marquess and your cousin have arrived, just as I said, Miss Bea."

Laurette found herself entangled in damp arms and squeals, not just from Beatrix but James as well. She drank in her daughter's face, pink from the sunshine with a smattering of freckles on the bridge of her nose.

She tugged on a thick red-gold braid. "You have not been wearing a hat," Laurette said, wanting to kick herself for the inanity.

James snorted. "You can't swim in a hat, Aunt Laurette. And Bea's becoming a capital swimmer, isn't she, Nico? She's almost as good as me."

"As good as *I*. Still full of Conover pride, I see," teased Laurette. "You have grown a foot since Christmas, James. And Bea—let me look at you."

Obediently the child stepped back. She was as slender as a reed, a bit taller than James, her usually pale face rosy. She dropped a curtsey and grinned with a freedom that Laurette had not seen often.

"I'm so glad you're here at last, Cousin Laurette. We've been having the most fun! There is the lake, and the caves, and Nico says the sheep are coming soon."

"Sheep?"

"Ryeland sheep, Aunt Laurette! That's R-Y-E-L-A-N-D. It's a bit of a joke on the family name. *My* idea. I read about the breed and told Father."

Laurette brushed his damp hair from his forehead. "Farmer James! I had no idea."

James looked smug. "I am an old hand at managing our properties. Mama took me with her around Conover lands when I was but a baby. I daresay I know more about our properties than Father does," he drawled.

"I daresay you're right." Con stood in the doorway. He had stripped down to his linen shirt and looked deliciously disheveled. "How do you do, James?"

There was no hugging now. James marched over to his father and held out his hand. "I do very well, sir. And you?"

Con shook the proffered hand. "I do very well now that we're here. I almost thought we wouldn't make it. That road is an abomination."

"It washed out in the spring flooding. Mr. Carter says he will be around to talk to you about it when he gets back."

James spoke like an adult. He *was* keen on property management, even at his tender age. Laurette watched the two of them, father and son, so alike yet so different. They were each wary of the other, like two dogs guarding their territory.

Beatrix stepped into the breach with another curtsey and a blush. "Thank you so much for inviting us to Stanbury Hill, my lord. We are having a splendid time, aren't we, James?"

"Yes." James shifted. "I am very wet. I believe I'll go up and change."

"An excellent idea," said Sadie, who had avoided Laurette's eye ever since she entered the kitchen with her charges. "Come, Bea. I'll get you sorted."

"And when you're done," Laurette said, "I want to talk to you."

"I was afraid of that," Sadie muttered.

"And so you should be," Laurette muttered back.

Laurette was left alone with Con in the kitchen, Nico having the good sense to disappear to search for his brother and escape the tension. Con headed for the bread and cut a chunk.

"Who is Mr. Carter?" Someone else to witness her fall, unless she was very careful.

"My caretaker," said Con. "Well, he's much more than that. He's my steward here and Yorkshire eyes and ears. A capable man. Ex-soldier. He'll manage the farm operation now that he's got the house to rights. He's gone for the sheep." He cut another piece and offered Laurette half. She shook her head and Con popped it whole into his mouth. When he was done, he leaned against the sideboard.

"You saw how he was. Polite but no more. As soon as I came into the kitchen he froze right up."

They were no longer speaking of Mr. Carter. "You've only had a year with him, and most of that time he was away at school."

"He dislikes me."

"Con, he's too young to understand what happened. Marianna never spoke against you, truly. She was as excited as a schoolgirl when your letters came and always shared them with James. I had a map—" She broke off, not certain her voice would work. "I had a map in the library at Vincent Lodge. When they came to visit, we marked your travels with little flags. We would read up on the countries." He would be surprised at the wealth and depth of her knowledge, for all she hadn't been at a proper school. It was never too late to learn, even when it came to the wisdom of her heart.

Con's face softened. "I never wrote to you. I couldn't bear to."

"I know. I think that's why Marianna brought your letters to me. She knew—" Laurette was not about to confess that news of Con controlled her life even when he was half a world away. "Your wife was really a most remarkable woman."

"Evidently." Con pushed his sleeves up. "I'm going to look at the outbuildings. Care to join me? As a friend," he added, as if reminding himself of his promise to her.

"I need to speak to Sadie, and catch up with Beatrix." In truth, Con's sadness had seeped across the kitchen, over-whelming her. Something must be done about James, but she had no idea what. A week wasn't very long to affect such a profound change, but it was all she was willing to give.

Laurette set about lighting the stove and put a kettle on. Nadia and Aram would be grateful once their conveyance finally lurched up the drive. The homey kitchen was immaculate and well-organized, fitted with every convenience thanks to the capable Mr. Carter. For an absentee owner, Con had lucked out with his servants. She wondered what Qalhata was doing in her own house, then realized with a pang she would never see the Nubian woman again, or her new friends on Jane Street.

Sadie bustled into the kitchen in a fresh apron, her graying hair neatly bound. "Here, Miss Laurie. I'll see to the children's tea."

"Where are they?"

"I told them to stay upstairs for a bit and have some quiet time. They are playing cards."

"They're getting on well?"

"Like brother and sister." Sadie flushed at her inadvertent honesty. "They fight tooth and nail but then make up. Like you and the marquess used to do at first when you came to live with your great aunt."

Aunt Henrietta had needed help, and had picked her impecunious nephew and his family to live with her and care for her in her old age. Laurette wondered if the old woman had ever been sorry, but, in the end she had left them the Lodge, more of a burden than a blessing—the house had been a shambles even then.

Laurette had half-forgotten the brief time Con had scorned her for being a girl, pulling her pigtails and teasing her, because he quickly found she was ready to share his adventures. She had followed him everywhere without hesitation, a shadow to the lonely boy he had been.

She sat down at the scrubbed pine table and waved her hand. "How long have you known about all this?"

"I know you're angry, but it was for your own good!" Turning from her, Sadie went to the cupboard, hauling out cups and plates.

"The tea can wait, Sadie. How long?"

Sadie gave her a long-suffering look, but Laurette was not to be swayed. Reluctantly, the maid dropped to a chair opposite and fiddled with her work-roughened hands.

"You do remember it was my idea to write to the marquess with your troubles months ago."

No wonder Con had been so accurate in sizing her new wardrobe. Laurette was stunned at the perfidy. "How could you?"

"We couldn't go on as we were. You know it. Master Charlie would have seen us all in the poorhouse. Lord Conover assured me he wanted to make an honest woman of you at long last. The man loves you."

Laurette snorted. Love was not blackmailing, trapping, unwrapping necessary secrets for all the world to see.

"You wouldn't have anything to do with him," Sadie continued. "All year you pushed him away. While I don't exactly condone what he did—"

"*Condone!*"

"He taught your brother a valuable lesson," Sadie retorted stubbornly. "You know as well as I the boy was on the road to ruination. He'll think twice before picking up a deck of cards and playing with money he doesn't have. He turned you into a beggar."

"You betrayed me."

"Nonsense. You always were a headstrong girl. Never would do what you ought. When the marquess proposed last year and you turned him down, I wanted to bend you over my knee. But now instead of a well-deserved spanking, you're going to be a marchioness." Sadie wore a satisfied smile.

Laurette could not smile back. "That is where you are entirely wrong. I will never marry him."

Sadie turned the color of the walls. "Don't tell me you've refused him again!"

"I did. Not that he really asked this time, just assumed, after all his spiderlike designs, I'd stick in his web. I have no need of Con or his fortune. We'll manage somehow. I dislike him immensely."

"Rubbish! And what about Bea? Here's your chance—"

"My chance to what?" Laurette asked, her voice a bitter whisper. "Tell her that I've lied to her her whole life? That she's a bastard?"

"I'll wash your mouth out with soap! Stop this now!"

The kettle whistled as Laurette sat, tears welling in her eyes. Sadie rose, lifted it from the ring and set it on a trivet. She continued to make up a tea tray despite the tears and sniffs of her own. It was her way to work through worry, so Laurette left her to it. She could not sit in this spotless white kitchen and pretend everything would be all right.

It would never be all right again.

Laurette got up and walked out the kitchen door, not really knowing where she was going. She needed to avoid Con until she got her raw emotions under control. Her head was whirling from the past hour's revelations. How could she endure being stuck here with the scheming marquess, his surly son, her innocent daughter, and hopelessly romantic Sadie for seven long days?

And the sheep, who were arriving any day. Despite her misery, Laurette laughed out loud and walked back up the hill to sit and think and watch for Nadia and Aram. It would serve Sadie right to be supplanted in the kitchen by someone else.

Two enormous trunks had been unloaded, each filled with toys and amusements for Beatrix and James. Con detected the slightest thaw in his son, for who could resist Chinese fireworks or Wellington's entire army of lead soldiers? Con had promised to reenact the Battle of Talavera, which remained unfortunately fresh in his mind. Although not officially attached to the army, Con had done his part for over two years before he was wounded. He had realized even then he took a deliberate risk to his life and courted danger, for in his youth he saw only the limits and bleakness of his marriage.

After his abbreviated honeymoon, he had stepped back into his home as a stranger. Unfamiliar faces and objects surrounded him. Footmen in proper livery raced about with the trunks and cases and crates that had followed them throughout Italy, multiplying at each stop like rectangular rabbits. The worn flagstone floor was now inlaid marble, the dark paneling painted white, a lacy-patterned pale blue paper on the wall. The effect was rather like walking into a snow fort in winter. He looked into the drawing room and saw a vast portrait of his wife hanging over the new mantel. This room, too, was pale and blue, just like his wife, who had been ill these past two weeks. She wanted to go home—she was very certain she was enceinte, she had said one morning cheerfully, before she rushed off to find a basin in their hotel suite. Con had stood uncomprehendingly still until relief washed over him. If Marianna was already carrying a child, his nights need no more be fraught with wine and fantasies of Laurette.

Con had never had much, hadn't missed it. It was not the lack of money that troubled him, but the loss of his freedom. He'd have to beg his wife so he could pay for a pint at the pub in the village, if she allowed him to go. She made him feel like a callow schoolboy. Yes, she treated him with deference in public. If anything, she was far more vested in his being a marquess than he had ever been. In private she was perfectly if dismissively correct. It was clear who held the pursestrings. Who was in control. His marriage had been a business arrangement, the agreement between his uncle and his father-in-law an insidious and necessary insult to his pride. But his wife had achieved her objective—rising to the peerage, mother to the future Marquess of Conover. He was the tool of her ambition, and much like a stud that had served his purpose, Con felt relegated to the pasture.

No, he was in the paddock, barbed wire fences all around.

It had taken years and miles of travel before he was at peace with his position. When it was past time to come home, Con had convinced himself he could rub along well enough with his wife if that was the only way to be part of his son's life. But it was too late. Marianna had died before his ship docked and his son would always view him with suspicion. The boy's heart would not be won over by trunkfuls of toys.

Nico and Tomas had helped the children haul their booty upstairs. Aram was inspecting the butler's pantry and rear ranging items he had deemed necessary to bring to the wilds of Yorkshire. Nadia and Sadie were squabbling cheerfully in the kitchen as they prepared dinner. He had no idea what Laurette was doing. Con swallowed the brandy that he had brought from London.

Dinner was an hour off. The children would be joining them. For the first time in his life, he would have the people he loved most together at one table, and it scared him witless.

He tried to take his mind off his problems by going over the exhaustive lists Jacob Carter had left for him. His confidence in the man had not been misplaced. Stanbury Hill Farm was miraculously different than it had been last November. The taint of his uncle was washed away by fresh coats of paint. Carter and his crew had not only spent the winter and spring decorating, but preparing and planting the fields for forage. He would make a success of the smallholding, might even turn a reasonable profit. Laurette and Beatrix would have something to call their own, if he could not persuade Laurette to become his wife.

A tap at the door made him drop the papers on the blotter. "Come in."

Laurette was a vision in a deep burgundy silk dress, even

though she had tucked a plain white fichu for propriety's sake into the bodice. Her own, no doubt, as he did not remember supplying Laurette with anything quite so proper. It took Con a minute to find his voice. "You look lovely."

"I daresay I'm a bit overdressed for dinner on a sheep farm." She flashed a brief wide smile. "May I sit?"

Con arose from his stupor. "Of course. After this afternoon, I'm surprised to see you here, Laurie."

"I *am* very angry with you."

Con examined her open, freckled face, the face he'd loved since they were children. He had tried to interest himself in clearer complexions, tidier hair, simpering smiles to no avail. No one else was Laurette. "You don't look angry."

"Looks are deceiving. You forget how long I've learned to lie. I am a mistress of deception."

"But no longer *my* mistress."

"Indeed not, and that is all your doing."

Con pushed an inkpot an inch to the left. "I'm sorry. It was not my intention to cause harm to any of us."

"I've already expressed my opinion of your intentions, my lord. I hear Hell is most inclement."

Con shrugged and tried to make a joke. "I've lived in the desert."

"That is what I've come to talk to you about."

She looked very earnest, as she must when she taught the village girls. "Pray, go on."

"Something you said earlier—about taking me to your favorite places. I believe that's a very good idea."

Con felt a wave of confusion. "I thought our relationship was at an end, Laurie."

She shook her head in impatience. "You misunderstand me. I'm not making myself very clear, am I? You should travel. With James. Take him out of school and show him your world. I know despite his reticence with you he was fascinated by your letters. You say you are writing a book for him, but what better way to explain things to him than to take him with you on the grandest of Grand Tours? You would be thrown together every day and bound to overcome your differences."

Con leaned back in his chair and closed his eyes. He couldn't tell her the only place he wanted to be was Ryland Grove with her installed in the Marchioness' suite. Not that he would let her spend even one night alone in it.

"I suppose your idea has some merit. Thank you for your concern. I shall consider it, once our week is at an end. Perhaps by then James and I will be friends and such a trip will be unnecessary. He's rather young, you know, to be introduced to the scandalous sights of the East."

"You've seen a great deal of wickedness then."

"A very great deal." Con chuckled inwardly. If she knew that he'd lived as a monk she'd never believe it. "And travel at present is dangerous. The Ottoman Empire is, I fear, in disarray, one of the reasons I chose a prosaic Yorkshire farm over my Greek villa. There's to be a war soon. My contacts have warned me there might be disruption to trade routes."

"Will your business be affected?"

"Perhaps. Even the largest bribes cannot stop an army. Don't worry. I've made adjustments. My fortune is safe."

"I care nothing for your fortune!"

"I know," he said softly. "I didn't mean to accuse you of avarice. No man has had a less demanding mistress. A mistress," he added with a grin, "who has volunteered to *cook*."

"Perhaps I wish to cause you harm. Poison you."

Her tone was teasing, almost saucy. It hurt worse than her frostiness.

"I would employ a taster so your murderous impulses came to naught. Nico or Tom would do most anything for me."

"They are both much too young and handsome to die."

"My dear Laurette, they are virtually children. Never tell me they've caught your fancy."

"No man will catch my fancy again, not even you." As if to prove her point, she looked away.

She'd brought their banter to a close with a thud.

She was withdrawing. Leaving in spirit even if she had a week left here. "What will you do when you go back home, Laurie?"

"My life is full enough. There are the village girls to teach and the house to maintain."

"What if Charlie wants to sell it once the renovations are complete?" Vincent Lodge was costing him a pretty penny—between it and Stanbury Hill and Jane Street, he was beginning to feel a slight pinch. But he would put the Jane Street house on the market—he'd never have use for it again.

"I suppose that's his right. He won't need it once he takes orders and finds a cozy vicarage to live in."

Con snorted. "I doubt seriously your brother will ever be anyone's idea of a parson."

Laurette's golden eyebrows raised. "Then why did you send him on his pilgrimage?"

"To get him out of my way, of course. It was all a part of my grand design upon you. As you said, I've been ruthless." He swallowed the last of his brandy.

"I have been thinking all afternoon."

Con raised his eyebrow, but felt his hopes rising as well. "And?"

"I understand why you've done all this. I cannot like it, but I understand it." She fingered the linen at her neck. "I thought, you know, perhaps when Beatrix was much older, I might explain. Tell her the truth."

"A deathbed confession?"

Laurette blushed. "Maybe." She stood up and walked to the long window. The sunlight set fire to the gold and amber in her hair "I am a coward, Con. For years I kept the secret because I feared Mr. Berryman. He was all that stood between us and the poorhouse. Beatrix has the advantages she does because of him. Then Marianna saw to her welfare when he died. She was very generous."

"You cannot thank them for keeping your child from you. From me."

Laurette turned to him. "Would you have stayed if you knew about her existence? You left James."

Three words. *You left James.* She cut him to the core.

"I didn't love Marianna. I loved you. I still love you." It took all his willpower to stay seated behind his desk rather than get up and take her in his arms. "At first I suppose I thought of James as the price I had to pay for my bargain. He didn't belong to me, not really. God knows I was grateful when I learned Marianna was pregnant. I felt like a male whore, Laurette, like a thoroughbred purchased to cover a mare. You cannot imagine the despair I felt every night when she expected me to come to her bed."

"But James is innocent in all this."

He swallowed back the bile. "I know. I was stupid. And twenty years old when I left. If you recall, I didn't have the best judgment. If I had, I never would have let you seduce me."

Laurette nodded, did not dispute the blame he placed upon her. She had been as determined to lose her maidenhead as the Berrymans were to buy his marquessate. "I did, didn't I? And you were not easy. But I never gave up. I was a fool."

Thank God for it, Con thought. She had given him precious memories to cling to when he had no hope. This last month had given him more. They were no longer children hurrying in the grass in fear of discovery, but adults who still savored each other, despite the broken promises.

"You always were a stubborn chit. Can we be friends again, Laurie?"

She brushed the curtain back. "I will try. But no more of your surprises or schemes. We shall do our best to provide the children with a holiday and then go our separate ways. It's for the best."

"I cannot agree, but will respect your wishes. If you should change your mind—"

"I won't."

"But if you do, I'll always be right next door." It would kill him to be so close to her, but what choice did he have?

Chapter 13

Laurette woke up to the bleating of one hundred sheep and lambs, the frantic bark of a dog, and the children's shouts. She wrapped her robe about her and went to the window. Judging from the sun in the sky, she had shamefully slept half the morning away. Everyone else seemed to be up and outside, busy driving the wooly parade down the lane into the enclosure.

The knots of tension were still in her neck. Dinner last night had been an uncomfortable affair, despite her and Bea's attempt at levity and civility. It had been hard work on her part, but Bea seemed like a born peacemaker. Laurette had six more days to try to affect a reconciliation between Con and James, six more days to love Bea before she took her home. Her Cornish cousins would not be expecting the child's return so soon—Con had bribed them generously to steal Bea away. Perhaps Bea could spend a few days at Vincent Lodge before they made the trip, although Sadie had said the house was in no state for company, thanks to the infusion of the Marquess of Conover's money. There was scaffolding everywhere. Con had employed thatchers, plasterers, painters. Laurette reckoned she'd scarcely recognize her old home when she got back. Her neighbors must be agog at the sudden improvement of the Vincent fortunes.

Laurette rubbed the back of her neck absently as she watched the activity below. She was more than a little ashamed that she had succumbed to Con's blackmail so easily, fell into his bed so easily, fell back in love with him so easily, no matter what she told him. The last few weeks had been a heady mix of frustration, lust, tenderness and boredom. She would have to keep her wits to get through the rest of their time together.

Con had made no real objection when she called their bargain over yesterday. Laurette thought of his face as he stood on the hill, the breeze blowing his midnight hair back to reveal all the hard planes and angles of his face. His lips had been set, as though he wanted to argue but was holding back. He had been reasonable, even affable last night when she found him in his study. So different from when he'd last broken her heart.

The standing stones were too far, the gazebo within sight of the back lawn of Ryland Grove—within the sight of Con's wife's very pale blue eyes. So Laurette had gone to their tree at its secluded spot on the river for two days, leaving little signs in its crook that she had been there, signs only he would recognize. Surely he would come on the third.

October had turned brisk. She layered herself in shawls under her cloak, slipping out the kitchen door down to the bottom of her garden. She dashed across the rock bridge as she had done as a child, then followed the rough path along the Piddle until she came to Ryland Grove's serpentine wall. It was a low, paltry thing, still easy to climb over where it wasn't tumbled down outright. Beyond it was a vast, empty down. She continued on the track until the lone twisted tree rose up from the chalk river bank in misplaced optimism, trying to reach the wood opposite with its gnarled arms.

Her talismans were missing. The flat pink stone, her skipping stone Con had given her and taught her to use as a child, and the little muslin bag of loose spangles she had picked off her wedding dress were no longer tucked into the seat of the tree. In their place was a small carved wooden box.

He had been here!

She scrambled up, fitting herself against the smooth bark and opened the box. Inside was a silver crescent pin of laurel leaves. Her hands shook as she pinned it onto her dress beneath the scarves. He had thought of her on his travels.

On his honeymoon.

She had thought of him, too—of no one else save Con. The weeks had lumbered by with painful slowness. She hadn't slept, hadn't eaten, felt she was literally dying of a broken heart. She told herself Con had had no choice but to marry and make good his debts, but a tiny part of her hated him for giving in. They could have run away together, disappeared. Now it was she who was to disappear.

The Vincent cousins would keep her until the summer. Until it was over. She would eat roast goose with them this Christmas and watch their jonquils burst forth instead of her mama's next spring. She would leave this box and the pin behind in Cornwall, something for the child to remember its real parents by.

She had been caught sometime before Con married despite their precautions, a punishment, her mother said, for her wicked willfulness. There had been a scramble, but at last her father had remembered a cousin and his childless wife in Penzance. They were willing to foster her child for their share of the Berryman fortune.

Laurette had endured a hideous interview with Mr. Berryman, who had made the financial arrangements with her father. The plan to have her removed from the neighborhood before Con returned was upset by the earlier-than-expected arrival of the marquess and his bride. But Laurette's trunks were now packed and she would leave tomorrow.

She had been forbidden to tell him. Mr. Berryman would stop Charlie's tuition and withdraw any support for the child's fostering. Con must never suspect she carried a child. She was thinner now than she'd ever been anyhow. Sadie told her once she got away from the Lodge and the daily recriminations from her parents, she'd bloom. But Sadie wouldn't see her. Laurette was to go to Cornwall alone.

Laurette waited in the tree, her eyes closed. He was coming, she knew it. She'd wait all day perched in the crook if she had to. Her mama had retired with one of her headaches and her father had shut himself up in his study with a bottle of second-best brandy. The Vincents were costing Mr. Berryman a fair amount, but rumor was he could afford to support her family and the whole of the village beside without so much as the blink of an eye. He had bought a marquessate for his daughter, after all.

She heard his footfall on the path but kept her eyes shut, as though seeing Con's brightness would burn her.

"Laurette."

The one word held all of his longing. She smiled and looked down on him. Everything yet nothing had changed.

"Hello, Con."

"May I come up?"

"Oh, yes."

She was snug in his arms in the crook of their tree. Suddenly her wraps were too warm for the dull autumn day. Con must have known, as his hands slipped under her old cloak, parted them and brushed her tender breasts.

"May I kiss you, just once for old time's sake?"

Laurette turned her face to his. His lips settled on hers with charming hesitation.

She opened her mouth to him, tasting him for the first time in weeks. A ripple of bliss spread from her scalp to the toes in her boots. His tongue was warm and seeking. She relaxed in his embrace, shutting her mind to the impossibility of the future as his hands skimmed her bodice.

She had today only. And desperate as she was, she couldn't manage to make love to him in a tree. She pushed him away gently and unknotted the strings of her cloak. Con raised a dark eyebrow.

Laurette kissed him quickly and hopped to the ground. She spread the cloak and shawls under the low branches, bare now. Anyone could come upon them. No green leaves and tall grasses would provide shelter. But it was unlikely Con's city wife would take a walk on such a gray day.

Laurette shivered with cold and anticipation. Soon Con covered her with his body, the scratch of wool against her bare flesh a welcome discomfort. She needed to feel every point of contact between them, no matter how harsh. There was no time for play, just the brutal business of two bodies joining for one last bite of pleasure. She was as fierce as he, writhing, nipping hard enough to draw blood and his wife's questions.

But Con belonged to her and no other, no matter what it said on the marriage lines.

She gloried in his hard grasp as he rode her toward heaven. There were no awaiting angels, just the devilish realization that this was the end. For now. Con's face was a mask of pain as he withdrew and spent into his hand.

"We cannot do this again, Laurie." He propped himself up at the base of the tree as she pulled her petticoats down.

"I know, silly," she tried to joke, arranging herself with misplaced modesty on the cloak. "I'll be away for months. But I see no reason why, when I come back, we cannot meet discreetly." She tried not to think of the possible consequences. Of what Mr. Berryman might bring them all to. She had to cling to the hope of it.

"There is every reason." His cheeks were flushed, but his lips were white. "Marianna is bearing my child. Now do you see? I am married. About to become a father. I've already lost most of my honor. Don't expect me to lose it all."

"A—a baby?" Laurette saw black swirls dance before her

eyes. She swallowed her breath and clutched at the fabric beneath her.

"Here, you're cold." Con shook the dry bits of grass from her scarves and wrapped them around her shoulders. "Get up, Laurie. I'm sorry. I only meant to kiss you. But, my God. I love you and there's no way out, none. I'm a bastard to use you like this."

Laurette stumbled as she rose, and Con caught her. He fingered the crooked pin at her breast. "Do you like it? I bought it on your eighteenth birthday."

A day that had gone unremarked by her parents, who were so angry with her. "It's lovely," she said woodenly. "Thank you."

"Don't thank me for anything! I've ruined your life!"

How dramatic he looked, his fashionably cut hair in disarray, his face all sharp angles, his eyes bleak. She noticed for the first time he was head to toe in new, expensive clothes, wrinkled now, boots scuffed where they had dug into the earth as he mounted her. He had been bought and paid for.

"N-nonsense. My life is not ruined." Just shattered into jagged points of reality. Laurette bent to lift the cloak from the ground and stilled, dizzy. She had hoped somehow he would not sleep with his wife, but have a true marriage of convenience, like other people in the ton. She could not imagine replicating what they had just done with any other man, ever. But Con had somehow made his marriage real. She felt his hands brush her as he fastened the cloak at her throat.

What an idiot she was. Her parents were right about so little, but they had been right about Con. She was young and so, so stupid.

From a great distance she heard Con tell her earnestly he had only ever thought of her when he made love to his wife, but that made it all worse somehow. She turned from his out-

stretched hand and hurried back down the path, moving as
swiftly as her leaden feet could carry her.

Tomorrow she would leave her home. Today was not too
soon to drive Con from her heart. In six months time, she
would entrust her cousins with the child and start anew. Her
life was not ruined. Her heart was not broken. Her tears
were not falling.

Laurette brushed away fresh tears. For over ten years she'd
pushed away these inconvenient recollections. But seeing
Con every day had brought the past to life again. She could
not help but remember the days when they were young—
when hope filled their hearts, when rules were meant to be
broken, mistakes were meant to be made. But Laurette could
never think of Bea as a mistake—one look at her shining face
in the midst of all those sheep proved that.

The children were being butted about, squealing in delight. Con towered above them in a white sea of wool, his
head thrown back, laughing. Another man, even taller than
Con, hung back at the edge, pulling his cap from his chestnut
hair, taking in the Mad Marquess and his charges. No doubt
he thought they were all a nuisance, city folk who had no
idea the noise they were making were disturbing the creatures. He barked out something to his dog, who sat down
reluctantly, waiting for the foolish people to stop their nonsense so he could do his job.

Laurette grinned at the spectacle below, wishing she could
be in the middle of it. She was a country girl at heart, and
had done her best for Penzance-reared and Bath-schooled
Beatrix to introduce her to pastoral life during her visits to
Vincent Lodge. Perhaps if she hurried, she could join her
family in the festivities.

Her family. Where had that inconvenient thought come
from? Her greatest desire was something that couldn't be, no
matter how much Con had manipulated everyone into position. She shook her head at her stupidity, then splashed some

water on her sleep-creased face. It took her no time at all to braid her hair back and slip into a simple dress and comfortable boots, suitable for sheep inspection. The dog had begun to yip again, so their progress to the paddock must be in train.

She dashed down the stairs and through the empty kitchen. Her stomach rumbled, but at this point luncheon was more probable than breakfast. When she stepped outside, she found Sadie and Nadia sitting on a bench in the tidy kitchen garden, shelling peas. They seemed to be in perfect accord, disregarding the "too many cooks" theory. Laurette waved off the offer of breakfast and headed for the children.

James was straddling the high stone wall as the small black-and-white dog and Mr. Carter confined the sheep beyond it. Bea's face was flushed with excitement as she chattered up to Con. Laurette nearly stumbled when she saw the expression on his face—he bore a look of unmistakable love for the child. He tugged at one of her pigtails, teasing her. She spun away from him laughing.

Just as she used to do. How could Bea not know he was her father? It was plain as day!

But no. Laurette knew what to look for. Perhaps a stranger might not notice. She hoped the sinking feeling in her stomach only meant she was hungry.

"Cousin Laurette! The sheep have come!" Beatrix cried.

"So I see and hear." There was an awful racket from the pen. *And smell.*

"Mr. Carter and Sam drove them all night because of the full moon. He says sheep would rather sleep in the daytime than at night anyway." Beatrix turned to Con. "Do sheep sleep standing up like horses?"

"It depends. If they feel safe, they'll sleep lying down on the ground. Sometimes some will serve as watchers for the herd, staying awake while the others nap."

"Watchsheep!" giggled Beatrix.

"How did you become so knowledgeable about sheep, my

lord?" There had been cattle at Ryland Grove before the drought claimed them.

"My son was quite convincing when he encouraged me to purchase the Ryeland sheep. I believe he's hit upon a successful scheme for Stanbury Hill. He's showing excellent business sense."

Laurette watched the tips of James's ears turn pink. It was his only response to Con's praise as he balanced on the rocks.

"And of course I bumped into a shepherd or two in the Holy Land. . . . Jacob!" Con shouted over the bleating of the sheep. "You must be dead on your feet. James and I will fill the troughs with water. Take the rest of the day off. You've earned it."

Con's farm manager ambled through a clot of sheep, his dog at his side. For a man who'd spent the night walking the drovers' path through the dales, he looked fit and awake. And remarkably handsome. He was a decade or so older than Con, lean and dark from time spent out of doors. Sunlight burnished the copper and silver in his close-cropped hair and his tweeds, though worn, were clean. He met Laurette's eye and nodded.

"Laurette, this is my caretaker and right-hand man, Jacob Carter. Jacob, may I present my Dorset neighbor and childhood friend, Miss Vincent. She is Bea's cousin and my son's honorary aunt."

Mr. Carter was well-spoken and not shy. "How do you do, Miss Vincent? It's a pleasure to meet you. The children have been looking forward all week to your arrival." The man extended a strong hand and after a moment Laurette realized she was expected to shake it.

"Lord Conover tells me you were in His Majesty's army."

"Just a sergeant. Put out to pasture now." The man grinned, revealing strong white teeth. His Yorkshire burr was blunted by years spent away from home. "Lord Conover needed a local man and I needed a job. Stanbury Hill Farm has been a challenge, but I hope I've been up to it."

"Don't fish for compliments, Jacob. You know I appreciate what you've done. But the road!"

"Aye, I knew you wouldn't like it much. But you don't have to sleep on it or eat it. I thought getting the house in order, haying and putting in a garden took priority."

Judging from his tone, he was certainly not one bit cowed working for a marquess. Con cuffed him on the shoulder. "Get some rest and we'll talk about it later. James, let's get cracking at the pumps."

Jacob Carter whistled for his dog and they headed back to the house. Laurette had seen the room he kept off the kitchen yesterday, a Spartan chamber meant to be the housekeeper's office. She imagined he'd spent the winter living in it and the kitchen, shooing off the birds and shutting up the rest of the rambling house. The property was completely isolated from any neighbors, and she wondered how he spent his time now that he wasn't repairing and renovating.

Beatrix reached through the fence to nuzzle a lamb. "I can help, too."

Laurette saw the stubborn set of her daughter's mouth and knew she was seeing a shorter version of herself. But as they were "cousins," that would explain the family resemblance to anyone who wondered.

"Bea, let's leave the men to their chores. I haven't had breakfast yet. I thought we might share some tea and have a coze. We haven't really had time to catch up with all your news."

Beatrix fitted her hand into Laurette's. "Oh, all right. Aren't the lambs the most darling things? Lord Conover says he'll get a few sheep for pets at Ryland Grove, so they'll be there when I visit next summer."

"I'm glad you're looking forward to next year already," Laurette smiled. "There might come a day when you're too much of a young lady to bother with me."

Beatrix frowned. "If you mean I'm to have a debut one day, my parents say they can't afford it."

Laurette felt a ripple of anger. Her cousins were well compensated for their care of Beatrix, and surely they knew that funds would be available for such an important event. Not that Laurette had cared about her own come-out, except to entice Con. She shivered. Perhaps it was just as well Beatrix would not be presented to society if it meant keeping her innocence a few years longer.

But she was being an alarmist. Beatrix was a sensible, sedate child, reared by good, devout people. She wouldn't be slipping into a shimmering dress, dancing the night away, and seducing anyone the next morning.

They entered the kitchen to find Mr. Carter not in bed but holding court at the scrubbed pine table, his dog Sam politely sitting at his feet. Abandoning the lunch preparations, Sadie and Nadia were flying about the kitchen brewing coffee and scrambling eggs. Laurette's stomach rumbled a reminder again.

"Here now, Miss Laurie. It won't do for you to wait until luncheon to eat. I know how you turn devilish when you're hungry." Sadie cracked another egg into the creamware bowl. "I'll bring a plate to you in the breakfast room."

"Don't be silly. If Mr. Carter has no objection, we'll join him." She eyed the chickens that were trussed and waiting on the sideboard. "Just a bit of bread for me. I promised Bea a cup of tea, too."

"And a raisin scone if there are any left from breakfast, please." Beatrix sat down and folded her hands, looking at Mr. Carter rather worshipfully. He winked at her.

"Don't know when I had my breakfast with two such lovely ladies. Not since I was a lad and my sisters were at home."

"Is your family nearby, Mr. Carter?" Laurette asked, buttering a half-slice of bread.

"A long day's walk. It's just my youngest sister left now,

and her man and children at the family place. They raise sheep, too. Not Ryelands, though. But Henry knew where I could find some."

"It seems you found plenty."

Carter shrugged. "Enough for what land's left here. His lordship's uncle sold off most of it ages ago, I understand."

Yes, Con's uncle had stripped him of every possession he could and beggared him into the bargain. "Did you know him?"

"He was a recluse, wasn't he? But everyone knew him hereabouts. Used to walk, rain or shine, grumbling to himself. I tried to talk him into hiring me to fix the place up, but he wouldn't hear of it. Shocking, this old house was. I remember when Miss Stanbury married his lordship's father here. I wasn't more than seven or eight, but all the neighbors were invited to the wedding and the big reception after. There were tents and tables on the lawn and all the ale you could drink, even though her old man had hit a bad financial patch. Sold off the best furniture, they say, for that party. The old gent died soon after. But his lass Katie looked like an angel to a boy like me." His eyes slid over to Beatrix. "There's a painting of her in the attic. Needs mending. Ripped in the corner, alas, and beyond my expertise. But she looked a bit like you, little miss."

Laurette's hands shook. She tore the crust off her bread to keep them busy. "It's said we all have a twin somewhere," she said tamping down her apprehension.

"True enough. I met a Frenchie that looked enough like me to be my brother. Had to kill him, though."

Beatrix's mouth hung open.

"Here now, I didn't mean to shock your delicate sensibilities." Carter grinned again, then tucked into his eggs. "Absolutely delicious, Miss Sadie. Don't know when I've eaten so well since you came."

"Go on with you, now." Sadie flushed at the man and not just from the heat of her exertions. Mr. Carter was a charmer.

Even Nadia, who was devoted to Aram, beamed at him as she topped off his coffee. Laurette found her bread difficult to swallow.

A trip to the attic was in order.

But not now. Now it was time for Beatrix, because there was so precious little of it.

Chapter 14

Once they finished breakfast, they rambled outside, Bea telling a comprehensive tale about her stay in the country so far. They climbed a hill and Laurette found herself short of breath. Too much city living had definitely spoiled her. They sat under a lone tree, spreading their skirts on the shade-dappled grass.

"You're getting on with James, then?"

Beatrix gave a long-suffering sigh. "He's all right. For a boy."

"And Lord Conover says he's all boy. I understand he gets into quite a bit of trouble at school."

Her daughter's face turned serious. "I think he wants to be bad enough so his father will have to come and get him. I don't know who James wants to cause more trouble for—his masters or his father."

Laurette's eyes widened in shock. "But he loves school! He's so bright and has always had high marks!"

Beatrix shrugged. "He'd rather displease his father just now. James is angry, you know. He wants to know why his father left him."

"Oh, dear." It was one thing to be resentful, but if James ruined his chances at an education, he'd hurt himself the most.

"You know, don't you? Why he went away when James

was born. You've known Lord Conover since he was a boy himself. He told me all about that when he came to visit me at school, how you were the best of friends."

Laurette studied her daughter's earnest little face. Her bronze-gold lashes framed hazel eyes that seemed older than her years. There were a few new freckles from the week spent out-of-doors with an active boy. Her half-brother.

A fact which she must never find out.

Oh, lord. What if Beatrix was forming a childish *tendre* for James? Now that they had been thrown together, what if it turned into something dangerous in the years to come? An unprecedented level of panic rose in Laurette's chest and she looked away.

"It's very complicated."

"James knows Lord Conover made a marriage of convenience. Most people in the ton do. But they don't abandon their babies." Bea looked disapproving, as well she should. Con had run away.

But so had Laurette. She'd felt she had no choice but to give Bea a better future, but what if she'd been wrong?

"Sometimes people do things that seem terrible, but they think it for the best. When they are very young—" Laurette's voice cracked, and she swallowed hard. This was territory that was far too dangerous. She wasn't sure she could excuse Con's behavior herself. And her own was beyond excuse.

Damn Con for throwing her into this and forcing her to pick at the scabs of her worst wounds. She was not ready to tell Beatrix anything. But Con was right. The child was smart. Laurette cleared her throat and began again.

"Lord Conover cares very much for James, and is sad that in the past he was not the parent he should have been. More than sad. Guilty. It's left him—a little unhinged, I think. Not—not in a dangerous way," she added, seeing Bea's look of alarm. "This holiday is a start meant to make up for the years he wasted. He knows a made a mistake with James. People make mistakes."

"I know that. Lord Conover said as much to me when we first met. He said he hadn't done his duty to his people. His neighbors. He was worried about all of you in Lower Conover."

Laurette tried to laugh. "He needn't worry about me! I'm perfectly content."

"Yes, but you're alone, except for Sadie. Your parents are dead and Cousin Charlie is a very poor sort of brother to you. He gets into worse scrapes than James and is old enough to know better."

"Beatrix Isabella Vincent! Who has been feeding you this gossip? My brother Charles is of no concern to you or Lord Conover! Damn that interfering man!" Laurette sprang up from the grass and brushed her skirts. Blast Con for whatever stories he told Bea. Sadie, too. It was time for another talk with them both.

But she had to tamp her anger down. It would not do to lose her temper any further and say something that Beatrix would remember and file away. "I apologize, Bea. You know I hate people meddling in my life."

"Please don't be angry with Lord Conover. He's just trying to be kind."

"By using you to tell his ridiculous tales?"

Beatrix looked alarmed again. "No, no. He didn't tell me anything ridiculous. He was most gentlemanly with me when he came to visit. Either Miss Davenport or Miss Emily were with us, and he could not have been more proper."

Propriety counted with Bea—she was a very proper girl, something Laurette had never been, much to her regret. "How many times did he come to Bath to see you?"

"Just three. And he didn't come to see *me*, exactly. He had business there. But he was very kind. When we first met I was a little shy of him—but then he told me funny stories about life at Ryland Grove and your village when you both were children." Bea dropped her lashes. "I think he likes you, Cousin Laurette."

Perfect. She was going to strangle Con for using their child so. "Don't go playing matchmaker," Laurette said tartly.

"James likes you too. A lot. Sadie says you could be a marchioness and then James could have a mother again."

Add Sadie to the strangulation list. "What nonsense! I'll have you know we're leaving here in a week. No, six days." She looked at the timepiece pinned to her dress. "Five and a half now. Lord Conover has overstepped his bounds by miles. The man needs to know he cannot have whatever he thinks he wants."

Beatrix paled beneath her freckles. "It's my fault. I've made you cross."

Laurette sat down again and clasped the child's palm. "No. Lord Conover and I agreed yesterday we would stay a week only. It isn't proper for us to be here."

"B-but I thought I was here for the summer," Beatrix said in a small voice. "And Sadie's here to chaperone." She looked crushed.

"Sadie, God bless her, is just as bad as Con," Laurette mumbled. "We won't go straight home to Penzance. I know you love the country. We can stay at Vincent Lodge for a few days. Weeks even."

"Sadie said the house is all torn up. And the lambs just came."

Bugger the lambs. It was as if Con knew just what soft-hearted Beatrix needed. She'd been mad for animals her whole short life, her cousins living in a small house in the middle of town with no room or tolerance to spare for a pet.

"There are the chickens at the Lodge."

"Sadie sent them all to the Cobb farm for the summer. Squire Cobb promised not to eat any of them."

"And Squire Cobb is very fond of roast chicken," Laurette smiled.

"He *is* very fat," Beatrix agreed. "As are his daughters." She covered her mouth. "I'm not being very nice, am I?"

"That's all right. The Cobb twins are not very nice themselves. Serves them right they look like stuffed hens." Neither woman, despite their parents' coddling or their substantial portion, had contracted a marriage yet. Laurette reflected that their joint debut at the Blue Calf Inn's assembly room all those years ago had brought none of the three of them the usual result. There was a high proportion of spinsters in their neck of Dorset, and Con, damn him, was not going to change that unless he married a Cobb twin.

"Well, I guess we can muddle through all the mess," Beatrix said. She bit a lip and looked forlorn. "I don't want to go home quite yet. Mama and Papa won't be expecting me for ages and ages. Perhaps the Marquess will let us live at the Grove. Oh, but I forgot, there are workmen all over there too." She gave a little sigh.

My word, but her daughter was dramatic, running through all her sad, wistful expressions in one sitting. Laurette was tempted to ask if she was performing in plays at school. She decided to take another tack. "I believe if we leave James and his father alone to their own devices, they may find their difficulties at an end. If you and I are not present at dinner to keep the conversation flowing, they'll be forced to talk to each other." Laurette teased Bea's pigtail as she saw Con do this morning. "I was very proud of you last evening. You tried very hard to engage them both. You're my little peacemaker."

Beatrix colored prettily. "It's only that I feel sorry for James. He wants to love his father but he cannot."

"Families are not always arranged as we'd like them. My own parents were sometimes unsatisfactory, just as I'm sure they thought I was an unsatisfactory daughter. But you get on with your mother and your father, do you not?"

"Oh, yes. Everything is as it should be, I suppose." Her lower lip quivered. Laurette wondered if more drama was about to unfold.

"But?"

"They are very strict, you know. We don't precisely have

fun. I think they're glad I am away at school for most of the year." She paused. "They didn't seem to mind at all when the marquess wrote to them and asked their permission for me to stay away for the summer."

Laurette closed her eyes. Her cousins were perfectly worthy people, if a bit dull. They were much older, probably finding Beatrix to be more spirited as she grew. Just the week at Stanbury Hill had transformed her quiet child, given her a sparkle Laurette had rarely seen. They would probably look at her now and see a Laurette waiting to happen.

To be reckless. Indiscreet. Shameful. All the things that had brought Laurette heartbreak. She could not bear for her daughter to be hurt as she was.

She could not bear her daughter's hatred if she learned the truth.

Con had probably promised her cousins more money if they allowed him to take Bea in and form this impossible family he planned. And her cousins must be tempted—Jonas Vincent's business schemes were invariable failures and his wife Mary always grumbled over economies.

The months Laurette spent in Cornwall waiting to give birth had been miserable on so many levels. Her cousins took their Christian charity seriously, but deeply disapproved of her unwed state. They had all been shut up in the dark little house, only Jonas escaping to go to chapel on Sundays and Wednesday nights. When Beatrix was born, passed off as Mary's, no one was the wiser. Laurette stayed to "help," nursing the baby until her first little crooked tooth heralded a switch to solid food and cups of milk. She had sat back as Mary was called mama, convincing herself that the situation was for the best.

And it still was, fun or no fun.

"I promise you some amusement when we go home. We'll get the chickens back, at the very least."

"All right." Bea's nose was still wrinkled. "Do you think Lord Conover will let Nico escort us?"

Laurette had not thought that far ahead. But surely Con would make arrangements for their protection. There were Nico, Tomas and their father Aram to choose from. "I shall let Lord Conover know your preference, but as his guests we will have to let him decide what's convenient."

Beatrix stood up and smoothed the wrinkles from her skirts. Her cousin Mary would be horrified that the child had sat in the grass, that she'd run wild for a week without a hat. That accounted for Bea's new freckles, nowhere near the number of Laurette's, but enough. Laurette knew from experience no amount of lemon juice or lotion would remove them before Bea's return to Cornwall.

"Well, if we're going to leave so soon, I want to spend as much time with the lambs as I can. There's a set of twins, you know. Mr. Carter said so."

Laurette thought that sheep by their very placid nature were entirely boring, but whatever pleased her daughter pleased her as well. "Of course, Bea. Go on, then. I think I'm going to stay up here for a while. Explore the territory."

Beatrix gave her a quick kiss and dashed down the hillock. Laurette cupped her cheek to catch the warmth of the kiss. There had been so few of them, and none as spontaneous as this one. As her daughter grew, they would be separated by miles and circumstance. She would treasure this week that Con had arranged, no matter the deceit on which it was based.

And now to enjoy herself. After being shut up in a carriage for days, it was time to see if her legs were still limber. Laurette decided the waterfall would be a good destination—just far enough away to test her unused muscles. The sound of the water would be a balm to her senses and she'd have some privacy to think, to figure out precisely how she would balance her emotions over the next few days.

She gave a bitter laugh. If she had known that the carriage ride yesterday morning was the last time she'd ever engage in sexual relations, she would have paid a bit more attention. She had nearly taken Con's attentions for granted, her body responding artlessly to his every touch. They had fallen into a pattern over the last two months that made most speech unnecessary. In fact, she was quite sure Con kissed her so often to keep her quiet. She had complained endlessly about her boredom until she befriended her unusual neighbors. She had, in fact, been something of a shrew, resentful of Con's control over her life.

And now it truly was at an end.

She hitched her skirt up and clambered over a stone wall that seemed to go on unbroken for miles. The prospect was very different from the gentle rolling downs of Dorset. The land here seemed vast, wilder. The peaks in the distance were still topped with snow even though it was summer. She wasn't sure where Con's land ended and someone else's began, but she'd not seen another house or person to get her bearings. The disputed road was in the distance, and she remembered just where Tomas had let them out, their bodies bruised from the bumpy ride on the rutted lane. But she needn't go that far—a narrow ribbon of water glinted ahead between green hills. If she followed it, she could find the waterfall.

Laurette stood still, listening. The countryside was never quiet—that was a myth city folk put about to excuse their frivolous natures. She heard the call of birds and the swish of the tall grasses in the breeze. Even the new sheep were bleating faintly behind her.

She imagined she could hear James and Beatrix laughing together. As long as they remained friends, there would be no harm to it. James needed a friend. Beatrix had a soft heart. Much like her own.

It had taken her years to harden it; she mustn't relent now.

It was a beautiful day, the sun high in the sky. She headed toward the rushing sound of water and was soon above the modest waterfall. Like Beatrix, Laurette hadn't bothered with a hat and she lifted her face to the rays. She'd been in such a hurry when she woke up she hadn't had much of a wash. Her face split in a naughty grin at her sudden idea.

The sunlight made rainbows of each water droplet as it tumbled over the rocks. The very air was veiled in shimmer. Laurette maneuvered down the grassy incline to where the stream foamed. Seeing the rocks in the river bed told her she would be in no danger of drowning. She'd have to stand beneath the noisy flow of water or only her ankles would get clean.

She unpinned her watch and removed the hairpins which held up her braid, tucking them into the pocket of her dress. It was simple enough to unfasten its ties, fold and place it far enough from the splash of the water so it wouldn't get wet. She hadn't bothered with stockings, either, so was down to her expensively embroidered demi-corset, shift and half-boots. She unlaced the front of her corset and then bent unsteadily to remove her boots. After a moment's deliberation, she unbuttoned her shift and tossed it into the pile.

She was now just as God made her, every freckle and flaw revealed. Fleshier than she'd been in years. This past month, she'd felt a bit like a force-fed French goose. Or one of the girls in North Africa, made to consume an endless supply of camel's milk so they would be attractive to their husbands.

One night over dinner, when she had complained to Con over his seeming desire to stuff her full of every conceivable delicacy Qalhata could cook up, he had explained the concept of *leblouh* to her. He had seen little girls with their fingers and feet pressed between wood to make sure they gorged themselves, as their countrymen prized a fat bride. Some women grew so obese they could barely move, but they were all the more worshipped for it.

Laurette had been horrified. She didn't want to be worshipped, fat or skinny. Once, she had deliberately used her

body to draw Con into her childish dream of a future together. She had paid the price for that ten times over.

She and Con had dined, and dined too well together nearly
every night in her weeks of captivity. He showed no signs of
overindulgence—his flat stomach and chiseled chin were just
as they had been. Every inch of him was—perfect. Even the
tattoo he had to cover up his scarred shoulder fascinated her.

He explained it was a reminder to himself not to go completely native in the East. No good Muslim was permitted a
tattoo. It was considered mutilation. Maiming. Con chose
the Jerusalem cross to ensure he was not tempted to change
his mind. It had brought him unwelcome attention occasionally, which suited his mindset at the time. Laurette was sure
he deliberately placed himself in harm's way for many years,
before he finally came around to realizing his responsibilities.

And now the idiot man wanted to take on more of them.
Sheep. Her daughter.

She shook her braid loose and stepped into the water,
wishing she'd brought a bar of soap. The rocks were sharp
and slippery against her bare feet but she welcomed the discomfort, just as Con had welcomed risk. Laurette wanted to
feel alive, separate from everything that had bombarded her
the past twenty-four hours.

Gingerly she stepped toward the splashing water until she
was beneath it, rivulets of chilly Yorkshire snowmelt pounding her head and shoulders. She gave a little yelp as her skin
contracted in gooseflesh. She hadn't expected to be quite so
cold. She tried to convince herself it was refreshing, but the
wisdom of her actions did not stand up to scrutiny. Ducking
around a jumble of boulders, she spied a large flat rock
bathed in sunlight. She would sit and drip dry on it before
she struggled back into her clothes.

The heat felt delicious on her bottom. After fingercombing
the tangles from her hair, she wrapped her arms around her
knees and closed her eyes. The pulsing sound of the waterfall

blocked birdsong and breeze. There was nothing but the rush and mist of the water and the warmth of the sun. If she chose, she could sleep her afternoon away as well as her morning. She felt the tension dissolve from her spine and took a deep, calming breath.

Chapter 15

A few yards away, Con watched his water nymph in her pool of sunshine. He had wanted to cool off under the waterfall since yesterday, and despite her scoffing, apparently so did she. She had no idea he was there, his manhood bedeviling him. Beads of moisture dripped from her wavy hair, sliding down her ripe breasts. Her clean-shaven cleft was visible, glistening. She was still as golden marble, her lashes fanning her cheeks, her lips forming the slightest smile. Her feet were flat upon the rock, her hands locked together around her knees. A purple butterfly came close to landing on her toes, and Con cursed it silently away. He wanted to look at her forever unobserved, or at least until she came out of her trance.

His hand reached for the fall of his trousers. He was iron hard. What would she do if she opened her eyes and saw him? Shriek and tell him to go away, of course, as though he hadn't seen her naked a hundred times. Could he persuade her to bed him one more time before she disappeared to Dorset? He knew he had to let her go.

It didn't mean he was giving up.

James would come around, too. They'd worked well together the past hour, hard enough for the scent of sheep and human sweat to be all over him. Nico and Tomas had taken the children for a swim in the lake before lunch. Con had not wanted to overstay his welcome and break the fragile truce with his son. When Bea had innocently said Laurette was out walking, his mind had been made up. He'd clean off here and find her somehow.

Getting out of Laurette's range of sight, he kicked off his boots and pulled a sliver of soap from his pocket. He shucked his trousers on the bank and pulled his dirty linen shirt over his head. He wasn't fit to touch her yet. With any luck, she would continue to sun-worship while he stood under the water and lathered up.

The water was bracing, to say the least. Con nearly bit his tongue in half to keep from crying out. But Laurette had braved it and so would he. He scrubbed until his skin was red beneath his perpetual tan. He had joined his tenants for the spring planting, was no stranger to hard work. James cared for the land as well. He would be an excellent steward when his time came.

And hopefully Con would pass at a very great age, his marchioness Laurette still alive and waiting to be buried next to him in the churchyard at All Saints. They would expand their family, have other children together. Raising sons and daughters from infancy would be a novel experience, one he was determined not to mismanage again.

He soaped his groin, his eyes closed, imagining Laurette stroking him, licking and suckling him. Her long fingers and beautiful mouth were made for sin, even if she was trying to turn starchy spinster on him.

He was chuckling at the memory of her lips around him when he stumbled back from the blow of a fair-sized rock.

"What the devil?"

"You!" Laurette was in front of him, her hands covering her bosom and mound, eyes blazing with anger. "You were spying on me!"

"Hardly. I cannot help it if we had the same idea. I left *you* in peace." He looked down at the mark forming on his chest.

"I suppose I should be grateful for your aim. A foot lower and we should all be sorry."

"Speak for yourself." He watched in amusement as she scrambled on the uneven stream bed, nearly falling. He caught her arm. "Let me help you."

"Stay away! What if the children should find us?"

"They're at the lake. We're alone. There's not a soul for miles." He tried to pull her closer, but she slipped from his soapy hands and headed for his clothes. *His* clothes, instead of hers.

Damn. He went after her but tripped and fell, slicing a knee on a rock. He watched in horror as she snatched his clothing in front of her. Surely she wouldn't leave him here naked. He would catch her, once he could stand up.

He looked down as the shallow water turned pink. Botheration. Someone might have to stitch him. Well, Laurette could just ride him, as he didn't think he should put pressure on his knee by embedding it in the grass as he covered her. Which he was going to do before she killed him.

He opened his mouth in protest as she balled up his shirt and threw it into the water. It rippled like a white ghost waving good-bye, then began its float down the current. As if struck by conscience, her hand dipped into the pocket of his pants before she threw them too and stilled.

He knew what she would find there. Good. He'd hidden them away long enough during his ridiculous imperial charade.

She had them in her hand now, his breeches dropped in a rumpled heap at her feet. Her golden brows were drawn together, her full lips rolled inward so only the barest pink showed in her suddenly pale face.

"They've been everywhere with me. They were the only things I took with me when I ran away." He lurched to his feet, glancing down at the rivulet of blood dripping down his leg. His shirt would have come in handy about now, but it had disappeared around the curve of the stream. She raised her eyes from her hand.

"You're bleeding!"

"Like a stuck pig. I don't suppose you'd loan me your shift."

As though the objects burned her hand, she dropped them to the ground and moved quickly over the grass to where she'd left her clothes. Her breasts bounced with each step, and despite his pain, Con's cock sprang to life again. She tried to tear the linen, but his blunt had paid top price for every inch of fabric he had clothed her in. With a frustrated groan, she pitched the whole garment at him as he climbed out of the water toward her.

"Thank you for not throwing my talismans away. And my pants, too, of course." He flopped on the grass, blotting up the blood. Laurette stood over him, biting her lip.

"I don't understand."

"Laurie. I've tried to tell you a thousand different ways. I admit I was wrong when I forced you to come to me the way I did, but do you think it was merely a game? Some whim? I have never stopped loving you. Look at me. Wretched and bloody and still hard for you." He admired the curve of her back and bottom as she went back to his trousers and bent to retrieve the flat skipping stone and the bag of tarnished beads. "You left them in our tree for me when I returned to Ryland Grove after—after I was away." He couldn't even say the word honeymoon. It had not been anything but a time of Hell. "I wasn't going to meet you. I talked my way around it for two days, but I came anyhow. I couldn't stay away. If I had known about Bea, I would have done something, I swear."

"You cannot tell her. Promise me."

"If you promise to consider my proposal again."

There was no sound save the rush of the water. She didn't say yes. She didn't say no. What she did do was clutch his charms in her fist as he had done so many times, as if to draw out some sort of magical power.

He'd found the rock for her when they were children, and

taught her how to skip stones on the river. Its salmon color was easy to find amidst gray and brown when they dove for it. She carried it around in her pinafore pocket until she grew up and stopped wearing pinafores. The glittery bag was a reminder of when he saw her dressed up for the first time, her cheeks glowing and gown sparking in the candlelight. And more importantly, their twilight pledge at the ring of stones. Both objects symbolized their childhood friendship and the love that grew from it. And now everything, both the physical specimens and the concepts they represented, was in Laurette's hands.

She sat down next to him slowly, seemingly oblivious to the fact that they were still naked. There was no further attempt to cover herself, and Con looked his fill. Her nipples had pearled and her hair lay in a wavy tangle as it dried. Mermaid hair. The sun burnished the short gilt hair on her arms, as though she was sprinkled with fairy dust. He longed to kiss the sheen on her body, to taste her, but he clamped the linen to his leg and waited.

"Why do you love me?"

He had not anticipated such a question and stalled. Was there even an answer he could articulate? Loving Laurette had been a given for so many years he couldn't remember life without her, or the idea of her. "Pardon?"

"Why, Con? You don't even know me anymore."

He frowned. "That's not true. I've learned a great deal about you over these past weeks."

"I have been horrible to you. Mostly. Except in bed."

She didn't look a bit guilty, and why should she? He had been just as determined to claim her as she was to push him away.

"I don't know if I can answer you." He ran a finger down her freckled cheek. "You are a part of me. I thought we were a part of each other."

She inched back from his touch. "Don't distract me. I want to talk."

"And I want to make love to you. One more time."

She was tempted. He saw it in the flush of her cheek and the way her top tooth bit her bottom lip. His eyes traveled to the pulse at her throat, which leaped. Her hands twisted nervously over his treasures.

Gently he pried her fingers open and plucked the rock and the bag from her palm. "Let's put these in a safe place. I should hate to lose them now. They have been with me through many trials. A bit of home. A bit of you." She glanced up at him, perhaps understanding what these odd objects meant to him still. "My pants are not going to join my shirt, are they?"

Laurette shook her head. Con limped to his trousers and slipped them back into a pocket. Lost in thought, she had not moved from the grassy bank, but had now enfolded herself so he was denied the joy of looking at her body.

"If we—" Her whisper was lost over the rush of the water. He leaned in to catch her words. "If we make love here now, Con, it will be the very last time. Forever. I cannot marry you and resurrect the past. There would be talk. It would hurt James and he would hate me. Blame me for you leaving."

Com weighed her words. There was not a soul alive in his two villages that did not suspect Laurette had been his lover before he married. She had spent years reclaiming her reputation, enough so she could run her little dame school.

Could he ever make James understand the bond that was between them? She had asked him why he loved her and he could not adequately explain even if he had Dr. Johnson's Dictionary handy.

Con didn't really believe in fated love. He had seen too much of the seamy side of the world, where women were sold as slaves and men took their pleasure when and where they could. Here in this country, most ton marriages were business arrangements. If mutual respect developed, all well and good and downright amazing.

But Laurette was his soul mate, absurd as it sounded. He

loved the girl she was, and the woman she'd become. If he lost her altogether it would be like cutting off his arm.

But he had a child to consider. Two, actually. And the woman he loved without reservation seemed to think that both of them would hate her if the truth were revealed. He couldn't agree, but had to acknowledge she knew them both better than he did. He pushed his wet hair back.

"I don't want to give you up, Laurie. I had to once and it almost killed me. I couldn't think straight."

"You are not thinking straight now, Con."

He managed a smile. "Ah. That explains it. The Mad Marquess strikes again."

She laid a hand on his forearm. "Look. I know you've moved heaven and earth to get us to just this spot. Together, under the sky, as we once were. But we have secrets wrapped in secrets now that should remain unspoken."

"Tell me one of yours," he said fiercely. "Tell me you still love me."

Her eyes were filled with pain. "Do you really need to ask? I tried so, so hard not to. You broke my heart once." She turned away from him and spoke to a rock. "I can't trust you with it again. You want more than I can ever give. Please find someone else to help you raise your son."

Con wanted to howl at the perfect sun that shone so perfectly on this perfect green Yorkshire hill, with its perfect rainbow waterfall. Instead he took the imperfect woman next to him in his arms. "If this is the last time, we must make it perfect."

Chapter 16

He felt a little like Adam to her Eve leading her carefully through the spray to the low flat rock behind the falls. It felt hot enough to bake something as he settled on its surface. Laurette stood above him, her face now devoid of emotion. She seemed fixed on the lazily drifting clouds that shadowed her eyes. He tilted her hips toward him, his hands looking brown against her pale, gold-flecked skin.

If she got her way, he'd never touch her like this again, never see the contrast between them, never fit themselves together as they were meant to be.

He'd make her regret that.

But no. He'd given her enough to regret already. Instead, he'd give her something she couldn't forget.

She overwhelmed his senses. Her skin tasted of rosewater and cold stream. He licked a path from her navel to her bare cleft, flicking within to find her plump button. The tip of his tongue pressed her flesh to his lips, where he indulged them both. To never taste her like this would be a sin.

Perhaps she thought so too. Her stiffness under his palms melted away, and her knees buckled a bit. He held fast. Twisting and tugging patiently, he was rewarded by her hitched breath and more unsteadiness, but he didn't stop. Couldn't. Her fingers dug into his scalp as she clasped him closer. He was imprisoned in her embrace and grateful for it.

She cried out, begging him to stop or continue, he couldn't tell which, but she didn't let go. Taking that as a welcome sign, he wrapped an arm around her bottom, settling her hip in the crook of his elbow. With his newly-free hand, he slid a finger into her hot, wet slit as his tongue traced lazy circles at her apex.

She truly came apart then, her scream rivaling the rush of the waterfall.

Boneless, she collapsed against him. He pulled her down to his lap and cradled her. She was so soft and warm in his arms, so *right*. His fingers wove in her damp hair as he brought her lips to his. She opened her mouth without hesitation. How many times had he kissed her? He tried to remember their first. She must have been about six. She had shyly pecked him on the cheek to wish him Happy Christmas and he'd made a great show of wiping his face.

A few short years later he had come home from school armed with the rumors of wet tongues tangling. She had airily informed him she'd seen her mama and papa engage in such an act and that it looked revolting. He had eventually convinced her otherwise.

After that they had kissed any chance they could, practicing artlessly. When he was seventeen and about to go to Cambridge, great guilt crashed over him for toying with her as her womanhood blossomed, but she had been the aggressor then, trailing after him until they went far beyond a kiss. He wondered if she was sorry now for bestowing the gift of her body to him. He had brought her nothing but pain when he meant to ensure her enduring pleasure.

Velvet honey. She always tasted so sweet. Everywhere. His tongue swept the roof of her mouth slowly, as though he had all the time in the world. She shifted into him, pressing her pliant breasts into his chest. Her hands slid through his hair, and he was glad he didn't follow fashion to cut it short. Her touch made even his hair feel alive. Her fingers stroked and tangled until his scalp tingled and a warm sensation lifted the hairs on his neck.

His fingers dipped down the even bumps of her spine until they came to the cleft of her buttocks. He lifted her bottom. Obediently, she swung her leg around and sank without resistance onto his shaft.

He held her tight, breastbone to breastbone. Pressed to him, her heart still thudded wildly from her orgasms. They were locked together, perfectly still, connected so completely it was almost painful. He longed to keep her in this position until they became a part of the landscape, two old weathered stones forever joined.

Laurette had other ideas. Gathering herself, she arched up. He let her do the work this time, watching her half-closed eyes narrow and her mouth dip down in concentration. He cupped her round breasts in his palms, rubbing the nipples with calloused thumbs, watching their color change from peach to raspberry. He feasted on one while his hand reached between them. He looked down to see her bare skin glistening, his cock and fingers busy. She set the rhythm, but her nails bit into his shoulders as she lost herself to every stroke.

He brought her over again. She threw her head back to the endless sky, her expression so blissful his heart nearly stopped. Con had given her what little he could, a respite from her lonely future. He was breaths away from going with her when he realized she could not be wearing one of her little sponges. Laurette had not expected him. Indeed, she had never thought to have sexual congress with him again. He meant to say something when her mouth came down upon his for the fiercest kiss. The Mad Marquess was rendered mute. Mindless. His only thought now was to prolong the exquisite friction between them as long as he could last.

Which proved to be a very short while. His seed spilled far up within her as she convulsed around him, kissing him senseless.

They clung together on their rock, panting, her legs still

wrapped around him. He was her more-than-willing prisoner. He always would be.

"I love you, Laurie."

He felt her shake her head on his chest, where her cheek
had come to rest. "Hush."

He lifted her chin. "I do. It's not enough, but I want you to
know it."

She gave a little sigh and snuggled back down. He thought
he felt the beginnings of a smile against his skin.

They sat in breathless peace, listening the steady tumble of
water over the rocks. Their world was finite, about to change.
His cock began its inevitable descent from her passage.

"You aren't perchance wearing a sponge?"

She leaped up, leaving his lap empty and his cock mournful. A look of horror flashed across her love-flushed face.
"Oh my God!"

"*You* hush. Don't worry. I'll wash you."

If a child came of this afternoon, wouldn't she finally give
in? He knew he would be over the moon. But he led her back
under the waterfall. His soap was stuck between two rocks
where he left it. Lathering his hands, he swabbed between
her nether lips, splashing water at her as she stood deathly
still. He tried to be clinical, keeping his fingers indifferent to
her folds, but apparently not indifferent enough. She snatched
the soap from him and scrubbed viciously. She was turning
blue with cold, her teeth chattering. He took the soap and
tossed it away, then pressed himself against her. "You'll wash
your skin off. Time to rinse."

She nodded, her eyes closed as if she couldn't stand the
sight of him. "In the sunshine. The water's warmer by our
rock."

Our rock. So it had become her world too. He propelled
her away from the waterfall. "Don't sit down yet. I don't
want you to cut that beautiful bottom." He reached down to
clear away the larger stones until she could sit on the silty soil
of the riverbed. He pitched them far down the stream, where

they made violent displays. Rock-throwing was no cure for his frustration, but it was the only activity at hand unless he tried to strangle himself.

She sat down in the shallow water, looking very much like a cross mermaid, her wavy hair glinting in the sun. "I am an idiot. You make me an idiot." She splashed water around her body, stirring up silt.

"And you make me an imbecile, madam. We are well-matched." He sank down beside her.

"Oh, Con, what are we going to do if I'm with child? I cannot believe we were so careless. Again! We are not children anymore. I've been so careful this time."

Con knew it and was sorry for it. Compromising her into a pregnancy would have been an easy way to make her his wife. He hadn't counted on her vial of preventatives when he first proposed she become his mistress.

He hadn't counted on a lot of things.

"It's most unlikely this last time will result in anything. Don't borrow trouble. But you will tell me this time, won't you? If anything happens?"

"At least you aren't married now," she said grumpily.

"I'd like to be."

She swatted him. "Stop it! We're done, really, truly done. You've agreed what's best for the children."

Con grimaced. "No, Laurie, you've agreed with yourself on what's best for the children. I simply respect your wishes. I don't think they'd be half so disapproving if they knew the truth. But I see from your thunderous expression I'm not likely to change your mind." The longer he sat her with her, the more he wanted to make love to her again. Words were unnecessary obstacles between them then. The more they talked, the further apart they grew. "Get dressed. I'll follow you back after a reasonable time. It would not do to have you return with a half-naked savage."

She swept the tattoo on his shattered shoulder with her forefinger. Did he see regret in her eyes? If there was, it was fleeting. She shook herself off rather like a golden puppy and tied her shift and dress on. She rolled her stays up under her arm and picked up her boots. "It's chicken for lunch," she called over her shoulder. "Don't be late."

He watched her walk barefoot over the rough grass, her back straight, her damp hair curling down her back like gilt serpents. He waited for her to turn, to wave, to come back and kiss him, and never leave. Instead, she disappeared over a hill as he sat in his cold mud, shriveling in body and heart.

This was not the end. It couldn't be. Somehow, he would do something, even if he'd quite exhausted his bag of tricks. He'd have to dig deeper, go further. He had the rest of his life to find a way back to Laurie's heart, or die trying.

Chapter 17

There. Had she seemed plucky enough? Insouciant? There had been a bad moment back there, when she realized they'd been careless again. Despair—and awful hope. If she were pregnant the decision would be out of her hands. There was no way she could deny another child its father, or bear to give away a part of her soul again.

She wouldn't have to wonder if she were doing the right thing for everybody, carrying the burden, keeping silent.

She was tired of doing the right thing. Tired of sacrificing.

But it would be disaster for Beatrix to learn she was a bastard. It would be disaster for James to know his "aunt" was his father's long-lost lover, the reason his mother never stood a chance despite her thousands and chocolate-box beauty. The reason Con had deserted his own child and wandered aimlessly around the world.

For a twenty-nine year old woman of average looks, Laurette had caused a lot of disaster, she thought ruefully.

But the past was behind her. She'd make the best of the future, starting right now. The day was absurdly perfect, golden and clement, the air fresh, the birdsong and ribbon of stream musical. She relished the feel of grass underfoot. It had been a long while since she had run outside barefoot, half-dressed, her hair a hopeless tangle down her back.

The more things changed, the more they stayed the same.

Once a hoyden, always a hoyden. She hoped she could set herself to rights before anyone saw her.

Luck was with her. She entered the house by the open front door and flew up the stairs. Someone had tidied her room. She'd left in a hurry this morning to inspect the sheep. If she were to pass inspection herself, she needed to do something about her wild, knotted hair. Her hairpins had fallen from her pocket somewhere along her tromp back to the house.

The contents of Con's pocket had been a revelation. It gave her a warm thrill to know her humble offerings had traveled the globe, pieces of home.

Pieces of her heart.

But Con was welcome to them, silly, sentimental man. Surely he would realize now how impossible a reunion would be, despite their undeniable lust for each other. That would end. That *had* ended. There could be no repeat of this afternoon.

Laurette removed her wet dress, donned a dressing gown and began the arduous process of brushing out her hair. She heard the slam of doors and voices below, the scampering of feet upstairs as the children returned from their swim. She was glad she closed the door as she listened to Sadie cheerfully bully Beatrix to change for lunch. Bea was far more obedient than Laurette had ever been.

Con was keeping country hours, with a big lunch in the middle of the day. They would join the children tonight for a nursery tea with all the trimmings. The awkward formal dinner of last night was not to be repeated, for which Laurette was supremely grateful.

She braided up her hair again and put on a fresh dress. Aside from the pink sunburn on her cheeks and nose, there was no trace of her earlier escapade. She was determined to spend a placid afternoon reading, or playing a board game with Beatrix, avoiding Con and his black eyes.

There was a tap. Bea's face peeked around the door. "I've been sent to fetch you."

"Excellent. I'm starved. Did you enjoy the lake?"

"It's quite cold, but once you move around a bit, you don't feel it as much. Are you sure we have to leave?"

"Quite. We'll dunk you in the Piddle now that you are a swimmer. Your mama and papa will not recognize you for the scales and fins once you go home."

Beatrix shifted around Laurette's expensive jars of paint and bottles of scent on the dressing table. "I'm not allowed to swim in the ocean, you know."

"Hold still." Laurette dabbed a drop of rose oil behind Bea's ears. "Oceans are vastly different from lakes and rivers, to be sure. I remember when I first visited Penzance, the ocean terrified me. It was so vast. And rough. Your parents are very wise not to permit you to go bathing." She pinned her mother's watch to Bea's collar, wondering if her mother would have loved her granddaughter or seen her as evidence of Laurette's sin.

How simple it would have been for Laurette to lose herself in the ocean all those years ago when she had been banished from Dorset. There had been one bleak winter day when the temptation had been strong. But the child in front of her had kicked in protest and the cowardly notion disappeared. Laurette had proved she was strong enough to live without her daughter, and now she had to be strong enough to live without Con.

She kissed the top of Bea's head. "Let's go downstairs, love."

The following days passed in a haze of sunshine. The children picnicked, swam, rode sturdy ponies, and fished. They explored the nearby caves under the supervision of Nico and Tomas, who were rather like big boys themselves. They marched up the hills with the sheep and cloud-gazed. Laurette made herself useful in the kitchens and the garden, while Con rode out with Mr. Carter to meet his neighbors, and arrange for the road to be repaired.

On Sunday the entire household rose early and, avoiding the rutted road, walked across the hillocks to the village and its humble church. Con, Laurette, the children, and their exotic servants weathered the curious stares of the small congregation as they filled the Stanbury pew up front and the row behind. If the homily referring to the Prodigal Son had been planned or was spontaneous, Con neither knew nor cared. He was beyond insult, or saving. In two days' time, Laurette, Bea, Sadie and Nico would be leaving Yorkshire.

He had done his damnedest to make Laurette change her mind. Never had he exuded so much charm and bonhomie. He was rewarded with Laurette's vague smiles and hasty departures as he entered a room. She chattered to the children at mealtimes but was pointedly reserved toward him. Con was sure she locked her bedroom door at night, not that he had the courage to breach her defenses at this point.

At least James was thawing. There were fewer silences in their conversation. He had taken Laurette's advice and proposed a trip abroad if James had a successful school year. The boy's eyes lit up. Con was still not beyond bribery.

When they exited the church, it seemed everyone had abandoned the thought of Sunday dinner and was milling about the churchyard, the better to see the fronts of the Conover party in addition to their backs. The cleric, a sturdy older man, vigorously shook Con's hand in welcome.

"We are delighted to see you and your family up north, my lord. I knew your great-uncle a little. He, alas, was not one of my success stories."

Con tried to picture this bluff, honest-faced man and his devious uncle Ryland in comity and failed. "I expect not. My Uncle Ryland was a bit of a sinner."

"As are we all, my lord, as are we all. Terrible business, his wandering off like that. I wrote to you in care of your good wife. You were, I believe, traveling at the time. Lady Conover, may I say how delighted I am to meet you at last? We thank you for your help with the bell tower and all the many other gifts to the parish. We are in your debt."

The vicar may have been informed of Con's absence, but he was not completely up to speed. Laurette looked stricken at the mix-up.

It was James who saved the day. "Father Andrews, I'm afraid you've made a mistake. My mama passed away more than a year ago. This is Miss Vincent, a very good friend of the family. She and her cousin have been our guests at Stanbury Hill."

The vicar raised his bushy gray eyebrows in surprise. "Do forgive me, my lord. I had no idea. Please accept my condolences. I should have made a visit once we heard of your arrival and then I wouldn't have put my foot in it." He glanced at an elderly woman hovering near a particularly elaborate headstone a few feet away. Con squinted and was not surprised to see the name Stanbury etched into the marble. His mother was buried at All Saints along with his father, but he supposed it was past time to acquaint himself with his mother's late relatives.

"You brought your own servants, I know, but old Mrs. Hardwick over there was housekeeper at Stanbury Hill Farm for many years. I think she'd like to talk to you about your mother. And your uncle, too, of course. It was she who reported him missing. I'll introduce you, if you can spare a moment."

Con had no interest in his uncle's final days, but he could barely remember his mother. She had grown up here, the squire's only living daughter, making a grand marriage to the younger son of a marquess. She had never expected to become a marchioness, and in fact, had not. She and her husband had drowned on the Dorset coast in a summer squall, orphaning Con when he was still in short pants. A few years later his entire family had been reduced to his great-uncle and himself. He'd love to hear a tale or two about his mother as a girl.

Father Andrews motioned the woman to come forward. Her face was wreathed in smiles, showing strong teeth despite her advanced age. Con thought she must be well past seventy. She must not have had an easy time of it looking after his uncle. Marianna had pensioned her off most generously according to the neat business records his wife had kept of his properties.

"How do you do, my lord?" Mrs. Hardwick dropped to a graceful curtsey. She turned to Beatrix. "I'd know your daughter anywhere. She's the image of your mother, she is. The same red hair. The same eyes. Aren't you a pretty thing?"

Time stood still. This time James did not step up to correct the woman, but cast Beatrix a puzzled glance. Con's tongue felt swollen in his mouth. He couldn't look at Laurette, who would be beyond horrified.

Beatrix blushed. "My cousin Laurette says everyone has a twin, Mrs. Hardwick. My parents live in Cornwall."

A wave of uncertainty washed across the old woman's face. "But—I could swear you are Miss Katie come to life. The hair—the eyes—"

"There, there, Nell. None of us have the eyesight we used to." The vicar squeezed her hand. "Perhaps now is not the time to discuss old times. Lord Conover is a busy man."

"I beg your pardon, my lord. I worked for the Stanburys when your mother was a girl. This little one—." She shook her head, fluffy tufts of white hair escaping around her ears and gave an apologetic grin. "As she says, twins. God saw fit to make two such little angels. Your mama was a lovely young lady, full of spirit but always thoughtful. When she married your da, it was a happy day for us all. Got married right in this church. Before your time, Father Andrews."

She nattered on. Con wanted the woman to shut up now. Laurette stood tense at his side, worrying her gloves. The children were inching back in boredom. When the housekeeper finally got around to talking about his uncle, he laid a hand on her arm. "Mrs. Hardwick, I'm sure you did everything possible for my uncle. You must know we were estranged. I'm sorry about the nature of his death, but I can't say I miss him."

The vicar blanched. Well, Con had no plans to settle here permanently, so hang his good reputation and the possibility of heaven. A few more weeks and he'd be back in London, James would be getting ready for school, and Jacob Carter would be king of his little sheep kingdom. Con doubted he'd ever come up here again. It was the site of one more spectacular failure.

James tugged at his sleeve. "May Bea and I start back, Papa? Nico and Tom will come with us."

Con saw his small staff, standing patiently under the shade of a giant beech tree. "Yes, yes, go on ahead. Tell the others they can leave us, too. Miss Vincent and I need no chaperone."

It was more than a quarter of an hour before they could make their escape, dodging the greetings and questions of a local populace with far too much time on their hands on this day of rest. He had no doubt his household would be the top topic around their dining tables. Mrs. Hardwick was not the only old soul who noticed Bea's resemblance to Katie Stanbury.

"I had no idea," Con began without preamble as they finally tore away from the churchyard. "Truly, I didn't, Laurie. I mean, I saw similarities, but I was so young when she died."

Laurette said nothing but walked at a pace even Con was having difficulty keeping up with.

"Bea didn't seem to take it amiss, though. Perhaps she'll forget about the whole thing."

"Oh, yes. That's just what children do when someone questions their parentage," Laurette said sarcastically. "There is a painting in the attic. We've got to destroy it."

"A painting? Of my mother?"

Laurette nodded curtly. "Mr. Carter mentioned it."

"We can't just throw it away. I have nothing of my mother's, not even the scrap of a letter."

"We'll have to hide it then." She stopped in her tracks. "You don't suppose they've run right home to look for it?"

"Don't be silly. Who'd want to play in a dusty attic on such a beautiful day? The lads will take them swimming while luncheon is being prepared, I'm certain of it."

"Oh, what do you know? You dragged us here thinking you knew what was best and look how it's turned out!"

She broke then, her careful composure shattering. He put his arms around her as she stifled a sob. "Laurie, Laurie. I'm so sorry."

How many times had he said this childish rhyme to her? She usually bashed him once and laughed. She was not laughing now.

"Look. Would it be so awful if Bea learned I am her father? I've met the joyless man who raised her, and I daresay I'm an improvement."

"You haven't listened to one word I've said, have you?" She *was* bashing him now, but he held her fast.

"Yes, I've listened to you. I've never agreed, but I've listened. She wouldn't need to find out about *you*. You could keep your secret."

"How would you explain the coincidence she was raised by *my* cousins? She's a smart little girl. Too smart. Damn it, Con! We've got to get back. Let me go!"

He dropped his arms and she flew away from him as if he were the very Devil. In her eyes, he was. He wished they'd come by carriage, but he hadn't wanted any of them to be subjected to the stomach-churning ride. A cobbled-together road crew was scheduled for the end of the week, after the Vincents left. Con planned to work right in the thick of them to ward off the misery he was already feeling.

He had read about forced military marches. Hell, he had even been in one or two, despite his unofficial capacity as a civilian aide to Wellington in the Peninsula. He was on one now, trailing in Laurette's wake. Perspiration dripped down his collar, unstarching the cravat Aram had taken such pride in.

And then he stopped. Froze his footsteps on the road, wondering if she'd look for him over her shoulder. She did not.

And then he knew. It was over. Everything he'd worked and wheedled so hard for this past year had come to nothing, like the dry road dust on his tongue. A dozen years of a dream that he should have awakened from long ago.

He watched her cut away from the track over the field, the feather on her flirty little hat trembling valiantly at every step. He let her go. Had to let her go. Had to let her live her life as she saw fit.

A life with no room for him.

Con felt a bleakness he had hoped to never feel again. But it was a selfish black emptiness he had no time for. If Beatrix had somehow discovered the truth, Laurette would need his help, whether she wanted it or not.

Chapter 18

The smudges of dirt on her daughter's face told her every thing she was afraid of. Bea's nose was pink and it looked like she had been crying. The children were waiting for her in the hallway, looking like two solemn sentinels. Between them both they had managed to find the painting and juggle it down three flights of stairs. Resting along the wall was a nearly life-size portrait in a chipped gilt frame.

Katie Stanbury, dressed in a golden-green panniered gown that matched her eyes, was posed outdoors with a collie that looked a lot like Mr. Carter's Sam. She appeared not quite old enough to put up her light red hair, but too old for Beatrix's braids. A large tear had split off one slender foot from the rest of her, and a glob of something stuck to the white of the dog's coat. The artist had written "Miss Katherine Desmond Stanbury" in the misty background. Laurette felt the blood drain from her face.

"My! Mrs. Hardwick was right. The likeness is remarkable, isn't it?" Her voice sounded amazingly normal, though a bit breathless from the near-run home.

Best just to seem absolutely unruffled by the proof listing against the smart new wallpaper. Have no interest in it. Treat it as insignificant, and Bea would think the portrait was nothing more than a fluke.

Bea shot James a triumphant look. Laurette half-expected

him to whip out a list of questions with which to interrogate her.

"She's *my* grandmother and I look nothing at all like her," he said doggedly. "This looks just like you, Beatrix Vincent. *If* that is your name."

Bea sniffed. "Of course it's my name! And you look like your papa, except for your eyes. You have Lady Conover's eyes."

The palest blue. Eyes that looked like they could pierce through the cobwebs to the truth with very little effort.

Marianna had always taken an interest in Beatrix when she came to Dorset for her week, and to Laurette's surprise had promoted a friendship between Con's children. James had considered himself too masculine to socialize much with a lowly *girl*—especially one who was taller than he—which made the friendship he and Bea had formed now in Yorkshire all the more bittersweet.

"Well," Laurette said briskly, "it's no wonder people thought you were a relation, Bea. Stand you next to Mr. Carter's dog Sam in a few years and we'll be seeing double." She laughed, but the sound was hollow to her. "I'm sure Lord Conover will thank you for finding this. He doesn't really remember either of his parents."

James looked through the open door to the crushed stone drive. "Where is he anyway?"

"I expect he'll be right along. Bea, I thought we could start packing. Come on upstairs with me."

"Now? Can't Sadie do it?"

"Sadie has enough to do without worrying about us, young lady."

Con had deliberately kept the staff to a minimum, only the people he trusted. Laurette supposed she should be grateful that her situation was not being bandied about from the Orkneys to Lands' End. She put her arm around Beatrix. "Come. I fear we're going home with much more than we brought. It will be a challenge to fit it all in our luggage."

"If it comes to that, James and I saw lots of trunks in the attic. We might borrow some. I'm sure his father won't mind."

"The coach will never get us down the lane as it is. Excuse us, please, James." Laurette smiled at him, but he didn't return it. Something about the stubborn set of his jaw told her Con was in for a grilling. The sooner she and Bea left, the better.

When Con entered the house a few minutes later, James sat on the bottom stair, his chin wedged into his fists. "I think, sir," the boy said, his voice not wavering, "you'd better tell me what's going on."

Con's eyes flicked from his son to the portrait beside him and his breath stopped. But any pleasure he might have had seeing his mother as a young girl evaporated when he looked into James's ice-blue eyes.

He tried to brazen it out. "Good Lord. No wonder that old woman was confused. Quite a coincidence, what?"

James rose. "I'm not a child. Well, I suppose I am in years, but I had to be the man of the family while you were off doing—whatever it was that you did. Bea's birthday is just a few weeks before mine. Mama always said I was a honeymoon baby." His tanned face flushed in embarrassment, but he continued. "You must have gotten some poor girl in trouble before you married."

Con tried to put his hand upon the boy's shoulder but James flinched away. Con saw the progress he had made the past week dissolving like smoke in the hushed hallway. "Not here, James. Anyone might hear us. We'll talk outside."

He owed the truth to his son—had in fact wanted to tell him—but how to keep his promise to Laurette to preserve her fiction? This was not the controlled atmosphere in which he had hoped to divulge the past. In his demented dreams he had seen them all in a meadow, laughing, *looking* like a family. When they discovered they *were,* roses would bloom and rainbows would banish any clouds from the sky.

Pure idiocy on his part. No wonder Laurette was disgusted with him.

They walked silently behind the house to the gate in the stone wall where the sheep had first been penned. The animals were dispersed now, fuzzy white dots grazing in the distance on his grandfather's land. Con shoved his hands in his pockets so he wouldn't be tempted to touch his son again.

James climbed atop the fence, putting himself almost at eye level with Con. It was probably an unconscious move, but Con was impressed. The boy would have made an artful negotiator. Although he was obviously bursting with questions, he waited for Con to speak first, another sign that Berryman blood was strong. Con was reminded of the old adage "He who speaks first loses."

Con had already lost so much. What was one more thing? He had a feeling he'd never have his son's respect. His son's love. He was undeserving anyway.

"This is a more than awkward conversation. Don't let your imagination run away with you, James."

"It doesn't take much imagination to put two and two together. Bea said you came to visit her at school this year a couple of times. Why would you do that if she's no relation to you? And why is she here now?"

A thousand thoughts whirled through Con's head. "This is not how I would have wished to have this discussion," he said at last. "Hear me out. You may judge me if you like. One more black mark to add against me on your list, but please don't judge Bea. Or her mother."

James looked him in the eye. "Who is she?"

Con shook his head, but kept his gaze upon his son's uncompromising face. "I will not name her. She was a girl I cared for a long, long time ago, when I was a boy myself. Someone I—someone I loved, James. Suffice to say, the affair happened before I was married. I never knew about Beatrix—didn't have an inkling—until I came back from abroad last year. I hadn't the first idea that I'd abandoned *two* children. One was enough to shame me."

He swallowed. "I know I let you down, James, and that it would be too much to ask you to forgive me. I was a young fool when I left England and very, very unhappy. Your mother and I did not—did not suit. It wasn't her fault, not a bit of it. It was an arranged marriage, conjured up by my mad old uncle and your grandfather. I—things were very bad for Ryland Grove financially. Surely she told you something," Con said, the desperation rising. How had he ever thought this was going to be easy?

"She only read me your letters, every one, even when they bored me to bits. That's all. Grandfather Berryman was furious with you, though. He called you a cheat."

"I was. But I was never unfaithful to your mother in all the years I was away. Not once."

James snorted. The breeze picked up the scent of grass and sheep dung. Bile rose in Con's throat and he wished they'd walked in a different direction. He brushed his hair from his brow with a shaking hand.

"You don't have to believe me. I can't expect you to. If it's any consolation, I have hated myself far longer than you've hated me."

"I don't hate you." Con heard the lack of conviction in his son's voice. James spoke out of automatic duty, not affection.

"Please get down from there. Why don't we walk to the lake? It will be cooler there."

James swung his leg over and slid down, catching his jacket on the wire. Con tried to get him free but James pulled away, causing a robust rip instead. Con reminded himself to respect the physical boundary between them his son was setting, although all he wanted was to give James a hug and tell him how sorry he was for bollixing up all their lives.

Instead he followed the boy down a grassy track, keeping a respectful five paces behind. They entered the deep shade of the woods path that led to the lake and Con unwound his sweat-ruined tie. "I was just nineteen when I married your mother, not even of age. I'm not making excuses, but my great-uncle as my guardian had to give permission for us to wed. I was deeply in debt to your grandfather Berryman. There were many people who depended on me and the estate, and I was next to bankrupt. My uncle had seen to that."

James had too much Berryman in him to ever be caught in so vulnerable a position, and Con was sincerely glad of it. His son would be spared from making decisions that rent his heart—if he had one—in two.

"Mama didn't like your uncle. She had to send him money all the time."

"She was wise, your mama. He and his brother, my grandfather, were always at odds, and when he inherited me and a ledger full of red ink, he saw his chance to stick it to the House of Conover. Whether it was all deliberate or a mixture of bad financial planning I'm not sure, but by the time I came down early from Cambridge, things were dire. My uncle had made a deal with your grandfather, and the marriage was arranged."

The glare of the sun on the silvery water was blinding. Con turned his back to it and sat down in a bed of rusty pine needles. James lowered himself opposite, his legs crossed Indian-fashion.

"I'd had a youthful attachment with Bea's mother. We—we weren't very sensible when we knew I had to marry someone else. I'm sure you've heard—you go to school—you know what's talked about in the dormitory. What happens between—"

"Yes, yes." James's face screwed up with disgust. Con nearly smiled. That would change in a few years. When he met the right girl.

When he met his own Laurette.

"Well, the girl and I broke it off and I married your mother. You know she was very pretty. Intelligent. She helped her father with his business. She was quite a bit older than I, and very—forceful. Marianna knew what she liked, went after it, and got it." He paused, reliving the crushing oppression he felt under the thumb of the Berrymans.

He had confessed to Laurette—that he'd broken his standing stones vows to her and was about to become a father. Con trudged back, hands in his pockets. He fingered the stitched inch-square of sheer cloth he'd found in the tree limbs yesterday, filled with silver beading from Laurette's come-out dress, the dress she wore to their "wedding." He remembered her walking through the garlanded door of the modest assembly room the night of her debut on her father's arm. The deep indigo of her gown had turned her eyes dark as she sought him out in the crowd of neighbors. Her hair gleamed bronze in the fading daylight. He had taken her virginity the next morning in the sheltering shade of their tree. The act had been too quick and awkward, but they had found their pace over the heat of the summer, contriving to meet as often as they dared. When they had made love after their stone circle wedding, their bodies had learned well.

He had lost her for good, now. The shock in her eyes told him he'd betrayed her for the last time. He had a duty to his wife and their child, duty to his dependents. He kicked a fallen branch savagely out of his way. Next year he'd get his allowance and be free of the Berrymans. He'd beg Laurette to leave with him. They could go anywhere in the world. He could follow in his feckless grandfather's footsteps.

By then, he'd have a son or daughter. Pray for a son, his father-in-law had told him, for until his wife delivered an heir to Con's misfortune, he was bound to Marianna Berryman by the complicated agreement his uncle had signed on his behalf.

Con suppressed his urge to tear something to tatters. One hand worked around the smooth rock in his pocket, the other pressing the bag of beads into his palm hard enough to hurt. Two worthless signs of years of love and friendship. He

*could toss them into the Piddle and be done with them, but
Laurette would not be uprooted from his heart so readily.*

*He entered the serene vacuum which was Ryland Grove.
The house was hushed, the workmen packed up. Marianna's
Town servants moved with impeccable grace as they handed
him off to his own chamber, a template for all that a noble-
man's bedchamber should be. Here at least was some color,
dark red bedcovers to match the dark red walls, fur rugs before the hearth, a painting of a stiff stag ever on alert. There
was no trace of Con's collection of stones or his grandfather's
books, the fleet of boats he'd carved with Laurette to set sail
on the river. Although it was full daylight, he threw himself
down on the bed, boots and all, and let the silent racking
sobs loose.*

James could not possibly understand what he had felt, so
he couched his next words. "I was resentful, I suppose. Felt
outmaneuvered at every turn. I was still a stupid boy and
your mother—she was a woman."

James nearly smiled. "She was bossy. She bossed me around
too."

"I tried to make it work, James." Con tasted the lie but
hoped James would believe it. "Your mother was very excited when she knew you were on the way. We both were.
But when you were born, I felt even more useless than I had
before. So I left.

"I didn't expect to stay away forever. But days turned into
weeks, and somehow months turned into years, and I didn't
go home. I—somehow couldn't."

At twenty, Con had felt trapped in amber, a bug beneath
the Berryman eyes, his every feeble attempt to twitch a wing
impossible. He had dreaded returning, fearing his hard-won
independence would soon evaporate under Marianne's cool
blue stare.

But he had a son. Con had come home for James, although
it was too late.

"I knew your mother would take good care of you, and

good care of herself. She was very capable, much more so than I was. I was ashamed that I left her on her own, but angry at the same time. I didn't want to have to depend on the Berryman fortune, so I set about making my own. I realize now how wrong I was, but I cannot change what happened. All the money I've made and the things I've done will never make up for walking away from you."

"What about Bea? What's going to happen to her?"

Con lifted a shoulder. "I don't know. I've been assured she is happy as she is."

"She *is* my sister," James said, forcing Con to nod in the affirmative. "I told her I thought so. And she cried."

There was too much smug satisfaction there for Con's comfort. "Please let it go, James. This is not the time to tell her. Perhaps when she's older."

"A few years won't make her any less of a bastard."

Con inhaled sharply. "Don't be cruel, James. She shouldn't be made to pay for my mistakes."

"I don't know if I can keep it a secret. She's not leaving until two days from now. She and Aunt Laurette are packing."

Damn. Laurette had kept her end of their deal to the day. Perhaps they could leave tomorrow. Today. He wasn't sure he could trust his son to keep so momentous a revelation to himself. He had given the boy power over all of them.

Power to hurt as he had been hurt.

"James, Bea is innocent in all this. And you like her. You're friends. Please don't say anything to her."

Con watched the calculation in his son's eyes. It was like seeing Marianna all over again as James deliberated his fate.

"Mama knew, didn't she? That was why she always tried to throw us together when Bea came to visit Aunt Laurette." A shadow crossed his face and he stood up abruptly. "I don't understand," he whispered. "They were *friends. Best* friends."

The last piece of the puzzle had snapped into place.

* * *

Con's words had been broken, his sentences fragments. He'd done his best to explain why every important adult in the child's life had lied to him, not that it made James's expression look any less thunderous.

At last, Con let him go. But he had managed to get his son's promise to keep Laurette's secret, offering to share Marianna's last letter when they returned home. When he read it, James would see his father was not a complete villain.

It was an extraordinary document, written in a spidery hand weakened by the fast-spreading cancer that ravaged her. Mr. Foster had remembered the letter's existence and given it to him too late—after Con had made his ill-fated proposal to Laurette. It was clear Mr. Foster didn't think Con deserved a word from his wife, but his attention to detail and loyalty trumped his antipathy to the man who had deserted his employer's daughter.

In it, Marianna had told him not only about Beatrix, but her role in keeping the child's existence a secret. More Berryman bribery, but he supposed even knowing he had another child might not have brought him home. Con wondered if Laurette would have answered differently if he'd had a plan for their child back when he first proposed. Probably not.

After he met with Foster, his fury had ignited all over again until he thought he saw a way to right the past. This year had taken a toll on his emotions and pocketbook, and still had come to nothing but resentment from his son, and Laurette's permanent refusal of his suit.

It was time he gave up, this time for good. There was no point harboring hope.

He started back to the house, sticking his hand in his pocket, absently rubbing the skipping stone. In Greece they strung stones together to ease the edge of despair; Catholics had their rosary beads. Con settled for his River Piddle rock, smoothed by the rush of water and blessed with childhood joy. He'd need something the size of the Rock of Gibraltar to tell Laurette that James knew everything now.

He trusted James. They had shaken hands, and if Mari-anna had done anything, she had raised their child as a gentleman. But it was an enormous burden to place on the boy. The sooner Laurette and Beatrix left, the better.

Aram opened the front door to him, an act of unusual pro-priety. Con had told the servants this was to be as much a va-cation for them as it was for his family, although Nadia and Sadie probably did not see it quite that way, as they turned out delicious meals in the newly-refurbished kitchen. But the atmosphere was relaxed, or he had meant it to be. Sunday lunch was to be a cold collation of greens from Mr. Carter's neat garden, rolls and cold sliced ham. Perhaps it could be wrapped up as a picnic so he wouldn't have to sit through what was bound to be a meal fraught with tension.

"Where is Miss Vincent, Aram?"

"I believe she is upstairs in her room, my lord. Packing." The older man emphasized this last word.

"Yes. My little scheme did not go as planned, I'm afraid, and it's bound to go worse. When Master James returns, could you see that Tomas or Nico—or both—distract him? They can take him somewhere with a box lunch. Anywhere. They can go riding. Caving. And have Nadia or Sadie look after Beatrix. Perhaps they can bake."

Aram looked at his master. "It is too fine a day to spend in-doors in the kitchens, my lord. And it is Sunday. The baking was done yesterday."

"Well, then, take her for a nature walk or something. I want her kept separate from James. There will be no formal luncheon in the dining room today."

Aram raised an eyebrow. He knew everything there was to know, and had urged Con to return home to his responsibili-ties for years. Aram's own sons were the light of his life. Con wished he had listened to him sooner.

He took the stairs slowly, each foot quite unwilling to step on the next tread. Smart feet. Laurette would give him hell in a few minutes and he supposed he deserved every epithet she was going to toss at him. But if she left tomorrow, perhaps disaster could be delayed if not averted altogether.

Her door was open. She stood over the array of muslins, silks and satins spread out on her bed and every available chair, a look of consternation on her face. "Oh! Con! You may come in, but please close the door."

He did as he was bid, wondering what she would say next. Had Beatrix plagued her about the portrait? He thought not. She seemed too calm, although she was in the middle of crinoline chaos.

"I cannot possibly take all this home. People would talk, and I truly have no use for such finery. Perhaps you can give them to Charlotte Fallon. My neighbor on Jane Street." Laurette blushed. "Of course, you can dispose of them any way you wish. It's just that Sir Michael won't buy her a stitch and she looks very shabby."

Trust Laurette to be thinking of another woman whose man let her down. She had plenty of experience in that area. He cleared his throat.

"They are yours to do with as you want, Laurie. I'll see to it. I have something to say to you. Please sit down."

Laurette looked around the room and suppressed a laugh. It looked as though her closet had exploded. She watched as Con bundled up an armful of dresses from the chairs by the fireplace and tossed them to the floor. She wanted to chide him for his carelessness, but since the dresses really belonged to him, she kept quiet and sat down. She watched the muscle in his jaw leap as he grasped the mantel and then turned to her. She was not going to sit still for a lecture.

"You're angry at me because I ran home. Well, don't be. Just as I thought, the children did find the painting, but everything is all right. I didn't make a fuss and Bea didn't ask too many questions. She's packing all the toys you bought for her now." She frowned. He still was as tense as she'd ever seen him. "You look like you're the one who needs to sit down. What is it? I thought we came to an agreement."

"We did. And now James is part of it."

Her heart stilled. "What do you mean?"

"He knows everything. And that means you've got to leave tomorrow."

"Everything?" Her voice was the faintest scratch.

"He guessed you're Bea's mother. I did not tell him, but I couldn't lie."

Laurette stumbled up. "Where is he? If he tells Beatrix—"

"He won't. He promised not to. He's off somewhere cooling his heels. I think he's disgusted with the lot of us, his mother included."

"Oh my God." Her mind whirred, too fraught to give Con a piece of it. Her instincts had been right, and now everything—*everything* she'd ever gone through to protect Beatrix was at risk. Laurette had come to terms with the past, or thought she had until Con managed to revive it.

"I know it's all my fault, Laurie. Every bit of it."

Laurette was sick to her soul. Her worst fears could come true at any moment. She sank back down in the chair, heart now pounding like a cannon.

"I can get him out of the way today, and you can leave at first light. If we limit his contact with Bea—with you—I think he can hold to his promise until he works it all out for himself."

How could an eleven-year-old boy keep such a portentous matter to himself? "What did he say?"

"A lot of hurtful things, at first. But I explained about Marianna. And his grandfather. He knows now the man was not a saint, nor, it turns out, was his mother. I had hoped to spare him."

"Marianna took lovers," Laurette blurted. She had never intended to speak against her friend to Con, for really, Marianna had tried hard to make up for the unhappiness she had caused. She had been generous to a fault with Laurette and her daughter. What did it matter if she sought what comfort she could in the face of her husband's abandonment?

"I know. People told me. I don't have the nerve to hold it against her. I was no husband to her and never would have been even if she had lived. You are—you *were*—the only woman for me." Con paced, his expression anguished. "But that's not what we talked about. We talked about how she and her father conspired to keep the truth about you and Beatrix from me. I was as blunt as I could be about the circumstances of my marriage, Laurie. Imagine if you're an eleven-year-old boy, hearing how you came to be, the result of desperation and guile. I don't think he'll ever forgive me."

For a moment Laurette wanted to go to Con and put her arms around him. Only for a moment. Instead she sat, staring into the empty fireplace, her blood thrumming. She could leave right now, if it came to it, leave the rainbow of her "mistress" dresses behind without a qualm, but she'd have a more difficult task explaining to Beatrix why it was necessary to pack and flee in a whirlwind. Tomorrow morning seemed so very far away. She knew she wouldn't sleep a wink tonight.

"We won't eat together. There's no use pretending everything is normal. I'll tell Sadie to bring a tray up."

"I'm not hungry." She swallowed. "Should I talk to him?"

"I don't think it will do much good. But you can't make anything worse than I have."

"I wish—" There was no point in complaining she wished Con had been honest with her from the first. If anyone had cause to protest secrecy and manipulation after all the Berrymans and his uncle had done, it was he. They would not be in this deceptively idyllic Yorkshire hell if Con had told her the truth, told her what he had planned. She would have never come, never allowed her daughter near him. "I'm sure it will be all right," she said, not sure of any such thing. "He's a smart boy. He'll come to see that none of this is really your fault."

Con gave her a bleak smile. "How can you bear to make excuses for me?"

Because I love you. I always have. I probably always will, but our time is past.

Laurette shrugged. "We're old friends, after all."

Chapter 19

James had already chucked his torn coat by the wayside, too hot to wear it another step. The sun beat down on his dark head. He may not have wanted his jacket, but a hat would not go amiss about now—the sun was fairly brutal. He swept his disheveled hair from his forehead, wishing he'd let Nico cut it.

The marquess—his father—had ridiculously long hair. He looked like a pirate. James cursed himself for trying to emulate the man, if only in his choice of hairstyle. His father was no one to copy. He walked away once from everything, and had let James walk away now.

When James was grown—well, he *was* already grown, even if he was still damnably short—he would honor his obligations. He kept his word and honored his promises even now, and that was what a real man did, wasn't it?

He could hold his tongue. He could hold his tongue forever, for how could he even utter what he had just learned? Beatrix Isabella Vincent was his half-sister. According to his father, his mother and grandfather and evil dead great-uncle had swindled Con out of his youth and his one true love.

That was not exactly how his father put it. James had watched him edit his words carefully in an effort to paint a prettier picture. There had been mention of duty and folly, devotion and finance. All James knew was that his father was in love with Aunt Laurette then and Aunt Laurette now. All this talk about helping an old friend during renovations to her house was just so much nonsense.

And Aunt Laurette was afraid Bea would hate her if she found out the truth—was terrified, according to his father. But James didn't think she would. Bea loved her cousin.

No, not her cousin.

Her *mother*.

Bea had done nothing but complain about her parents since she and Sadie had joined them on the road to Yorkshire. It was something she and James had in common, something that brought them closer. While it was acknowledged between them that James had the greater grievance—his father had gone missing for a whole *decade* and all James had to show for that time was a bunch of rubbishy stained letters—Bea's parents were deemed more than unsatisfactory as well.

They were unbelievably strict. They didn't let her go anywhere or do anything when she was home from school. He'd had to teach her to play cards, for heaven sakes—they thought games of chance were wicked. The Vincents spent all day Sunday on a hard wooden bench in chapel, expecting Bea to sit there with her hands folded in her lap and her eyes raised to heaven.

They even forbade her from participating in dance instruction at her school. She was forced to lounge on a settee at the edge of the ballroom and watch while every other girl in her class practiced with Monsieur Lucien. The way Bea said his name led James to believe Bea had a silly *tendre* for the dancing master, but his own school lessons on Napoleon were far too fresh in his mind to fall prey to the dubious charms of the French, no matter how well they danced or how long their eyelashes were. Girls were so stupid sometimes.

James sat down hard on a rock. He was spoiled for choice—the field he had tromped on grew them like big gray weeds. He uprooted a fistful of daisies and ripped the petals off, still angry at his father, and now his mother as well. He wished there was someone to talk to, but who would that be? Sometimes a fellow was best on his own.

James had been away at school since he was eight. The masters were all right; he was heir to a marquessate, after all, had a courtesy title of viscount besides. At an early age, he'd learned to lift his eyebrow and look down his nose when necessary. But when his mama died, he had no one. His father didn't come for weeks and weeks. Only Laurette was at his side for the funeral, and had wept when he could not.

She told him his mother was her best friend. How on earth could they have been friends after what his father had just told him? Women, like girls, were stupid too.

He would never befriend an enemy. Never. It was why he held himself aloof from his father, no matter what the man bought him or where he pledged to take him. The Marquess of Conover could not come waltzing back into James's life like a French dancing master and expect him to open his arms wide in welcome.

James had pride. Consequence. He didn't need anyone. Couldn't, evidently, *trust* anyone.

He pulled up a clump of grass, watching the tiny black ants scurry for cover. He couldn't sit here all day roasting in the sun, but he couldn't go back to the house either. Not yet. He felt—he felt *sleepy* all of a sudden. Like a puling baby who needed a nap. His brainbox was chock-full of contradictory ideas, and it would be much easier to push them away, curl up and sleep until he was all grown up to make sense of everything. If that were even possible.

To hell with luncheon. He couldn't eat a morsel, watching his father's earnest face across the table. Aunt Laurette would be nervous—*scared* of him. Bea would wonder what was wrong when he stuffed his mouth with disgusting vegetables so he couldn't talk. He would just stay away for a bit. Worry his father like he'd been worried.

Of course a few hours were nothing like ten years.

James dusted the dirt from his trousers and set to climbing the hill. He'd be up high so he could see to hide if anyone was coming after him from Stanbury Hill Farm. With luck he might come across another cave to get out of the sun and lick his wounds.

He and Bea and Aram's sons had already found several on the property. Nico said some caverns went on for miles and miles, calcite crystal roads beneath the earth. Of course when they'd gone caving, Nico and Tomas had brought lanterns and rope, even though Bea was too miss-ish to go in very far. She was afraid of everything.

James took the starched handkerchief out of his pocket and wiped his face. It was getting blasted—bloody—hot. Just like the summer his father had told him about all those years ago, when the grass caught fire, and the crops and animals and people died. The summer when everything changed. The summer that was the reason he stood here to feel the sweat trickle down his neck.

His eyelids felt heavy against the glare of the sun. How had his father managed in the vast desert, with black-eyed Saracens waiting behind every sand dune to slice his throat? Of course, the Marquess of Conover might have been mistaken for one of them, bearded and turbaned as he was. His father's friend Mr. Bankes had sketched him into a corner of one of the letters he'd sent home. When his mother had shown it to him, James had refused to believe at first that the man in the picture could be his long-lost papa. That wild savage? Scandalous.

He reached a ridge and sat down to catch his breath and wipe his brow again. Below him was a deep green vale, the earth rippling irregularly as if the grass was a wrinkled blanket cast off in haste by a giant. A thin ribbon of water winked in the sunlight. And between a grouping of rocks, James thought he spied the mouth of a cave. At this distance it was impossible to tell how big it was, but it would be cool and dark, perfect to while away the afternoon in privacy.

He scrambled down the steep bank, losing his footing and sliding ignominiously on his arse, until he caught a root with a grubby hand and braked himself. His bum hurt like hell.

"Fuck!" he said, experimenting. Some explorer he'd make; he couldn't even stay on his feet. He'd never be wearing this suit of clothes to church again, even if he retraced his steps to find where he'd discarded his torn jacket. James felt the back of his pants. They were shredded, but his hand came back clean of blood.

It took him much longer than he thought to get to the stream at the bottom. The route was uneven and there were more than enough half-hidden jagged rocks for him to stub his toes. He began to question the wisdom of his judgment at coming so far from Stanbury Hill Farm—he wasn't even sure if he was still on his father's land, and said the word "fuck" several more times, as men were wont to do when irritated. There was no trace of the regimented drystone walls that bisected the property, just undulating grasses and sinkholes and scores of rock outcroppings.

James's face was fiery and perspiring, and he could smell something most unpleasant—himself. He splashed some cold water on his face, cupped his hands and drank greedily, and upon brief consideration, sat right down in the shallow stream. The burn on his bottom felt better immediately. He soaked his handkerchief and tied it around his neck.

There. He felt one thousand percent better. He stood, the water squishing out of his boots. His old nanny Mrs. Pulsifer would have given him the devil for his disarray, but Conover had dismissed her almost immediately after coming home to Ryland Grove. James had been upset by that too, but allowed his father had the right. He was too old anyhow to be coddled by a nanny during breaks from school, and the woman had been disrespectful, calling his father a "heathen" right to his face. Conover had just laughed—a frightening sight, his feral white teeth splitting his brown face, paid Pully off, and that was that. Nico became James's valet / companion when he was home and they rubbed along well enough together.

James wished Nico was here now.

But no. He had thinking to do, and couldn't begin to discuss his family's tattered history with a servant. James walked along the stream until he slipped under the overhanging rock and stood still, his eyes adjusting to the dimness inside the cave. The ceiling rose well above his head so he didn't need to crouch, but the floor seemed uneven so he stepped carefully. Without light, he wasn't going to venture far. His hand brushed against the pitted wall. "Hallo!" he shouted.

His echo was not endless. Arm outstretched, he followed the curve of the wall and found himself inside a small chamber, with a narrow passage to the right that he was too big to fit through. He edged along, stumbling over loose rock, until his foot hit air.

It happened so quickly he didn't have a chance to scream. James pitched forward, trying to grip the damp wall as he went down, feeling his fingernails scrape at the limestone. Before he could stop himself, his body was wedged into a deep split in the cave floor, a rugged finger of rock tearing his shirt, the last article of clothing he wore that had not been ruined, and the skin beneath it.

Two falls in one day. He was a lummox. He tried to wiggle up, but to his horror, rock crumbled and he slipped down another foot. Wary now, he extended his booted toe but felt nothing under it.

How deep was this fissure? James swallowed down the panic that was building inside him. It wouldn't do to lose his self-control. He'd been in this pickle less than a minute.

But what if he was to be trapped here all day? Several days? When would his father decide to come looking for him after their row, and how on earth could he ever find him?

Nico said there were hundreds of caves in Yorkshire. He'd read travel guides before their trip north, and had entertained

Sadie, Bea and him with stories of his own trips to Greece and other places.

James wanted to travel too. He had been promised a trip with his father if he behaved in school this year. But, suddenly, James thought he might never have the chance to go anywhere. Because he would never get to school to behave. Because he would die right here, jammed in this crack in the earth.

Alone and in the dark.

His face was wet, but he couldn't move his arms just yet to wipe the tears away. There was no one to see or hear him when he forgot he wasn't so grown-up after all.

"Fuck." Somehow the word seemed less than satisfactory, but it was all he could think of to say.

Chapter 20

It was well after dinner time, although this far north the summer sky would be light for hours yet. Con had moved restlessly throughout the house all afternoon, finally winding up in the library. An uneaten sandwich, its edges curling, lay on the desk just where Aram had placed it, giving him a look brimming with pity. Laurette had chosen to eat upstairs in the nursery with Bea, and he hoped they were deep in their plans to leave.

He had flipped through and abandoned a stack of crumbling books, not sure whether they reflected the tastes of his grandfather Stanbury, or his uncle. He'd have to tell Carter to box up the lot and burn what the mice and bugs hadn't eaten. It was unlikely Con would be returning to Yorkshire after the debacle of this trip. The house was repaired and once the farm turned a profit, he could sell it off or save it for his daughter.

There had been no sign of James since he'd stomped off down by the lake, and Con was worried. The boy must be starving by now, with only his pride to fill his belly. Con had already sent Nico and Tom off to "bump into" the boy.

He had promised himself to give his son time, but when he closed his eyes, he saw James's white face, heard his angry words, and saw his stiff back as he marched away from him.

There might not be enough time in the world to mend this difficulty.

When Con was a boy, he would have gone straight to Laurette if something upset him. James had nobody.

Con felt a searing pain in his chest. He wondered if it was possible to die of heartbreak, no matter how noble one's intentions were. But now that half of the truth was out, he and his son could perhaps find the way to each other.

If not, life would not be worth living. He had lost Laurette. He'd never had James to begin with.

Con was in a hell of his own making. The choice he made at twenty had poisoned whatever future he had with his only son. It had taken him a night halfway across the world to realize it.

Con's heart squeezed. He had done to his own son what had been done to him. He had mastered the fury he felt toward his uncle and the Berrymans some years ago. His pride had been nicked, his love thwarted. He had seen too much of the world now to imagine himself the center of the universe.

He had been faithful writing to James, but had purposefully made himself a nomad with no fixed address. Perhaps half the missives he had sent had been lost or delivered months late. Marianna had probably turned the boy's mind against him, and who could blame her? Con had deserted her, and worse, had abandoned his son.

And now his son had abandoned him. He looked up from his melancholy thoughts to see Beatrix standing in the doorway.

"May I come in, my lord?"

"Of course, Bea. You are a welcome diversion."

"Cousin Laurette tells me we are to leave tomorrow instead of Tuesday. I just came to say good-bye. And to thank you. I've had a lovely time." She smiled shyly up at him.

She was so lovely herself, all pale copper hair and sun-blushed cheeks, a different child entirely from the first time he met her at school. "I have an idea, Bea. I'd like to give you the portrait of my mother, but not until it's cleaned and stitched."

A look of uncertainty crossed her face. "Are you sure, Lord Conover? That doesn't seem right. And Mama and Papa— well, the picture is rather large and our house is small. I don't think they'll know what to do with it."

"I'm sure your cousin Laurette can keep it for you at Vincent Lodge until you grow up with a house of your own. That old place has plenty of room." *And she can look at it when she misses you.*

"Thank you, Lord Conover. That's very generous of you. You've been awfully kind to me."

He heard the unspoken *Why?* "I know you mean a great deal to your cousin. Your summer visits mean the world to her. She is—she is my oldest friend, you know. I've known her since she tugged on my coattails, and I've been chasing after her ever since."

That was too much, too close to the truth. But Bea took his words in placid fashion.

"I have known James a long while too, although we were never so close as you and Cousin Laurette. But we have become better friends since coming to Stanbury Hill Farm. I want to say good-bye to him too until next year. Where is he?"

Con winced. "I'm afraid he and I had a bit of an argument. Nothing serious," he lied. "He'll be home soon, I'm sure."

Suddenly he doubted the veracity of his words. James would *not* be home. It had been hours, and the golden ball of sun was dropping behind the peaks. His son had run away.

Con sprang out of his chair. "If you will excuse me, Bea, there's something I've just remembered."

She curtseyed. "Certainly, my lord. Good-bye and thank you again. Will I see you at school this year?"

No. It would be like stabbing myself with a rusty knife. "We'll see. I may be very tied up with my business interests. I may even have to go abroad again."

"Oh." She looked disappointed. He was grateful for the scrap of her affection.

"Get a good night's sleep. You'll be off with Nico at dawn." His nails bit into the palms of his hands. How far could James have gotten by now? He'd have Aram saddle up his horse so he could ride out.

Bea stepped forward. "I should like to give you a good-bye kiss, my lord."

Con bent down. Bea stood on tiptoe. She smelled like starch and flowers. The first and last kiss from his daughter, and he was too wild with worry to appreciate it.

When she left, he went to the kitchens. Jacob Carter, Sadie, Nadia and Aram were at the table, finishing the last of their dinner, Sam under the table testing his luck. The usual bantering atmosphere was missing. Two covered plates remained on the sideboard for the boys.

"They're not back yet?"

"No, my lord." Aram looked at him keenly.

"I think he's run away."

"No!" Sadie breathed, blanching. "He's a sensible lad. He wouldn't do anything so foolish."

"I don't know, Sadie. He's been pushed to his limits today. He's only eleven, for God's sake." Con shoved his hair back in agitation.

Jacob Carter was already on his feet. "We'll find him. There's a map of the property in my room. We'll each take an area. There's plenty of daylight left."

"When Nico and Tom come home, give them their dinner and send them back out. With lanterns. Find every lamp and candle stub you've got," Con told the women.

"Perhaps we should wait. Find out where they've already searched." Aram sounded calm, but Con saw his hand working at the Greek worry beads in his trouser pocket.

"I can't just sit here. I'll go mad. Aram, could you saddle my horse? I'll ride out on the main road. If he's walking, I'll find him." Unlikely, with the head start James had. And if someone had picked him up along the way—Con suppressed a groan. Why had he waited so long to realize that James was truly missing?

He had to find Laurette. Tell her what he feared. If they didn't find James tonight, there was no way she'd be leaving here tomorrow. He'd need Nico, and, if it came to it, her and Bea too to help with a search.

If he got his hands on James—he'd hug him instead of cuffing him. Kiss him. If he had finally kissed his daughter, it was past time he kissed his son.

Laurette was alone, her trunk and bandboxes stacked neatly in a corner. Her clothes for tomorrow were laid out on a chair. She sat on the window seat, staring at the misty blue mountains and swath of green and sheep, when Con burst into the room without knocking.

"What is it?" Her voice was sharp. She could have been undressed, ready for bed although the sun was still pale in the sky. Con had seen every freckled inch of her a thousand times anyway. But it had been a long, dreadful day. She had a long dreadful day ahead tomorrow as well and had sent Bea to her room to try to go to sleep.

"James has run away."

"Surely not. How do you know? Perhaps he's just *staying* away. To make you suffer a little."

"Believe me, I'm suffering. He's been gone the whole damned day. Missed two meals. Something's wrong."

"He could be at a neighboring farm."

Con shook his head in impatience, looking more upset than she had ever seen him. Laurette herself was not convinced. James had his share of imp in him, especially at school, but it was not like him to be thoughtless. Even if he had had the shock of his young lifetime today, she thought he would be stoic and steady. Eventually. He had always been old-headed, considering himself the man of his family in his father's absence.

"I came to tell you I'm going to look for him. Jacob and Aram and the boys too. If we don't find him tonight, I'm afraid you'll have to stay here until we do."

Laurette could hardly argue. James's safety was far more important than her desire to flee from her past. She rose from the window seat. "I'll come with you."

"Thank you, but no. I'm riding out, Laurie."

"I can ride! Astride even, or have you forgotten?"

"I've never forgotten a thing. But I think you should stay with Bea. I've already told her James and I had an argument. She'll be worried."

"She also might know where he went, where his favorite spots are. Let me ask her."

"Fine. If she says anything useful, tell Jacob and Aram. I'm going up to the main road. Check if anybody's seen him. Put the word out. If he's not back by tomorrow—" Laurette watched him swallow the lump in his throat—"we'll organize a full-fledged search party." He paused. "They never found my uncle."

"Con! Don't think like that! James is probably safe and sound in some farm wife's kitchen, eating biscuits."

"I hope so."

She couldn't help herself. In seconds she was in his arms, smoothing the lines at his eyes with a shaking hand. "You'll find him and everything will be all right."

"Will it?" He looked down at her, his dark eyes unfathomable.

Her lips found his, giving him a fierce quick kiss of promise. If something bad happened to James, she knew Con would not be able to bear it. Nor could she.

She was left alone in her pretty room, counting her heart-beats until they slowed. She smoothed her hair back absently and went to talk to Bea. No matter what Con said, she couldn't wait around while the others looked for James.

Tomas's face was incredulous. He and his brother had been shoveling food in their mouths at a breakneck pace so they could continue looking for James after their quick supper, when Laurette made her proposition. Laurette hoped they wouldn't choke. Their father and Mr. Carter had already left to search the spots Bea had remembered. A map of Stanbury Hill Farm was spread out on the table, anchored with a jam jar and a clean knife. On it someone had drawn a quadrant with a red oil pencil. Other marks and circles indicated where Nico and Tom had already been and where they were to go next. A grouping of lanterns and candlesticks was amassed on the sideboard. Though the sun was still gilding the mountains, the sky was turning from hazy blue to turquoise.

"We're about the same size, Tom. You're a bit taller, but I could roll the cuffs up. I can't go out in my skirts. They're not practical."

"My lord won't want you to go out at all, Miss Laurette," Nadia scolded. "What if you get lost too? There will be hell to pay. And wearing gentleman's trousers? No and no and no."

Sadie winked at Laurette. "It wouldn't be the first time for her, Nadia. Let her go. We can take care of Bea until the men come back."

Bea sat in a rocking chair by the cold stove, twisting her long white fingers. She was still in her night rail, having taken to heart Laurette's suggestion she go to bed early. Her face had lost all the color two weeks in the country had put there. "I could go with you."

Laurette smiled at her daughter. "No, love. If James comes home on his own, you'll be here to yell at him for us. I don't trust Sadie and Nadia to do a proper job of it. They'll probably fix him all his favorite foods and hug him senseless."

Bea gave a wobbly smile back. Laurette's heart ached for her. When she told Bea that James was missing a half-hour ago, the child looked as if she might faint.

And then Bea had said a most unsettling thing. "All this is about the painting and what he told me, isn't it?"

Laurette lied to her. Again. "No, not at all. You know how James and his father are always at odds."

"Oh. I thought he may have quarreled with his father because of the silly story he made up about me."

Laurette had to ask, although she thought she knew the answer already. "And what was that?"

"He teased me up in the attic. Told me I was a changeling child, that I was his secret sister stolen away by Gypsies and sent to live with evil trolls in Cornwall. He is such a *boy,*" Bea sniffed in disgust.

Laurette could almost hear James now, mixing a joke with the very real suspicion he must have felt seeing his grandmother's portrait. Piecing together bits of the mosaic, snatches of adult conversation, servants' gossip. Perhaps James had always known the truth on some level.

Laurette arrested her wayward thoughts. When this night was finally over, she would deal with Beatrix. Gather her up out of the rocking chair or her bed and hold her tight and tell her *something.* But now she followed Tom upstairs to the room he shared with Nico. Taking the first clean shirt and trousers that came to hand, she hurried to her bedchamber to change. Braid her hair so the pins wouldn't fall, leaving a trail on the ground.

A trail. Maybe James had left a clue to his whereabouts behind—a handkerchief or something. She closed her eyes and tried to remember what he had worn this morning. He'd looked a proper little gentleman in church.

"Bea! I want you to go to the drive and gather up all the small rocks you can, white or very light ones only." Tom and Nico looked as if she were mad again. "You two help her. We'll each leave stones behind so we can find our way back in the dark. Drop stones to the right and left every twenty paces to mark a path."

Bea's face lit up. "Like *Hansel and Gretel*. That's a brilliant idea, Cousin Laurette." She dashed out the door barefoot.

"We'll need some bags, Ma," Nico said to Nadia. "Some water jugs and a bit of food too, in case James is thirsty and hungry. For each of us, whoever finds him."

James could be miles away by now, but somehow Laurette didn't think so. He was probably in some cave, holding out and waiting until the very last moment to come home. He must know how wild they all were to find him.

Another quarter of an hour passed while the little party was outfitted for their trek. Sadie slung a heavy canvas satchel across Laurette's chest. Between the stones and the provisions, she might have trouble staying upright. Dusk had fallen and the lanterns were lit. Laurette had pinned her watch on Tom's shirt pocket, promising to return before midnight.

Con had told them James left him at the lake. The boys had already passed that way today, but they returned to the shore. The water was flat and glassy, reflecting the lavender sky. They kept together on the path until they came to a sloping open field, then split up on their assigned routes.

It wasn't quite time to start dropping stones, so the bag dug into Laurette's shoulder and bounced against her hip. "James!" she shouted. She could hear Aram's boys doing the same in the distance. By the time she crested the hill, she was sore and sweaty. She reached into the bag and dropped two oval rocks, counting twenty long strides before she dropped two more. The grass had been mowed quite recently, and what the scythe hadn't caught, the sheep had. Each stone looked like a pearl sewn on emerald velvet.

Counting kept her mind from embracing the worst. She didn't have to think of James being snatched up by some predator, human or otherwise. She didn't have to think of his twisted body at the bottom of a ravine. At each point she dropped her rocks, she called his name. She was getting hoarse and tired already. She raised her eyes to the darkening sky and made a wish on the first star she saw.

And then she tripped. Fell down in an ungainly thump, the lumps in her bag digging painfully into her chest. The lantern spluttered out, then flared back to life.

Mercy. That would teach her to watch her step and depend on children's fairy tales. Even wearing trousers, there were difficulties walking in the country. She sat up, catching her breath. Her foot was tangled on something soft.

James's jacket. "James! Nico! Tomas!" She screeched like a banshee. The boys were probably too far away to hear her, but James might be near. She listened, but heard only the pulse of her own blood rushing in her ears. Should she return home and wait for the others to come back to bring them to this spot? Squinting at her little watch, she saw it was just after ten, the sky still pale gray. She left the jacket where it was, weighting it down with extra stones. If they should come this way, they would know that she'd been here, found it.

She continued on, lured by the hope that James had walked before her. Trying to take the straightest path so she could leave her own stones, she picked her way around the large rocks jutting randomly from the field. They looked as though they were thrown by some unseen hand in a demented dice game. The land was uncompromising, harsh in the twilight. Shadows loomed and the silence was palpable.

She was thirsty herself now. She set her lantern down and

sat, uncorking the water jug to take a swallow. Not too much—James might need it, although there was bound to be a stream out here somewhere. A few stars twinkled feebly in the sky. How she wished for a full moon—any sort of moon at all. The lantern would not last forever, nor would she. Her arm was tingling from holding the light at the proper angle. Laurette estimated she had another half-hour before she needed to head back. It wouldn't do to have them all hunting for *her* as well.

As she walked through the stone garden, a flash of white caught the corner of her eye. Next to a flat rock, a sad pile of torn daisy petals lay in the grass. Total destruction. James again—she was sure of it. She left a fistful of smaller pebbles and climbed the hill ahead.

She was truly winded now, a piercing stitch in her side. She held the lantern high. Below her was a little valley, too steep for her to navigate unless she slid down on her bottom as if she were on a snow sled. With her luck, it would be *her* twisted body at the bottom of a ravine. The gentle rush of water was the only sound. "James!" she screamed. "James!" Her voice echoed back, lonely.

She sank down, fighting the tears that were threatening to overtake her. She needed to turn around, if she could summon the energy. Instead she sat very still, her aching legs outstretched in Tom's nankeen trousers.

This was her fault. Every single thing that had caused her so much unhappiness was her fault and hers alone. As a girl, so she was so determined to seduce Con, he never stood a chance. Even when she knew he was to marry, she went to him, night after night. She had given the Berrymans control over Beatrix and her future. She had refused Con's offer of marriage.

Oh, she'd told herself it was because Marianna's death was too fresh, but that was a lie. She was afraid to tell him they had a child together, denying herself the happiness she didn't deserve. How could she form a normal life with him when their daughter was in Cornwall?

When he had finally confronted her about Beatrix, she had forbidden him all contact. Laurette had practically forced him to ruin her brother to get to her. And now when Con had tried to cobble together a family, she extracted promises to keep her secrets, promises which made James disappear and doubt every single thing he knew.

She allowed herself one frustrated sob. Just one. Feeling sorry for herself was not going to find James. She called out one last time, then reached for the bag, much lighter now.

Her hand froze. There was the faintest noise from below.

"James!" Seconds later her own voice came back to her, but there was something else underneath, apart from the sound of the water. "James! It's Laurette! Can you hear me?" There was a muffled tapping in the distance. Steady, like a metronome. Not a sound to be found in nature, unless there was a particularly regulated woodpecker. "James! Where are you?"

The tapping was more urgent now, in sets of three, coming from somewhere far below. Laurette couldn't see well enough to make out the shadowy shapes on the incline. Scrubby trees. Boulders at the bottom. She could take a header and kill herself.

"Tap twice if you hear me," she bellowed. There was something, but she wasn't sure. "Again, James, please!"

Two distinct raps. Rock against rock. *Thank God.*

"I'm coming down to get you, James. It may take me a little while. Are you hurt?" He was silent. "Two taps for yes, four taps for no."

She waited. Slowly she counted. One. Two. And then three.

He was hurt, then, but being brave about it. She could be brave too, on her bottom all the way down this ghastly cliff, which was far from the typical rolling dale. She dumped out the rest of her stones in a little pyramid, blessed Tom for the loan of his breeches, and scooted down inch by inch, her lantern flickering at each bump. Every few feet she called out to James that she was on her way. Her voice was so cracked she hoped he could still hear her. The tapping remained reassuringly steady.

The narrow stream glinted ahead. Suddenly the lantern extinguished, and she was in gloom.

She put it down and rubbed her arm. "Damn and blast. James, keep tapping. I've lost my light."

Sound came from across the riverbed. Her eyes adjusted to the deepening night. The stars were stronger now, silver sprinkles spilled across the sky. It seemed safe enough now to stand up and walk the rest of the way. By God's grace the water would be shallow enough for her to walk through it.

"I'm crossing the stream now, James." Sloshing, she kicked up a commotion so James could hear her advance. To her right was a jumble of boulders. James's signals were louder now. Laurette hoped he wasn't trapped under rock. "James, can you talk?" There were four quick taps.

Wherever he was, he'd probably been yelling his head off. She could barely articulate herself; her throat was raw.

Somewhere she had heard that the most beautiful, calming sound to a person in distress was their own name. She imagined Con at her ear, murmuring "Laurie," holding her fast.

"James, I see rocks, James. Big ones. Are you near them?"

He tapped twice. She lost her footing and stumbled. Catching herself, she smoothed the rock's surface with her hand, waving through empty space. "This is a cave! You're inside a cave aren't you, James? Are you trapped somehow?" Two taps. "Under stone?" Four taps. Not a cave-in then. But something.

She heard desperate rasping. There was nothing for it but to duck under the arch. She set the bag down near the entrance with a clunk. It had been growing dark before, but now inside it was ink-dark. A fevered series of raps came from a place below the cave floor. Laurette let out a little shriek as something soft brushed her cheek and flew by her. Bats.

"I'm all right, James. I'm right here, but I can't see a damned thing. Is it safe to walk?" Four very loud raps. Immediately she fell to her knees, then flattened her body on the cold ground. "James, I'm going to crawl toward you. Can you talk at all?"

"N-not really." The barest whisper.

Laurette had never heard anything so wonderful in her life. She inched along the uneven surface on her belly, pausing now and again to listen. Bats whirred above her head, and from the snuffling she was fairly sure James was crying in relief. But she hadn't reached him yet, and had no idea how to get him out of whatever situation he was in. There was no light and she had no tools. Brushing away a pile of rubble, she reached forward, fingertips touching rough edge. The floor had collapsed and she felt nothing in a two foot wide radius. Somewhere within this narrow chasm, Con's son was stuck and hurt.

"I'm right above you, James. Can you see me? I can't see you, I'm afraid. Don't try to talk, just tap."

"I'm all right. I can whisper."

She shoved her arm down in the hole but touched nothing. "Can you reach up to me?"

"No. I've tried, but I can't get my hands up past my shoulders. I keep sliding down every time I move."

Who knew how deep this crevice was? James could fall to his death as she dithered above him.

"Stay put then. Let me think." She could go back for help, but without light, her little white rocks were just so many smudges in a blur. There was a knife in her bag. If she cut Tomas's voluminous white shirt, she might be able to tear it in strips to dangle it down, but the well-washed fabric would never support James's weight, even if he could figure out a way to hold onto it. She should have thought to bring rope instead of cheese.

"Are you thirsty, James? I've brought water, and food, too, but I'm not certain I can get it down to you."

"Thirsty."

Laurette pulled the shirt from her breeches and over her head, slipping her useless watch in her pocket. Beneath the shirt, she wore a short shift, and she shivered automatically. If she were cold after just a few minutes in this cave, James must be frozen. She'd try the shirt first without cutting it. Sleeve to sleeve it measured at least five feet. If that wasn't long enough, she'd try the pants next. The fabric on the sleeve was thin enough to loop into the jug's handle. "I'm going to get my bag, get the water." She stood up, ducking quickly as another bat whizzed by.

She couldn't leave him alone all night, even if she could find her way back to the farm in the dark. They'd come tomorrow morning at first light. Con would come.

She secured the stone bottle to the shirt. "I'm going to take the cork out for you. I'm sorry, you may get wet as it comes down. I'll try to be steady." She lay flat again, leaning in as far as she dared, holding the bottom of the jug with one hand and the sleeve with the other. She released the bottle and it hit rock with a sickening chinking sound. "Did it break over you, James?"

"No." She heard wriggling and rustling and dreaded the consequences. "I've got it."

Her arm strained under the weight of the bottle. It seemed forever before she heard the slurping sound. She closed her eyes in relief. Eyes opened or closed, she was truly in the dark. But dawn came early to Yorkshire. There were only a few more hours to get through.

"Th-thank you."

"You're most welcome. Do you want more or shall I reel it up?"

"More."

She felt the blood rush to her head as she bent into the opening, felt dizzy. Ashamed she was so weary, she took a deep breath. She would talk James through the night and hope he didn't slide any deeper. She had many things to tell him, and they weren't going anywhere.

Chapter 21

Con had cursed in English, Greek, Arabic and schoolboy French. What in *hell* was that bloody woman thinking, wandering out in the dark? The others had returned an hour ago, their search for James as fruitless as his had been. He sent them to bed for a few hours while he waited in all his riding dirt for Laurette to return.

But he couldn't wait any longer. He splashed some water on his face, picked up a lantern, and left the house and went into the barn. His own horse was spent, but he'd procured a sure-footed pretty little filly for Laurette as well as ponies for the children. The animal seemed agreeable to being awoken and saddled and stood patiently as he packed a bag with whatever came to hand. There were random tools and rope hanging on hooks along the wall which might become useful.

Con usually traveled light, but tonight he stuffed as much as he could into the saddlebag. He walked the horse down the path to the lake. Con knew he had to look for Laurette's Hansel and Gretel crumbs every twenty paces and could not do so from horseback. Once he found her, she could ride back and fall into bed. She was bound to be as exhausted as he was.

If she wasn't hurt.

If she wasn't dead.

He promptly squelched those thoughts, but he could feel silver sneaking into his dark hair. Between his son and his lover, he would truly be the Mad Marquess by morning.

The night was alive with noise, from the hoot of an owl to the lap of the lake, to the ladylike whickering of the horse. He added to it, shouting Laurette's name every few footsteps. Her path had been well-marked, each silvery stone catching the glow of the lantern.

As children they had perfected just such a system, when they escaped of an evening and went exploring. Laurette had even painted stones with whitewash for this purpose, until Sadie discovered her cache and hid all the house keys, locking her in. The maid had been more alert to their mischief than the Vincents, but she hadn't been able to tame Laurette's wild nature.

Somewhere under the starlit sky, his wild Laurette was striding around in Tomas's breeches looking for his son.

At least he hoped she was on her feet. He couldn't think of her crumpled on the ground, injured somehow. His worry over James was too fierce.

He'd stopped at every dwelling for miles this evening. No one had seen a handsome dark-haired boy on the road this afternoon, and they would have noticed. It was Sunday. Traffic was non-existent after church services, either by foot or on horseback. Everyone was enjoying their hearth and home with their families, spending a quiet sunny day thanking God for His blessings, just as they should.

Con received promises of help in the morning if the boy didn't turn up. He had soon gotten tired of the knowing chuckles and the "boys will be boys" platitudes he heard all evening. Something was wrong and he knew it.

Nico thought James might be holed up in a cave somewhere. He'd been a keen potholer the past two weeks, and had begged Nico to camp out overnight after he and Bea arrived at Stanbury Hill. However, nothing could induce Bea to sleep out of doors with bugs and bats, and bright-eyed creatures of the night. The idea of James curled up sound asleep on a cavern floor was an appealing one, but one Con couldn't quite believe.

The horse shied and shifted and Con held her reins. He lifted his lantern and saw James's folded jacket, a neat row of rocks marching up the front like buttons. His heart leapt. "Good girl," he murmured. The horse preened, but his praise wasn't meant for her. He slowed his pace now, scanning for the double stones, getting off course several times before he came to the scattered daisies. *He loves me, he loves me not.*

Con loved his son even if James didn't love loving him back right now.

He led the filly up a rise. There was no way the horse could go any further; the way down was steep and gnarled with rocks and roots. He walked a few yards and found another pile of stones. Quite a lot of them, as if Laurette had dumped the whole bag open.

"Laurette! James!" His voice came back to him, the sound of its need so strong no one could fail to know how desperate he was.

James couldn't credit it. He'd fallen asleep for a bit, that big finger of rock still poking him in his gut, his body aching from head to toe with damp. He'd finally dropped his signaling rock, and had listened to it skitter down a fair distance. A long way down, then. Good thing he was trapped between a rock and a hard place, no matter how much it hurt.

Above him he could hear Laurette's breathing. *No.* No point in beating around the bush. Her snores. The wuffles were magnified by the acoustics in the cave. He shouldn't be surprised that she snored. He expected he did too when he was lying down in his own soft bed, not wedged between limestone slabs.

They had talked for a long time, and his head was a bit

clearer now. His father would come for him. Laurette wouldn't leave James alone tonight, but if rescue didn't come by early morning, she would go back and fetch help. He could manage a few more hours smashed in the dark.

He shifted slightly and undid the placket of his trousers. He had an urgent need to relieve himself. The water still dangled against his chest from the shirt and a bit of leather strapping that Laurette had cut from her bag and anchored with a heavy rock. She'd dropped food down on him too. He'd been pretty lucky getting anything into his mouth. He imagined he reeked of piss and cheese and ham in equal quantities.

He had just finished his business when he heard a low mournful sound, kind of like a trapped bear. That's all this adventure needed, for them to be discovered by some wild beast, and be eaten as a midnight snack. There wasn't even any food left to fob an animal off with; he'd consumed every crumb that rained down on his shoulders.

"Laurette! Wake up! There's something out there."

And then he knew it was *someone*. He heard his father shouting, first Laurette's name, then his, over and over. "It's my father! Wake up, Laurie!" he croaked.

She made a peculiar snort and then spoke in a sleep-softened voice. "I'm awake. What is it?"

"It's my father. I heard him shouting."

Before she ever got up, she screamed, "Con!" His father's name reverberated around the arched cave roof. James heard Laurette scramble to her feet and shuffle across the floor in the pitch black. She screamed again and James's head ached. His own voice was coming back to him but he was glad she was there to do the screaming for him. She sounded like one of the three Furies, although she certainly was a lot prettier. Very pretty, in fact. And very nice to him. Always had been. He shut his eyes, squeezing the tears back. He was to be rescued.

* * *

Con took off down the cliff, his lantern swinging wildly. He had found Laurette at least. From the sound of her cries, she was some distance away.

"I found James! He's trapped in a little cave. The floor gave way and he slid down. I can't reach him, but he's safe for now. Oh, I see you, Con! I see your light. Thank God."

He couldn't see her yet, and could barely hear her raspy, breathless voice. He understood enough to stop his descent. "I have rope, Laurie. Let me get it. I'll be right there."

He'd climbed worse cliffs than this, but not in the dark. Not when his heart was pounding. Not when the relief he was feeling threatened to put him on his wobbly knees in thankful prayer. He left the lantern wedged against an out-cropping of rock and used both hands to propel himself up. How the devil he was going to get up it again later with Laurie and James, he had no idea. Maybe they could take the long way home.

He allowed himself a breath. His son was alive and the woman he loved was resourceful and safe. He was deter-mined to kiss both of them—sloppy, emotional kisses that left no doubt how much they meant to him. Laurette might want to keep her distance, and James probably thought he was too old for such a display, but Con would prevail. Just this once. He threw himself over the bank, rolling onto the grass.

The horse stood a little ways away, just where he left her, untethered in his hurry to get down. She whinnied at his folly, ambled over him, and dipped her velvet nose to his face.

"That's a girl." He reached into his pocket for a lump of sugar and tied her reins to a twisted root, then removed the saddle bag. Slinging it over his shoulder, he started back down the slope trying to keep his balance.

Laurette flew out of the dark at him, clad in buff trousers that revealed every sweet curve, her braid unraveling, her chemise so thin he could see her honey-colored nipples. His mouth dried and he struggled to keep his eyes on her worried face. He placed a hand on her shoulder to steady her and himself.

"Is he all right?"

"I think so. Mostly. He got scraped up as he fell into the shaft, and then hollered himself hoarse. We have to cross a little stream to get to the cave. Your boots will get wet."

"Is that what happened to your shirt? I must say, I find this new fashion quite fetching."

She gave him a stern look. "I'll be most happy for the loan of *your* shirt, my lord. Tom's is doing water-bearer duty."

Con stroked her arm. "You're cold as ice." He handed her the heavy bag while he stripped off his coat.

"What's in this? Rocks?"

"No, my clever girl. That was *your* bag. Brilliant, by the way. Made me feel like a boy again." He wrapped her in his jacket. Laurette shrugged into it gratefully.

"I'm fine, really. But James is freezing. His teeth keep chattering. When he fell he was wet from head to toe. He took a bit of an impromptu bath in the water but forgot to remove his clothes."

Con followed the sway of her delicious backside as they walked down the hill and over the slippery riverbed. He was amazed and grateful Laurette could have found his son in this most inconvenient of places. "How did you know to look here?"

She shrugged. "I found his coat at first, then just kept going. It's a bit of a miracle, really."

It was that and then some. "Where is your lantern?"

"Went out."

Con was incredulous. "You found him in the dark?"

"I heard him before I lost the light. He was banging a rock."

He grabbed her elbow and squeezed it. "You've saved his life, Laurie. I don't know how I'll ever thank you."

"Just get him out of that hole." She stopped at the cave's

entrance. "And don't be too hard on him," she whispered. "He never intended to cause anybody this much worry. We had a very good talk."

As if Con would ever say a cross word. James would have a free pass for ages, at least until he reached his teen years and tried the patience of a saint, as all youth were wont to do. Con dodged into the entry, casting light in the interior. Laurette shuddered as a few bats objected to the invasion of their playground.

"Over here. Mind your step."

Con knelt at the edge of a substantial drop, his heart constricting as he looked down into his son's pinched white face. "Hello, James. I'm awfully glad to see you."

"I didn't mean for you to be inconvenienced, sir," the child said in a gravelly voice.

"Hush. Don't talk. Laurette said you've strained your throat."

James shook his head. "I'm sorry for all the things I said."

"I've forgotten them, James. I'm just so happy you're all right. Alive. Now how are we going to get you out?"

"I kept slipping down. I'm on sort of a shelf now, but I can't get my arms up through the gap. I've tried."

And was probably bloody to prove it. "Tight quarters, eh? I brought a hammer along. Suppose I come down and knock about?"

Laurette shook her head. "Con, you'll never fit. I'll do it."

He raised an eyebrow. "It makes much more sense. You can lower me in with a rope and hold me. I doubt I could hold you."

"We're talking about rock here, Laurie. Are you strong enough to chip it away?"

"Pooh. It's limestone. Relatively soft as rock goes. And I don't have to quarry a huge block of it, just break off a few chunks. Some of it was loose enough for James to do it with his bare hands to make his signaling stone."

Con chuckled. "You really are a marvel. All right, we'll try it your way. Feet first or head first?"

"I think I'd have more leverage if I went feet, but I'd wind up too high to be useful."

Con uncoiled the rope while Laurette buttoned up his jacket, tucking her braid under the collar. He looped the rope securely around her slender waist, then tied the other end around his, wrapping the excess around one fist. "We've got plenty of play. He's not down all that far, just jammed. Let me know the minute you want to come back up. You've been heroic enough. If this doesn't work, I can go back for Tomas or Nico." He nudged a good-sized rock with his foot to help stabilize the rope once she was down.

She swung the tool in an arc, testing its weight. She looked like a Valkyrie warrior, loose tendrils of golden hair catching the lamplight.

"Ready?"

"As I'll ever be."

She hung over the edge, giving Con an unobstructed view of her derriere. In his opinion, if all women wore pants, the world would be an entirely different place. She flipped into the opening, Con unspooling the rope inch by inch. She wriggled through a narrow passage, angling her shoulder.

"Stop! Hello, James!" Her voice was rich and mellow in the tunnel. Con slipped the rope under the rock but held firm anyway.

"Mind your eyes, the both of you. James, you should close yours altogether."

"James, how about I put your kerchief around your eyes?" Con waited anxiously while she struggled with the knot with one hand, the other clutching the hammer, her feet seeking a toehold along the walls. Finding the task impossible, she stuck the hammer under her chin and covered James's eyes. "Just like blindman's bluff, but you can't touch me yet. You will shortly."

Her strikes on the rock were at first tentative. A few chips flew up and James coughed.

"Sorry."

Con watched as she switched her strategy. Holding the hammer with both hands, she increased the speed, swaying alarmingly at every blow.

He should stop her. This was madness. Instead he held the rope and light as steady as he could, watching her body twist and turn with her efforts, and occasionally seeing the top of James's head. Limestone was porous and full of seams; if they were lucky she'd find a flaw. Soon.

He tried to imagine how his son felt encased in a stone cocoon for hours. Shivers raced up and down his spine. Con had done his share of tomb raiding with William. It was never pleasant underground in the dark and dust and damp. Throw in the fact that James was alone, thinking his whereabouts would be unknown forever, and Con felt his own panic ratchet. He'd never liked enclosed spaces; even on ships he spent most of the time on deck. This episode might scar James permanently, beyond whatever injuries he'd sustained in his fall.

Laurette's whoop and the sound of rocks and metal clattering down ripped him from his thoughts.

"Progress?" he asked.

"Success, I think! But dash it, I've dropped the hammer. James, can you get your arms through now?" Con couldn't catch the exchange. They spent an eternity talking and then Laurette said, "Pull me up, Con."

She was dead weight as he hauled her up, squeezing her limbs as close to her body as she could. When he finally got her out, her arms were shaking with fatigue, her face bright red and slick with sweat.

"Are you all right?"

"Don't worry about me. Just take the rope off. I'm afraid I can't manage." She collapsed on the floor and tried to force the feeling back into her fingers. Con got on his knees, loosened the knot and slipped the rope up over her torso. Her voice was pitched too low for James to hear. "He's nervous about moving from his little seat down there. There's quite a drop below. But his arms are free and I think he's fit enough to get the rope around himself. It will be tricky though. I'm so hot." She tried to unbutton Con's jacket but her hands were too numb. Con did it for her, slipping the coat off her freckled shoulders. "Should I have stayed down there and pulled him up myself? I didn't think I could hold on."

"You did the right thing. The perfect thing, Laurie. I love you."

She looked right at him, shadows from the lantern flickering across her face. "I love you, too."

Chapter 22

There. She'd said it aloud. She hadn't uttered those words in twelve years, just kept them locked in a chilly corner of her heart while she distracted herself with life. But she did love Con, always had, always would. How she was going to live out the next forty years or so she hadn't a clue, but now was not the time to hammer out the details. For the time being, she was done with hammering. She brushed Con's startled mouth with her own. "Get him out, Con. Now."

Con lurched up as if he were drunk. She had shocked him, with words and touch. Listening as he explained what to do to James, she admired his patient tone. He was meant to be a father, had the requisite mix of humor and strength that so many men lacked. Her father, for example. She could have benefitted from some adult supervision. But then she might not have grown up to run around the countryside in the dark, wearing men's breeches. Or hang upside down like a spider for what felt like hours, chiseling away at sedimentary rock.

She felt every muscle inside her scream for a hot bath and a soft bed. She wasn't sure how she could possibly climb that benighted cliff and walk all the way home, and knew James couldn't. Con had brought her horse, though, if the creature was still somewhere up there waiting.

He'd urged her to give it a name, but she had refused. She

was not going to get attached to an animal for a week, and she had been so very determined to stay only a week, and not a minute more. Those plans were by the wayside now. She wouldn't leave until she knew James had recovered from his ordeal. She wasn't sure but that he might need stitches on an ugly gash on his shoulder. The blood had seeped through his wet shirt and showed bright red. She pulled the watch from her pocket. Just two hours left until dawn. The sun rose early and set late in summer in Yorkshire. She wondered if Con would wait until it was light before they left the cave.

"Cinch yourself tight, James, as tight as you can," Con urged. "There's no rush. Take all the time you need. Just tell me when you're ready for me to reel you in like a fish. I had the lake stocked for us, you know. When you're up to it, we'll go fishing."

Prosaic words to alleviate anxiety. Con was chatting as though they were around the breakfast table planning their day. James said little as he struggled to get the slipknot over his chest. Laurette had tried to brush off most of the dirt from his face and neck with his handkerchief, but he'd been so pale. She counted off the minutes as Con leaned over the shaft, biting her tongue from speaking. The sooner James was free, the happier she'd be. She would never, ever step foot in a cave again in this lifetime, and would absolutely forbid Beatrix from ever going caving again.

At last James said he was ready. Con braced himself, a look of concentration on his face. Laurette stood up and placed a hand on his cheek, rubbing the black bristles with her thumb. "I can help, too."

"You've done quite enough for one night, my darling. But thank you."

He'd removed his shirt after he pulled her up and wiped her face with the fine linen, so he looked like a half-naked god to her. Staying at his side, she watched his muscles cord as he worked the rope, his lips set in a grim line. The dark cross on his shoulder gleamed as he strained backward, sweat pouring off him. The cold of the cave danced across her skin, or perhaps it was simply desire. Her nipples puckering, she quickly covered herself with Con's jacket right before he tugged James up over the edge.

"I've got you, I've got you." Con hooked his hands under James's armpits and dragged him onto the bumpy surface. James lay limp, his eyes blinking against the light.

"The water bottle, Laurie."

It was still attached to her makeshift strapping, and nearly empty, but she passed it to Con as he positioned James in his lap. James spluttered a bit as he drank it all.

"I'll get more."

Con nodded. "Take the lantern."

She wouldn't leave James in the dark after all he'd been through. "I'll navigate by starlight. Be right back."

She stood outside the entrance for a moment, gulping air. It was almost over. The stars overhead winked with promise. Bowing her head, she gave thanks that her prayer was answered.

The gentle spill of the water reminded her she had at least one more job to do. She cupped her hands and drank in the sharp taste of the wild, then filled the bottle for James and Con.

She bent to enter the cave, then stepped back unseen. They wouldn't need the water quite yet. They were wrapped in each other's arms, clinging fast. Both were crying, their sobs muffled by ragged clothes and bare skin. Tears of reconciliation and relief. Laurette's heart lifted.

She waited a few minutes. Clearing her raw throat as a warning, she ducked under the rockface. Con was putting his ruined shirt back on as James toyed with the rope that was still coiled around him.

Their moment was over. Men, in her experience, were odd creatures, keeping their vulnerability secret as though it were a crime. Boys were even worse, victims of their pride.

"James tells me he's game to get back tonight. This morning, rather." Con took the water from her, took a quick sip, and handed it off to James. Con reattached the other end of the rope to his waist and snapped it.

Laurette was not feeling game at all. "Isn't there any other way?"

"The other side is just as steep. And your faithful steed awaits us, my lady." He scooped James up as if he didn't weigh a thing. "When I can't carry you anymore, you can climb up after me. I won't let you fall."

James made no objection.

"What about the saddlebag? The tools?" Laurette asked.

"Leave them for the next unfortunate soul who wanders this way. Even though we're not on Stanbury property anymore, I have half a mind to put up a danger sign. Just carry the lantern for me, Laurie. We won't need it much longer anyhow."

She led the way across the stream, and started up the rise, dreading every step. Her back and legs stiffened in protest each time she raised her knees. If only she could climb *up* on her bottom—well, why couldn't she? She'd kissed her dignity good-bye some time ago.

She put the lantern down, where it promptly rolled down the incline and went out. *Wonderful.* It could get together with its mate and have a merry old time. "Sorry. You two go on ahead. I'm going to scuttle up the hill like a crab."

She thought she heard James laugh, but it was too dark to see his face.

"I'll come back for you if you get stuck. Just let me get James settled."

"Of course."

They trudged by her as she sat in the damp grass. She made fair progress going backward until the angle changed and she thought she'd be more efficient crawling on her hands and knees. Every so often Con would shout down to her and she'd shout back. The stars were fading in a pearl-gray sky. This night was almost over.

* * *

The household had finally quieted down again, just when it should be coming to life. Con had bathed James himself, trusting Nadia to sew up the slash on his shoulder and Sadie to rub an herbal concoction on his scrapes and bruises. James had eaten a little—and vomited it all up, and was now sleeping, mummified in his sheets and just as white. A dozing Beatrix kept him company in an armchair in the corner of his room. She had pleaded with Con to let her sit with him, wanting to do her part in his rescue and recovery. Laurette had disappeared upstairs to clean up. To spare the servants any more work, he'd gone to the lake with a bar of soap and swum with near violence, as though he hadn't been up all night and was a decade younger. The physical challenge was a punishment.

He'd come so close to losing his son.

James had once been a bit of an abstract concept. At birth he'd been red, wrinkled and hungry, belonging entirely to Marianna and her breast. Con felt like a rather useless appendage, forbidden even from holding his son. He had been shut out, including when it came to choosing the child's name. His father-in-law had pranced about Ryland Grove as if the child were *his,* crowing to the countryside how he'd set his grandson up for life. The next Marquess of Conover seemed more Berryman than Ryland to Con's twenty-year-old self, one more figure moved to the Berryman side of the ledger in the Berryman accounts book. The first week of James's existence showed Con all too clearly how the next years would enfold, and he couldn't stomach it.

He had a son, but did not feel like a father. So he left, wondering if he would be missed. He thought not. One thing led to another until it was too late to return. But now he was here, his son a flesh-and-blood boy who needed him, who perhaps could love him in time. That would have to be enough for now.

He slicked his long hair back, dried off and dressed,

watching the pale yellow sun shimmer up over the distant mountains in the east. After the exercise in frigid water, he was as weary as he'd ever been, his arms aching from retrieving Laurette and James from what James had dubbed "the pit of despair." The lad would have a story to dine out on all his life, and a scar to prove it. Con kneaded his own sore shoulder, the cross-covered scar tissue courtesy of Monsieur Bonaparte's troops rough beneath his fingers.

He'd sent everyone back to bed, so was not surprised to enter an empty kitchen, save for Sam, who wagged his tail from under the table. A loaf studded with raisins and currants had been left on the sideboard. He was not really hungry, although he should be. Cutting off the heel, he took the backstairs to his room. The door was shut, which was surprising. What—who—was inside surprised him even more. Laurette lay beneath the woven coverlet, tendrils of wet hair tangled on his pillow. Her lips were parted, her golden lashes fluttering as she dreamed.

It seemed criminal to wake her. It seemed criminal not to. Con warred with his instant erection. Perhaps she had just come to talk and had fallen asleep waiting for him to swim himself into sanity.

"Laurette."

She sighed and turned, exposing a very naked back.

Not to talk then.

Con undressed quickly, wondering why God was so good to him today. He sank into the feather ticking, drawing her to him. Her breast was in his palm, his lips at her ear, her bottom cushioning his manhood. If he never moved for the rest of his life, he would be perfectly content, although it seemed Laurette had other ideas. She reached behind and cupped his balls, her fingers cool. Each pad tantalized his skin. All thoughts of sleep and bread vanished.

They made love without a sound, slow, languorous, their exhausted bodies taking turns gentling and teasing each other. No one was master. No one was mistress. They fit together in a seamless whole, just the way Con had dreamed for so many years, only better. This was real. Her velvet skin was against him, the floral scent of her in his nose, and the sweet taste of her in his mouth. Laurette loved him as he loved her, and somehow he would make this work for everyone.

Beatrix shook James's elbow gingerly. She didn't dare to be too bold because of his injuries, but his cries were alarming. He was smack in the middle of a bad dream and no wonder. After the time he'd had, he'd probably have lots of bad dreams for the rest of his life. She shivered to think of being wet and trapped and hurt, with no light and no hope and *bats*.

Well, he'd gotten his wish to spend the night in a cave, only not exactly how he wanted to.

"Wake up, James. It's only a dream."

His pale blue eyes jerked open. He stared at her as if he'd never seen her before and not spent the past two weeks tormenting her in his James-way. It was all because he was shorter than she was, Sadie said. And that would change. Gentlemen were almost always taller than ladies.

He wasn't really mean, but moody sometimes. Bea felt sorry for him because of his parents. Lady Conover had been very nice to her when she visited Cousin Laurette in Dorset, but very *managing*. Everything had to be done just her way. Or else. Of course, now she was dead and James had a stranger for a father. Bea hoped they'd made up their fight and things would be better between them now that Lord Conover had saved James's life. Well, Lord Conover had said it was Cousin Laurette who was the heroine. Bea was just happy that James was alive to stare at her, cross as a bear, no matter who was responsible.

"What are you doing here?" he croaked.

"Playing nurse. Sadie and Nadia have other things to do."
They had fixed up the chair for her so it was quite comfort-

able, with some pillows and an afghan throw. She had not slept much last night, waiting to hear from the search party. She was still in her nightgown, barefoot.

"Where is my father?"

"Asleep, I would think. Are you hungry? I can go downstairs and get you something."

James wrinkled his nose. "Sadie gave me oatmeal. It was vile."

"I rather like oatmeal. With cream and plenty of sugar."

"Glue," James mumbled. "Go away."

Bea felt a stab of hurt. "Are you ill?"

"I'm all right. I just don't want to talk to you."

The way he said "you" was very odd, as though he'd be happy to blab to everyone else in the world except her. She stood up, the knitted blanket falling on the floor. "Very well, then. I don't wish to be where I'm not wanted." She gave him her most supercilious look, hoping to make him squirm, the worm. To think she'd lost sleep over this rude little—

James struggled to sit up. "I promised I wouldn't."

"Wouldn't what?" He was making no sense, gawping up at the ceiling as if there were words written on it. Perhaps Cousin Laurette had hit his head with that hammer as well as the rock.

"Talk," he said at last. "It's—it's my throat, you see. Damaged from the screaming."

"Oh." She sat down again, folding her hands. "I could read to you."

He shook his head, his gaze wandering everywhere around the room but on her. He seemed very uncomfortable. Almost—guilty.

He should be, remembering the way he teased her yesterday when they found that painting. He had made her cry and then called her a *girl*, as if it were a curse word. Gypsies and trolls, indeed. Maybe his brush with death would be good for him, if it taught him to be kinder.

"Your father has given me the portrait we found in the attic, you know."

If possible, James grew even paler.

"Are you feverish?" Bea got up and felt his forehead. He was warm, but only from sleep.

"Um."

"You were rather a beast about it yesterday."

"I'm sorry."

He did indeed look stricken. Maybe she should leave him alone, or send Nico or Tom in.

"You're not my sister!" His voice cracked on the last syllable.

"Of course I'm not. Although I wouldn't mind, even if you are a *boy* and quite impossible sometimes. Having a brother might come in handy some day."

James didn't seem to appreciate her joke. He looked truly wild now, his face turning crimson and back to snow. "James, you *are* ill. Let me get your father."

"No! He'll think I broke my word. To talk. Vow of silence." His lips snapped shut and he lay back down on the pillow.

"Let me get you some tea with honey for your throat."

He nodded, looking vastly relieved that she was leaving. She wondered when she would be leaving for good. Last night had made today's departure out of the question, for which she was secretly glad. She loved it here, with Sam and the sheep, the bright green of the dales and the gentle mist in the morning. She had learned to swim in the calm lake and had bested James in a rainy-day card game. Altogether it had been a wonderful holiday.

The voices in the kitchen told her the quest for tea would be successful, although she was perfectly capable of boiling water. Sadie and Cousin Laurette had taught her all sorts of useful things when she visited. She stopped just outside the doorway to listen. If Nico or Tom were in there, she really should not turn up in her nightrail. Bad enough they saw her last night, although they had been too busy eating and worrying to notice her impropriety. Last night had been an emergency, but this morning was not. Her mother would have a fit to think Bea was such a hoyden.

"It's about bloody time." That was Sadie. She sounded gleeful. Bea's mama would not approve of such language from a servant. Or from anyone, for that matter.

"So you think Lord Conover's plan has worked?" The gentle, accented voice of Nadia.

"Well, she's in his bed again, and that's a start. Now, if she can just get up the courage to tell Bea the truth, last night will be worth all the fuss. Laurette's a stubborn lass, always has been. But she loves her daughter. The marquess has plenty of money to buy her back from those cousins. The poor mite can have a proper life with her real parents. People at home might talk at first, but they like Conover. And they love Laurette."

Bea flattened herself against the wall, heart racing. Her mama had always told her it was wicked to eavesdrop. You heard just what you deserved. Her mama was right.

Her mama. If she understood Sadie correctly, her mama wasn't her mama at all.

She bit the inside of her cheek, hard, just to check if she could feel anything. She tasted blood. James knew. That's why he was so nervous around her. He lied to her too. She was the bastard child of Lord Conover and her cousin. Not her cousin. No wonder her papa and mama looked at her the way they did sometimes, like she was dirty.

She went upstairs to her room, forgetting the tea. But she could not forget what she had heard.

Chapter 23

Laurette lay in his arms, right where she should be. He supposed he should get up and check on James before too long. It was late morning already, time to start the day and a new life. Con wasn't quite sure how it happened, but Laurette seemed altered as well. She was his. She would marry him. She hadn't said so yet, but he knew in his heart.

"What did you say to him last night? He seems much altered."

Her lips tickled his shoulder. "That I knew Marianna and why she did what she did. That people aren't all good or bad. Not you, not his mother. Not me."

She slipped out of his embrace and pulled the sheet up around her. "I'm going to tell Beatrix, Con. I realized last night that life is too unpredictable to continue to lie. I even lied to myself. Told myself I was protecting Bea, but I was only protecting me." She gulped a breath. "She will hate me."

"She won't." He played with the spill of taffy-colored hair that fell across her shoulder. "You're doing the right thing. I've already approached her parents." He winced. He and Laurette were her parents. Would somehow make up the years they missed. "The Vincents. It's my impression they'll feel relief to be rid of her." He hurried on as he saw the alarm on Laurette's face. "Oh, they haven't been bad parents to her. They've done their duty. But she's not a baby any longer. So biddable."

"They worry that she'll turn out like me," Laurette said wryly.

"I hope she does. You are the purest soul I've ever known."

"Oh, Con. I wish that were true. From the moment I decided to make you mine, I've flown awfully close to the sun. My angel wings are singed."

"You were so young, Laurie. We both were. Can you imagine even being so young again? But I wouldn't change a thing—not one—if it meant you would not be here in this bed beside me. Marry me." He was hasty again, but he couldn't help himself.

"I already did, Con. At twilight one August night." She smiled wistfully at him.

"In a church this time. Here or in Dorset, I don't care which."

She was so quiet he felt the sourness rise up his chest, but then she spoke.

"Yes, I will."

"Thank God." He closed his eyes to keep his tears at bay. When he opened them, he saw Laurette's own tears sliding down her cheeks. "Look at us. I'm already called the Mad Marquess. You'll be my Mad Marchioness. Between the two of us we're blubbering idiots."

Laurette wiped her face with the back of her hand. "I don't dare to feel happy yet."

"Do you want me to be there when you tell her?"

"I don't think so. It's something I have to do myself, as you did with James. Thank you for offering, though."

Con rolled out of bed and got back into his clothes. "I'm going to see James. If you need anything—"

"I know."

And she did. He would do anything and everything to honor the vows they made to each other that evening in August.

*   *   *

Laurette felt a little like a spy, poking her head out of Con's room to see if the coast was clear. The hallway was empty. And endless. She tied her robe tight and headed for her room. The house was quiet, probably in deference to the invalid and because its inhabitants were so very tired. She had slept for perhaps an hour in Con's arms, and wondered if she was thinking clearly. She was going to marry the man— again—and tell her daughter that she was her mother. Two rather life-changing decisions that perhaps should be made tomorrow instead of today. But tomorrow her old cowardly self might resurface.

Her room had been straightened, the bathwater and Tom's filthy clothes removed, and her bed turned down. Laurette looked at it longingly, but got dressed instead. She donned a sea-blue dress that Con had ordered to match her eyes, then spent an inordinate amount of time brushing the snarls out of her hair. She wished she had a brush for her stomach, which clenched in knots with every thought. When she was presentable, she stepped a few doors down to Bea's room and tapped.

"Come in."

Bea was on her window seat, still in her ruffly white night-gown.

"Good morning, sleepyhead. Or is it afternoon already?"

"I wasn't sleeping."

"You've been sadly neglected with all the to-do about James. Shall I help you dress?"

"I don't care."

"Bea, what's the matter? Are you feeling all right?"

Bea curled herself up in a ball and leaned against the glass. She gave Laurette the most curious look, then turned her face away. "When are we going to leave here?"

"That's partly why I've come to talk to you. I know you want to stay for the summer."

"I don't care," Bea repeated.

This was not one bit like Beatrix. While she was naturally reserved, this morning she seemed very distant. "You must be very tired. Thank you for sitting with James. I haven't seen him yet. How is he?"

"I forgot his tea."

"His father is with him now. I'm sure he'll take care of it. Poor James lost his voice and tea will do him good. Tea cures everything." Laurette was babbling, but something felt wrong. Surely James hadn't broken his promise. He couldn't really talk, after all. But if he was feverish—

"Beatrix, may I sit down? I have something important to tell you."

Bea didn't move. Her face was still pressed against the window, her hands around her knees.

"I'm not sure how to begin."

"At the beginning," Bea muttered, still facing away.

"Yes, well." Laurette's knees were weakening and her heart thumping. "If I begin from the beginning, my story will take a while." She dragged a chair over the carpet to the window seat. "Do you suppose you might look at me while I speak?"

Bea turned a fraction of an inch.

She knew. Laurette didn't know how, but she would swear on her life that Beatrix already knew the truth and was punishing her for it already. Between the uncanny painting and Con's attention and James's teasing talk of Gypsies, Bea had put it all together.

So Laurette got right to the heart of it. "I am your natural mother, Bea, and Lord Conover is your father. We both love you very much." She wasn't going to apologize for her "sins," for loving Con had been the only thing she *could* do, both then and now.

She had Bea's full attention now, and, inconceivably, the smallest of smiles.

"I know."

Laurette felt the air whoosh out of her lungs. "Did James tell you?"

"No. He couldn't wait to get rid of me. I overheard Sadie and Nadia talking."

"Oh, my poor Bea. I'm so sorry." Laurette was afraid to get up and touch her daughter, so she sat, stiff in her chair, her fingernails digging into the armrests.

"I'm illegitimate."

Laurette closed her eyes. "Yes. In the eyes of the law, perhaps. But not to God. God loves us all. Con and I loved each other. We planned to marry when he came of age, but then we couldn't. He was forced to marry James's mother instead. But before that wedding, we spoke our own vows in our own private ceremony. At the standing stones at home. I have felt married to him since I was seventeen and he nineteen. I've loved him much longer. I love him now. We're going to marry, Bea. In a church this time."

"Where do I fit in?" Bea asked, her voice cool.

"We would like nothing better than if you would come to live with us. Con wants to become your guardian."

"Would everyone know? I'll never be able to enter society if they do."

Her very practical child had just uttered Laurette's worst fears. A bastard son might be able get on in the world, but a bastard daughter would be prey for every unscrupulous man in England. Bea would be shunned, have no friends. No matter how high her dowry, she would be met with repugnance on the Marriage Mart. The unfairness of it made Laurette furious, but females were always blamed for Eve's sins.

"No. We can keep this secret to ourselves. We don't want you hurt any further. I know this has been a terrible shock." Though Bea was handling herself with far more poise than Laurette expected. Or deserved.

"What about James?"

"Con and I both have spoken to him. He knows you are his sister. I think he understands the need to be discreet." Laurette sighed. "I have been living with lies for so long I suppose it doesn't matter to go on doing so." She swallowed hard. "I was afraid you'd hate me, Bea. Judge me. I couldn't blame you if you did, but couldn't bear it if you do."

"I don't know how I feel." Bea turned back to the window and opened the latch. Warm fragrant air swirled in, with the scent of fresh-cut grass and summer. Laurette felt homesick for a moment, but now home would be wherever Con was.

She could give her daughter up again if she must. She had once.

"It's your decision, Bea, what to do. Where to live. I don't expect you to tell me now. You probably want to talk to your parents."

Bea raised a copper brow but said nothing. Laurette felt a hot flush sweep across her throat. "You haven't been unhappy with them, have you? I know they are strict, but I'm sure they did the best they could." Another layer of guilt surrounded her. The Vincents had been rather joyless in comparison to her own hard-drinking, careless parents, but Laurette had welcomed that. Her daughter would be raised to be the proper lady that she was not.

"I think they kept me for the money," Beatrix said quietly. "I've heard them arguing about it. Wanting more. Lady Conover paid them, didn't she?"

Laurette felt her heart splinter. "Her father first, then when he died, she did, yes. I had nothing to give you, Bea. But they—the Vincents—love you. I know they do. When you were a baby, they wrote to me regularly. About your first step. Your black kitten. How you taught yourself to read. They were proud of you. *Are* proud of you."

"It doesn't matter. I live at school most of the year now. With the charity girls. My moth—they told me it was too expensive to have me come home between terms. Or they are off somewhere on one of Papa's business schemes. They don't really want me."

"Oh, Bea. My darling girl. That's not true." But hadn't Con said as much earlier? Laurette couldn't hold back any longer. She joined Bea on the window seat and stroked her cheek.

Bea drew back from her touch. "I know you and Lord Conover mean well. You're not bad people, but I just can't think right now."

"I understand. I am so sorry, Bea. So very sorry to cause you distress. This is exactly why I never wanted to tell you."

"I'm glad you did, Cousin Laurette. Really. But I'd like to be alone now."

Cousin Laurette. Laurette stood up reluctantly. When James had been left alone, the earth had swallowed him up. But Bea didn't seem angry, just sad. And all her clothes were packed. She wasn't apt to run off in her nightgown. "I'll look in on you later, then. Do you want a tray sent up?"

"I think I'll go back to bed."

"Sweet dreams, then. I love you, Bea."

Beatrix dipped her pointed little chin and nodded.

Laurette shut the door, tamping back her sorrow. It had gone much better than she had hoped, yet still was one of the worst days of her life. There had not been many, but enough. The day Con married Marianna. The day she left her daughter behind in Cornwall. And now the day she found that daughter, perhaps to lose her forever.

She needed Con, needed to tell him—what? Everything was still unsettled. It might almost have been better for Beatrix to scratch and spit at her, and hate her, than to see the sad resignation on her precious face. No child should have the rug pulled out from under them like this, and she and Con had done it to both the children in the span of twenty-four hours.

The truth shall make you free. Con had quoted those words to her, but Laurette felt far from free. As she approached James's room, she heard the unexpected sound of his raspy laugh, which went a little way to ease her. James was propped up on a pillow mountain, his midnight hair— his father's hair—sticking up every which way. The white bandage on his upper arm and shoulder showed a pale stain, not the scarlet of before. His father leaned back on a chair beside the bed, his stocking feet propped up on the bed coverings.

"How is our brave patient?" Laurette asked, managing a smile.

"Laurette!" Con scrambled up and went to the doorway. He lowered his voice. "What happened?"

"She knows. She's thinking."

"How did she take it?"

Laurette shook her head. "She was remarkably composed. But so sad. I have no idea what she'll do."

"What are you two talking about?" complained James. He sounded much stronger, the sandpapery quality of his voice healing.

Con gripped her hand and dragged her into the room. "We're talking about our family. All of us."

James looked wary.

"Not now, Con," Laurette whispered.

"It's all right," James said. "I expect you're going to tell me that you're getting married. I have no objection."

The rug had been pulled out from under the adults this time. Con's expression was a priceless mix of chagrin and relief that he was spared one more confession.

"Thank you, James," Laurette said.

"Have you told Bea? Everything? I swear, I kept my promise, but it was hard."

Laurette sat in Con's chair, suddenly exhausted. "Yes. She

saw the repercussions to her reputation immediately. If she chooses to live with us, I promised it would be as an adoptive daughter only." She saw the resistance on Con's face. "It's the only way, Con. As it is, people at home will suspect."

"Then we'll go abroad. To my villa in Greece," he said stubbornly.

"You said a civil war is brewing. And you have an obligation to your estate. If you want to win Bea's heart, in this one thing you must compromise. You will know the truth, and that will have to be enough."

His fingers slid through his hair in frustration, making it nearly as disheveled as his son's. They were both in desperate need of some barbering. "Very well. I want what's best for Bea. For James. For us. That's all I've ever wanted."

"I know. I haven't always approved of your methods, but I understand." One truth James was not going to learn was that his father had taken her as his captive mistress. There were some things that were simply too truthful to tell.

James yawned. "Tell Bea to come visit me later. I had better go back to sleep for a while. My head is fuzzy."

Laurette could relate. She brushed her lips on the boy's forehead. But she was too keyed up to sleep herself. And realizing as her stomach rumbled, hungry too.

Con chuckled and led her out of the room. "Come. We'll pack a picnic basket and find a quiet spot."

Laurette thought of lunch and love al fresco. Tempting, but it was time to be practical. "I think we should visit with the vicar instead. Have the banns called. We can marry here within the month."

She was swept up in Con's arms, twirling around perilously close to the stairway. After her little shriek, he put her down and kissed her. "Are you sure you don't want to marry from home?"

"Everyone I love is right here. Except for Charlie, and I can't wait until he comes back." She bit her lip. "Even if Bea decides to go back to Cornwall, I can deliver her and be here in plenty of time. I don't want any fuss made, just a simple country wedding."

"You'll have to argue with Sadie over that. And probably Nadia, too. They'll want to invite all the neighbors."

"No. This is for us, Con. Just like last time."

Her words gave Con an idea, but he held his tongue to put it in Laurette's sweet mouth. His bride. His wife. His life.

Chapter 24

When James woke up, Beatrix was sitting in the chair again, only this time she was dressed and looking rather grim. "They said you wanted to see me."

"So," he said, cocky. "I was right. But no Gypsies were involved."

"You are insufferable. How can you joke about such a thing? My whole life is ruined!"

"Don't be such a girl." He caught the feral gleam in her eye and retrenched a bit. "You've never shut up about how beastly those Cornwall people are to you."

"That's because all you did was complain about your father! I was only complaining in sympathy!"

James shook his head. He was still feeling woozy and the movement did not help matters. "You know that's not true. As I understand it, you'll just be my father's ward. Nobody ever needs to know the precise circumstances of your birth. I won't tell. I don't even want a sister."

"And I don't want you for a brother, you rude little pig! You are arrogant and diabolical and . . . and. . . ."

Good. She seemed to be at a loss for words, an extremely rare occurrence. She had given him a headache for two weeks with all her talk. But he did like her, and felt sorry for her. Her secret was worse than his secret, at least in society's eyes. Everybody's parents married for money and hated each other. All his mates at school said so. He supposed growing up in a cold marriage with people fighting was much worse than growing up with a mother who loved him, and gave him everything, and an absent father who was making up for lost time now. When he was allowed out of bed, James planned to ask for a horse of his own, not a babyish pony, and he had every expectation of Conover caving into him. *Caving.* An unfortunate choice of words. He shivered.

"Look. I know just how you feel, but don't go running off. They've had enough excitement for one holiday."

"I won't run away. I have more sense than you."

He'd like to wipe that smirk off her face, but a gentleman never hit a lady, no matter how provoked. He was pretty sure that applied to sisters, too, or his father would think it did.

"I didn't run away. I went off to think. There's a difference." He shifted his pillows.

"And what conclusion did you come to, Socrates?" she sneered.

James looked her straight in the eye. "I fell in that hole and thought I would die. Then it didn't matter so much what happened a dozen years ago."

That shut her up for a while. But his luck didn't hold.

"Everything we thought we knew was a lie."

"They lied to protect us. And themselves, too. They're not perfect. Laurette said something interesting to me before my father came. She said she could never think that she had made a mistake with him, because she couldn't think of you as a mistake. She loves you a lot, Bea."

"I don't know what to do." Her voice was snuffly. Damn it, she was crying again. But he had cried himself quite recently, and much more vigorously, so it wasn't fair to tease her this time.

"You don't have to do anything. Go back to that poky little house in Penzance. Go back to school. Come to Dorset for a few weeks next summer."

"You really *don't* want me as your secret sister."

"I just said that. I didn't really mean it. I suppose if my father and Laurette get married, there might be another sister, although I'd prefer a brother."

"James! They're too old."

James gave her a scornful look. "Do they teach you nothing at your school? I could draw you a picture—"

"You are disgusting!"

He grinned at the compliment. Beatrix promised to be a thorn in his side for the foreseeable future. He could almost guarantee it.

Con sat rigid in a threadbare chair in the mean little parlor counting to one hundred. He wondered what these people had done with all the money they had received for Beatrix's upkeep over the years. There was no evidence of it anywhere, from his chipped teacup to the battered old doll Bea had shyly shown him. He got all the way up to eighty-seven when he stood up abruptly and walked out into the busy street. Perhaps he was a coward for leaving the girls he loved to manage without him, but if he stayed inside, he would commit murder and they'd have to do without him permanently.

He walked to the quay, a blast of briny sea air clearing his head. He had his son to thank for Bea's decision to throw her lot in with the Conover clan. She had been closeted with James that Monday afternoon for hours. When she emerged, she was pale but resolute. She would consent to Con's guardianship if the Vincents agreed to it. When Con asked his son what had transpired, the boy had merely shrugged and said they played a game of cards. And that he'd won. Con hated to think that Bea's future had depended upon a game of chance, but he was grateful nonetheless.

He couldn't endure one more minute with Jonas and Mary Vincent. Beatrix had gone up to pack her meager belongings, so was spared the hypocritical proselytizing. While pleased by a lifetime income far exceeding any amount they had ever dreamed, they were nevertheless vocal in their disapproval of the upcoming nuptials. In their opinion, those who had sinned deserved no happiness. All their hard work with Beatrix would be undone.

But he disagreed wholeheartedly. The sooner he could get her away from these grasping, heart-shriveled zealots, the happier he'd be. In less than an hour they would be on the road again, back to his sheep farm and a wedding. They would return to Ryland Grove when Laurette was ready. If she was not accepted as his marchioness, he was prepared to live somewhere where she was.

The children would keep to their school schedules no matter what happened. As hard as he'd considered hiring a tutor and a governess for the Grove, James and Beatrix could fight as though they'd been siblings all their lives. There would be no peace for the Conovers if they lived together year-round.

Things were not exactly how he planned, but they were good enough and would get better. Or worse. He laughed out loud, pushing his wind-blown hair from his face. Each day with Laurette was a gift he didn't deserve.

Guilty, he retraced his steps to the door of the dreaded cousins to rescue his girls.

Chapter 25

Very early on the morning of her wedding day, Laurette crept down the long hallway from Con's room, avoiding the squeaky spot right before the landing. This was her last time to sneak around, although perhaps everyone knew where she'd spent her nights anyway. She'd had a ghastly "birds and bees" talk the other day with her daughter, who was being cheerfully corrupted by her mischievous half-brother. James reminded her so much of Con at that age that it brought a smile to her face.

But today was a day for seriousness. She was to be married to the man she'd loved most of her life. Turning the door handle of her room, she entered the dim chamber and opened the curtain to let in the dawn. What she saw spread on her bed stunned her.

There was her wedding dress, not the yellow confection she'd planned to wear, but the stiff midnight-blue satin gown covered with moons and stars she had worn at seventeen at the standing stones.

"Sadie, what else does Mama have in her trunks in the attic?"

Mrs. Miller took the knife out of Laurette's clumsy hand. "There'll be nothing left to eat if you keep that up. Just sit still and do your talking."

"Well?" Laurette prompted.

Sadie screwed up her face. "There's nothing fit up there for a young miss."

"Excellent. Let's go upstairs. Mrs. Miller, you are done with us, are you not?"

The cook sighed in defeat. "Go on, then. You won't stop plaguing us until you get your way, and you murdered that carrot."

Laurette pulled Sadie up the back stairs to the top floor, throwing open the door to the attic. Pails and pans were placed strategically across the slanted wood floors in case of rain. The smell of heat and dust and mice was overwhelming. Sadie sneezed.

"Just tell me which trunk it's in and we'll go right down to my room."

"Don't know as I recollect."

"Pshaw. You were just up here."

"The dress I'm thinking of belonged to your great-aunt, not your mother. Might be in the black trunk in that corner."

Laurette darted between the containers and the mouse droppings and lifted the lid. Beneath a layer of linen sheeting was the most exquisite midnight blue dress she had ever seen, trimmed in tarnished silver lace, embroidered with silver threads and beads and spangles, tiny glimmering moons and stars scattered across the fabric. Yards and yards of fabric, the skirts gathered up with silver ribbons to reveal more graying silver lace. This gown was very old. But gorgeous.

Laurette brought it downstairs to a patch of sunshine, loose stars and moons and circles sparkling in her hand. She tucked them into the apron pocket and fetched her sewing box. It took her some time to unravel a spool of dark blue thread, not quite a match but close enough. Silver thread would be better, but she knew none was to be had at the village shop.

Carefully, she swept her hand over the front of the gown, discovering what held fast and what was relentlessly determined to detach. She threaded her needle and anchored the strands of silver back into the gown at tight long intervals. No doubt Sadie would have unstrung and restrung every single bead, but they did not have time for that. It was tedious work, but the end result would be worth it, stabbed fingers and all.

Sadie would have to do the rest. Laurette sucked on her injured thumb, imagining the look on Con's face when he saw her walk through the flowered archway to the little ballroom at the Blue Calf Inn. If he thought to keep resisting her, he was mistaken. This dress was pure magic.

And its magic had worked, just not in the way Laurette expected. She had worn it twice—to her debut and her secret wedding to Con. But she'd need some of its magic this morning—she doubted very much she could get into it. She was no longer the slender girl she'd been, and the new baby growing inside her had thickened her waist and plumped her breasts to the point that even Con had noticed. He was pleased, thinking she was finally eating more.

She hadn't told him yet. That would be her wedding gift to him tonight. She didn't think he'd mind that she had kept this secret to herself for a few days. But there were to be no more secrets between Lord and Lady Conover.

She turned the dress over and saw that Sadie, blessed Sadie, had added a panel of almost-matching fabric, with tiny tarnished beads stitched over it. Laurette remembered the little muslin bag Con had carried with him everywhere and closed her eyes.

Con had thought of everything to surprise her, even, she saw, a hat with blue and silver ribbons and silver slippers. But she had a surprise for him too, and hers was better.

If you liked this book,
try Donna Kauffman's OFF KILTER,

available now from Brava!

"**M**an up, for God's sake, and drop the damn thing."
"We're not sending in nude shots," Roan replied
with an even smile, as the chants and taunts escalated. "So I
don't understand the need to take things to such an extreme—"

"The contest rules state, very clearly, that they're looking
for provocative," Tessa responded, sounding every bit like a
person who'd also been forced into a task she'd rather not
have taken on—which she had been.

Sadly, that fact had not brought them closer.

She shifted to another camera she'd mounted on another
tripod, he supposed so the angle of the sun was more to her
liking. "Okay, lean back against the stone wall, prop one leg,
rest that . . . sword thing of yours—"

" 'Tis a claymore. Belonged to the McAuleys for four cen-
turies. Victorious in battle, 'tis an icon of our clan." And
heavy as all hell to hoist about.

"Lovely. Prop your icon in front of you, then. I'm fairly
certain it will hide what needs hiding."

His eyebrows lifted at that, but rather than take offense,
he merely grinned. "I wouldnae be so certain of it, lassie.
We're a clan known for the size of our . . . swords."

"Yippee," she shot back, clearly unimpressed. "So, drop
the plaid, position your . . . sword, and let's get on with it. It's

the illusion of baring it all we're going for here. I'll make sure to preserve your fragile modesty."

She was no fun. No fun 'tall.

"The other guys did it," she added, resting folded hands on top of the camera. "In fact," she went on, without even the merest hint of a smile or dry amusement, "they seemed quite happy to accommodate me."

He couldn't imagine any man wanting to bare his privates for Miss Vandergriff's pleasure. Not if he wanted to keep them intact, at any rate.

He was a bit thrown off by his complete inability to charm her. He charmed everyone. It was what he did. He admittedly enjoyed, quite unabashedly, being one of the clan favorites because of his affable, jovial nature. As far as he was concerned, the world would be a much better place if folks could get in touch with their happy parts, and stay there.

He didn't know much about her, but from what little time they'd spent together that afternoon, he didn't think Tessa Vandergriff had any happy parts. However, the reason behind her being rather happiness-challenged wasn't his mystery to solve. She'd been on the island for less than a week. Her stay on Kinloch was as a guest, and therefore temporary. Thank the Lord.

The island faced its fair share of ongoing trials and tribulations, and had the constant challenge of sustaining a fragile economic resource. Despite that, he'd always considered both the McAuley and MacLeod clans as being cheerful, welcoming hosts. But they had enough to deal with without adopting a surly recalcitrant into their midst.

"Well," he said, smiling broadly the more her scowl deepened. " 'Tis true, the single men of this island have little enough to choose from." The crowd took a collective breath at that, but his attention was fully on her. Gripping the claymore in one fist, he leaned against the stacked stone wall, well aware of the tableau created by the twin peaks that framed the MacLeod fortress, each of them towering behind him. He braced his legs, folded his arms across his bare chest, sword blade aloft . . . and looked her straight in the eye as he let a slow, knowing grin slide across his face. "Me, I'm no' so desperate as all that."

That got a collective gasp from the crowd. But rather than elicit so much as a snarl from Miss Vandergriff, or perhaps goading her so far as to pack up and walk away—which he'd have admittedly deserved—his words had a rather shocking effect. She smiled. Fully. He hadn't thought her face capable of arranging itself in such a manner. And so broadly, with such stunning gleam. He was further damned to discover it did things to his own happy parts that she had no business affecting.

"No worries," she stated, further captivating him with the transformative brilliance of her knowing smile. She gave him a sizzling once-over before easily meeting his eyes again. "You're not my type."

This was not how those things usually went for him. He felt . . . frisked. "Then I'm certain you can be objective enough to find an angle that shows off all my best parts without requiring a blatant, uninspired pose. I understand from Kira that you're considered to be quite good with that equipment."

The chanting of the crowd shifted to a few whistles as the tension between photographer and subject grew to encompass even them.

"Given your reluctance to play show and tell, I'd hazard to guess I'm better with mine than you are with yours," she replied easily, but the spark remained in her eyes.

Goading him.

"Why don't you be the judge?" Holding her gaze in exclusive focus, the crowd long since forgotten, he pushed away from the wall and, with sword in one hand, slowly unwrapped his kilt with the other.

He took far more pleasure than was absolutely necessary from watching her throat work as he unashamedly revealed thighs and ass. He wasn't particularly vain or egotistical, but he was well aware that a lifetime spent climbing all over the island had done its duty where his physical shape was concerned, as it had for most of the islanders. They were a hardy lot.

The crowd gasped as he held the fistful of unwrapped plaid in front of him, dangling precariously from one hand, just on the verge of—

"That's it!" Tessa all but leapt behind the camera and an instant later, the shutter started whirring. Less than thirty seconds later, she straightened and pushed her wayward curls out of her face, her no-nonsense business face back. "Got it. Good! We're all done here." She started dismantling her equipment. "You can go ahead and get dressed," she said dismissively, not even looking at him.

He held on to the plaid—and his pride—and tried not to look as annoyed as he felt. The shoot was blessedly over. That was all that mattered. No point in being irritated that he'd just been played by a pro.

She glanced up, the smile gone as she dismantled her second tripod with the casual grace of someone so used to the routine and rhythm of it, she didn't have to think about it. "I'll let you know when I get the shots developed."

He supposed he should be thankful she hadn't publicly gloated over her smooth manipulation of him. Except he wasn't feeling particularly gracious at the moment.

Treat yourself to a preview of MY FAIR HIGHLANDER, the next from Mary Wine,

coming in August 2011!

A rmed Englishmen riding across Scottish land only meant one thing, and it had nothing to do with friendship.

As she had just learned. They would use violence to gain what they wished without any remorse. She looked at the dirty plumes crowning the English knight's helmet and decided that they fit him well.

"If ye've any sense, ye'd start for the border before Ryppon discovers what ye were about with his sister." Laird Barras leaned down over the neck of his horse. "And if I see ye again on my land, I'll not leave ye drawing breath to test my good will again."

His voice was hard as stone, leaving no doubt that he was a man who would not hesitate to kill. He looked every inch the warrior, but Jemma discovered herself grateful for his harshness, even drawing comfort from it. The man was saving her life and sparing her a painful death too. The English didn't wait but began walking towards England. It was humbling to set armored men on their way without their horses, but to return the animals would see the men becoming a force to be reckoned with once more. Laird Barras proved to be merciful by sparing their lives, but he was not a fool.

He turned to look at her. The night sky was beginning to fill with tiny points of light and that starshine lit him. It cast him in white light, making him appear unearthly, like a god from legends of the past. A Norseman Viking that swept across the land, unstoppable because of his sheer brawn.

A ripple of sensation moved over her skin, awakening every inch of her flesh. It should have been impossible to be so aware of any single person's stare, but she was of his. His stallion snorted and pawed at the ground a moment before he pressed his knees into the sides of the beast. Lament surged through her, thick and choking as she anticipated his leaving.

But he pulled the stallion up alongside her, a grin of approval curling his lips up when she remained in place without a single sound making it past her lips. Jemma found herself too fascinated to speak. Too absorbed in the moment to ruin it by allowing sounds to intrude.

"Up with ye, lass. This is not the sort of company ye should be keeping."

He leaned down, his thighs gripping the sides of his horse to keep him steady. Her gaze strayed to his thighs and she stared at the bare skin that was cut with ridges of muscles, testifying to how much strength was in him.

"Take my hand, lass. I'd prefer not to have to pull ye off the ground again."

But he would. She heard that clearly in his voice. That tone of command that spoke of a man who expected his word to be heeded no matter what her opinion might be.

Of course, staying was not something she craved. She lifted her hand and placed it in his outstretched one, only to pull it away when his warm flesh met her own. That touch had jolted her, breaking through the disbelief that had held her in its grasp. Her body began to shake while her face throbbed incessantly from the blow that had been laid across it. She suddenly felt every bruise and scrap, her knees feeling weak as the horror of what she had faced sunk in deep to torment her mind with grisly details of what the English had been intent on doing to her. The idea of touching any man was suddenly repulsive and she clasped her hands tightly together.

"I thank you for your . . . assistance . . . but I will return to . . . Amber Hill."

Jemma looked around for her mare, but in the night it was difficult to determine which horse was hers in the darkness. The younger boys had several horses each and she couldn't decide which one belonged to her. She suddenly noticed how cold it had become and the darkness seemed to be increasing too, clouds moving over the sky to block out even the star shine.

"Give me yer hand, lass. 'Tis time to make our way from this place."

His voice was low now and hypnotic. Lifting her face, she found his attention on her, his eyes reflecting the starlight back down on her. Jemma lifted her hand but stopped when she felt her arm shaking. The motion annoyed her but there seemed to be nothing she might do to banish it.

"Do it now, lass. This is nae a safe place to linger."

"But is going with you a safe thing to do?" She truly wondered because he looked so at ease surrounded by the night. All of his men sat in their saddles without any outward sign of misgivings or dread for the deepening darkness. Her words didn't please him. His expression tightened and something flashed in his eyes that looked like pride. A soft grumbling rippled through his waiting men.

"I will nae strike ye."

Which was better than she might expect from the horseless Englishmen standing nearby. For all that they were her countrymen, she discovered more trust inside her for the Scots. There was no real choice, she hungered for life and the Scot's offer was her only way to hold onto that precious thing.

Lifting her hand, she placed it firmly against the one offered. Barras closed his hand around her wrist and she jumped to help gain the saddle. He lifted her up and off the ground to sit behind him.

"Hold on to me, lass."

There was no other choice. She had to cling to him, press her body up against his in order to share the saddle with him. Her thighs rested against his and the motion of the horse made her move her hips in unison with his. The thick scabbard strapped to his back was the only barrier between them. She actually welcomed the hard edges of the leather scabbard because it kept her from being completely immersed in his body. There were several things she should have been dwelling on—the English left behind in the night, or the way her brother was most likely going to have her flogged for riding so late in the day. There was also Synclair to consider. The knight was going to be far more than unhappy with her for slipping out the moment his attention was taken away from her. He was not a man that made the same mistake twice.

Instead she was completely focused on the man she clung to. Her arms reached around his slim waist. It was amazing how much warmth his body generated. Holding so tightly against him kept the chill of the autumn night from tormenting her. The wind chilled her hands on top where the skin was exposed, but her palms were warmed by the man she held onto.

Her head was tucked along one of his shoulders, one cheek pressing against the wool of his doublet. His sword was strapped at an angle across his back, the length of his plaid pulled up over his right shoulder helping to cushion the weapon. Suddenly, the Celtic fashion of dressing was not so odd. Instead it was quite logical and useful. That bit of thinking made him seem less of a barbarian and more of a very efficient warrior.

Her heart accelerated and that increased the tempo of her breathing. She drew in his scent and shivered. It was dark and musky, touching off a strange reaction deep inside her belly, a quivering that became a throbbing at the top of her sex. Each motion of the horse sent her clitoris sliding against the leather of the saddle, and the scent of his skin intensified the sensation somehow. It was unnerving, and she licked her lower lip because it felt as dry as a barley stalk. Every hot glance he had ever aimed at her rose from her memory to needle her with a longing she hadn't truly admitted she had for the man. Now that was pressed against him, part of her chastised her for not jumping at him. No matter how often she had listened to other women talk of their sweethearts, it had never been something she longed for. Now, her body refused to be ignored any longer, it enjoyed being against him.

If Barras noticed, he made no comment, which she felt herself being grateful for. Sensation was rushing through her, filling every limb and flooding her mind with intoxicating feelings that seemed impossible to control. Her fingers opened up, just because she failed to squash the urge to see what his body felt like. Tight ridges of hard muscles met her fingers, they covered his midsection and even his clothing did not disguise them.

His men closed around them, the sound of horses' hooves drumming out everything else. But a slight turn of her head and her ear was pressed against his shoulder, allowing her to hear his heartbeat. Another shiver raced through her, rushing down to her belly where a strange sort of excitement was brewing. Her mouth was dry and her arms tightened around him because she feared she might lose her hold on him due to the quivering that seemed to be growing stronger along her limbs. It was a strange weakness, like too much wine gave to a person. Even her thoughts felt muddled.

A rough hand landed on top of hers. Jemma flinched, her entire body reacting to the touch. His fingers curled around hers, completely covering her small hand in his. But it was his thumb that she noticed the most because it slid around her wrist to the delicate skin on the underside. That tender spot felt the rougher skin of his thumb stroking across it before pressing against the place where her pulse throbbed. It was a strangely intimate touch, and she yanked her hand away from beneath his and curled her fingers around the wide leather belt that kept his kilt in place. She felt his chest vi-brate and knew that he was chuckling, even if the wind carried the sound away before she heard it.

Jemma snorted, enjoying the fact that she could make whatever sounds she wanted. But his head turned to cast a sidelong glance at her and she realized that he'd felt the sound just as she had felt his. Jemma was startled to discover that she was communicating with him on some deeper level.

A much more turbulent one, her thoughts returned to the way he'd looked at her in the past.

They rounded a hill and a fortress came into view. It was almost black against the night sky, with thick towers that rose up against the hills behind it. A wicked-looking gate began to rise, the grinding of metal chain cutting through the pounding of the horse's hooves. Her breath froze as fear tapped its icy fingertips against her.

This was not Amber Hill.

It was not even England.

She shuddered, unable to contain the dread creeping through her. It stole away the excitement that had been making her so warm, leaving her to the mercy of the night chill. Indeed life might become very frigid if she awoke in a Scottish fortress without there being any marriage agreement. The gossips would declare it her own fault for riding out without an escort.

Laird Barras rode straight under the gate and into the courtyard without hesitation, his stallion knowing the way well. But he had to rein the horse towards the front steps instead of the stable. The animal had not even fully stopped when he turned and locked stares with her.

"Welcome to Barras castle, lass."

Keep an eye out for Sylvia Day's
PRIDE AND PLEASURE,

coming next month from Brava!

"And what is it you hope to produce by procuring a suitor?"

"I am not in want of stud service, sir. Only a depraved mind would leap to that conclusion."

"Stud service . . ."

"Is that not what you are thinking?"

A wicked smile came to his lips. Eliza was certain her heart skipped a beat at the sight of it. "It wasn't, no."

Wanting to conclude this meeting as swiftly as possible, she rushed forward. "Do you have someone who can assist me or not?"

Bond snorted softly, but the derisive sound seemed to be directed inward and not at her. "From the top, if you would please, Miss Martin. Why do you need protection?"

"I have recently found myself to be a repeated victim of various unfortunate—and suspicious—events."

Eliza expected him to laugh or perhaps give her a doubtful look. He did neither. Instead, she watched a transformation sweep over him. As fiercely focused as he'd been since his arrival, he became more so when presented with the problem. She found herself appreciating him for more than his good looks.

He leaned slightly forward. "What manner of events?"

"I was pushed into the Serpentine. My saddle was tampered with. A snake was loosed in my bedroom—"

"I understand it was a Runner who referred you to Mr. Lynd, who in turn referred you to me."

"Yes. I hired a Runner for a month, but Mr. Bell discovered nothing. No attacks occurred while he was engaged."

"Who would want to injure you, and why?"

She offered him a slight smile, a small show of gratitude for the gravity he was displaying. Anthony Bell had come highly recommended, but he'd never taken her seriously. In fact, he had been amused by her tales and she'd never felt he was dedicated to the task of discovery. "Truthfully, I am not certain whether they truly intend bodily harm, or if they simply want to goad me into marriage as a way to establish some permanent security. I see no reason to any of it."

"Are you wealthy, Miss Martin? Or certain to be?"

"Yes. Which is why I doubt they sincerely aim to cause me grievous injury—I am worth more alive. But there are some who believe it isn't safe for me in my uncle's household. They claim he is an insufficient guardian, that he is touched, and ready for Bedlam. As if any individual capable of compassion would put a stray dog in such a place, let alone a beloved relative."

"Poppycock," the earl scoffed. "I am fit as a fiddle, in mind and body."

"You are, my lord," Eliza agreed, smiling fondly at him. "I have made it clear to all and sundry that Lord Melville will likely live to be one hundred years of age."

"And you hope that adding me to your stable of suitors will accomplish what, precisely?" Bond asked. "Deter the culprit?"

"I hope that by adding *one of your associates*," she corrected, "I can avoid further incidents over the next six weeks of the Season. In addition, if my new suitor is perceived to be a threat, perhaps the scoundrel will turn his malicious attentions toward him. Then, perhaps, we can catch the fiend.

Truly, I should like to know by what methods of deduction he formulated this plan and what he hoped to gain by it."

Bond settled back into his seat and appeared deep in thought.

"I would never suggest such a hazardous role for someone untrained," she said quickly. "But a thief-taker, a man accustomed to associating with criminals and other unfortunates . . . I should think those who engage in your profession would be more than a match for a nefarious fortune hunter."

"I see."

Beside her, her uncle murmured to himself, working out puzzles and equations in his mind. Like herself, he was most comfortable with events and reactions that could be quantified or predicted with some surety. Dealing with issues defying reason was too taxing.

"What type of individual would you consider ideal to play this role of suitor, protector, and investigator?" Bond asked finally.

"He should be quiet, even-tempered, and a proficient dancer."

Scowling, he queried, "How do dullness and the ability to dance signify in catching a possible murderer?"

"I did not say 'dull,' Mr. Bond. Kindly do not attribute words to me that I have not spoken. In order to be acknowledged as a true rival for my attentions, he should be someone whom everyone will believe I would be attracted to."

"You are not attracted to handsome men?"

"Mr. Bond, I dislike being rude. However, you leave me no recourse. The fact is, you clearly are not the sort of man whose temperament is compatible with matrimony."

"I am quite relieved to hear a female recognize that," he drawled.

"How could anyone doubt it?" She made a sweeping gesture with her hand. "I can more easily picture you in a swordfight or fisticuffs than I can see you enjoying an afternoon of croquet, after-dinner chess, or a quiet evening at home with family and friends. I am an intellectual, sir. And while I don't mean to imply a lack of mental acuity, you are obviously built for more physically strenuous pursuits."

"I see."

"Why, one had only to look at you to ascertain you aren't like the others at all! It would be evident straightaway that I would never consider a man such as you with even remote seriousness. It is quite obvious you and I do not suit in the most fundamental of ways, and everyone knows I am too observant to fail to see that. Quite frankly, sir, you are not my type of male."

The look he gave her was wry but without the smugness that would have made it irritating. He conveyed solid self-confidence free of conceit. She was dismayed to find herself strongly attracted to the quality.

He would be troublesome. Eliza did not like trouble overmuch.

He glanced at the earl. "Please forgive me, my lord, but I must speak bluntly in regard to this subject. Most especially because this is a matter concerning Miss Martin's physical well-being."

"Quite right," Melville agreed. "Straight to the point, I always say. Time is too precious to waste on inanities."

"Agreed." Bond's gaze returned to Eliza and he smiled. "Miss Martin, forgive me, but I must point out that your inexperience is limiting your understanding of the situation."

"Inexperience with what?"

"Men. More precisely, fortune-hunting men."

"I would have you know," she retorted, "that over the course of six Seasons I have had more than enough experience with gentlemen in want of funds."

"Then why," he drawled, "are you unaware that they are successful for reasons far removed from social suitability?"

Eliza blinked. "I beg your pardon?"

"Women do not marry fortune hunters because they can dance and sit quietly. They marry them for their appearance and physical prowess—two attributes you have already established I have."

"I do not see—"

"Evidently, you do not, so I shall explain." His smile continued to grow. "Fortune hunters who flourish do not strive to satisfy a woman's intellectual needs. Those can be met through friends and acquaintances. They do not seek to provide the type of companionship one enjoys in social settings or with a game table between them. Again, there are others who can do so."

"Mr. Bond—"

"No, they strive to satisfy in the only position that is theirs alone, a position some men make no effort to excel in. So rare is this particular skill, that many a woman will disregard other considerations in favor of it."

"Please, say no—"

"Fornication," his lordship muttered, before returning to his conversation with himself.

Eliza shot to her feet. "My lord!"

As courtesy dictated, both her uncle and Mr. Bond rose along with her.

"I prefer to call it 'seduction,' " Bond said, his eyes laughing.

"I call it ridiculous," she rejoined, hands on her hips. "In the grand scheme of life, do you collect how little time a person spends abed when compared to other activities?"

His gaze dropped to her hips. The smile became a full-blown grin. "That truly depends on who else is occupying said bed."

"Dear heavens." Eliza shivered at the look Jasper Bond was giving her. It was . . . expectant. By some unknown, godforsaken means she had managed to prod the man's damnable masculine pride into action.

"Give me a sennight," he suggested. "One week to prove both my point and my competency. If, at the end, you are not swayed by one or the other, I will accept no payment for services rendered."

"Excellent proposition," his lordship said. "No possibility of loss."

"Not true," Eliza contended. "How will I explain Mr. Bond's speedy departure?"

"Let us make it a fortnight, then," Bond amended.

"You fail to understand the problem. I am not an actor, sir. It will be evident to one and all that I am far from 'seduced.' "

The tone of his grin changed, aided by a hot flicker in his dark eyes. "Leave that aspect of the plan to me. After all, that's what I am being paid for."

"And if you fail? Once you resign, not only will I be forced to make excuses for you, I will have to bring in another thief-taker to act in your stead. The whole affair will be entirely too suspicious."

"Have you had the same pool of suitors for six years, Miss Martin?"

"That isn't—"

"Did you not just state the many reasons why you feel I am not an appropriate suitor for you? Can you not simply re-iterate those points in response to any inquiries regarding my departure?"

"You are overly persistent, Mr. Bond."

"Quite," he nodded, "which is why I will discover who is responsible for the unfortunate events besetting you and what they'd hoped to gain."

She crossed her arms. "I am not convinced."

"Trust me. It is fortuitous, indeed, that Mr. Lynd brought us together. If I do not apprehend the culprit, I daresay he cannot be caught." His hand fisted around the top of his cane. "Client satisfaction is a point of pride, Miss Martin. By the time I am done, I guarantee you will be eminently gratified by my performance."